Matthew Ryan Davies is a freelance copywriter and editor, mostly for the healthcare sector. He ghostwrites non-fiction books, edits university textbooks for medical and nursing students, and writes scripts for educational videos and documentaries.

Matthew is also the author of *Things We Bury*, which has been optioned for television, and the young adult novel *This Thing of Darkness*. He lives in Melbourne with his wife and two grown children.

To find out more about Matthew and his work visit www.matthewryandavies.com.

Also by Matthew Ryan Davies

Things We Bury

Matthew Ryan Davies

THE BROKEN WAVE

MACMILLAN

Pan Macmillan Australia

Pan Macmillan acknowledges the Traditional Custodians of Country throughout Australia and their connections to lands, waters and communities. We pay our respect to Elders past and present and extend that respect to all Aboriginal and Torres Strait Islander peoples today. We honour more than sixty thousand years of storytelling, art and culture.

This is a work of fiction. Characters, institutions and organisations mentioned in this novel are either the product of the author's imagination or, if real, used fictitiously without any intent to describe actual conduct.

First published 2023 in Macmillan by Pan Macmillan Australia Pty Ltd
1 Market Street, Sydney, New South Wales, Australia, 2000

 A catalogue record for this book is available from the National Library of Australia

Typeset in 12/16 pt Bembo MT Pro by Post Pre-press Group

Printed by IVE

The author and the publisher have made every effort to contact copyright holders for material used in this book. Any person or organisation that may have been overlooked should contact the publisher.

 The paper in this book is FSC® certified. FSC® promotes environmentally responsible, socially beneficial and economically viable management of the world's forests.

For Tom,
my childhood friend

'A writer writes . . . because he is driven by the need to communicate. Behind the need to communicate is the need to share. Behind the need to share is the need to be understood.'

— Leo Rosten

The white sun is my first memory of Australia. It was under those dazzling rays that, at twelve years old, I became who I am. For good and for bad. It was there that I learned the value of true friendship, family and simple pleasures. And where I learned about loss.

It was there that I sipped my first beer, reeled in my first flathead and discovered that there's no better sight in the world than sunrise over the bay at Queenscliff.

And the beach. Ah, the beach. I remember how, after the tide went out, it would leave a thin film of water glistening on the shore. I remember the salty wind whipping through my hair as I rode my bike along the tideline, the tyres kicking up sand behind me.

And him. Most of all I remember him. The day we met he was standing on a pontoon, a fishing pole in his hands, tugging

1

on the line like his life depended on landing that fish. That's how I like to picture him still.

I could never write about that time. Or about him. Maybe that's all I ever write about. Eliot, my literary agent, once told me that I was blocked—that I had to work out what it was I *wasn't* writing. 'It might mean wading through some shit,' she said, 'but it'll be worth it.'

I'm not sure it would be. I'm not sure I could stand it. But sometimes we have to confront the things that have wounded us the most so we can deal with them and 'move on'.

Sometimes this makes us stronger. Sometimes it destroys us.

1

I pushed my chair back from the desk and peered through the window. Outside, powdery snow blanketed my front lawn, the large sugar maple beyond it starved of leaves.

The winter of 2018–2019 was shaping up to be the costliest for Minneapolis in a decade—snowplough drivers working overtime and the tens of thousands of tons of sand and salt needed to keep our roads and sidewalks functional.

My laptop sat open on the desk. I stared at the blinking cursor, flashing impatiently after the 'D' in THE END as if challenging me.

They say writing your second novel is infinitely harder than your first because there is now expectation. You have a readership. Can you match the brilliance of your debut?

'Second novel syndrome' was different for me. If this one didn't sell, that would be it. Eliot would drop me and it would be too hard to find another agent. Two failed novels doesn't look good on a résumé.

I leaned forward in my chair and scooped up the fishing lure that sat on the windowsill, three inches long and in the shape of a finless sardine. The vibrancy of its golden scales had dulled since Tom handed it to me on a pontoon in Queenscliff twenty-six years ago. 'For luck,' he'd said.

The memory of that day rose up, vivid and bright, as dazzling as the Australian sun. Or maybe it was a mix of memory and extrapolation. We spent so much time at the beach that summer that maybe my mind was playing tricks on me, creating memories born of repetition. Either way, in the screening room of my mind Tom wore bright-coloured board shorts and no shirt. He wasn't wearing shoes either. He hardly ever did, except for school. He had a year-round tan, the sun so imbued into his skin you imagined it would always be warm to touch.

I squeezed the lure, cold from the windowsill. 'Fish are lucky,' he told me. But it didn't prove true. Our luck ran aground that year.

Outside, the day had died as I sat there turning Tom's lure over in my hands, remembering. I liked winter, even the unforgiving winter of Minneapolis. Something about the snow burying everything, driving us all indoors, appealed to me.

I flicked on my desk lamp, illuminating the book-lined walls behind me. The snow disappeared from beyond the window, the lamplight turning the pane black.

I toggled back to Facebook. Tom's wife, Tia, had posted about his death eight hours before. It must have been the middle of the night in Queenscliff then. I pictured her, not yet asleep, her eyes empty of tears, hunched over her phone in the dark, the kids tucked in bed.

Our beautiful husband and father, Tom, passed away yesterday in a boating accident. Our hearts will be forever broken.

Below the post she'd attached a picture of him on his cruiser, the boat he used for work. His dark hair, flecked with grey, ruffled by the breeze. He hadn't shaved in what must have been a week and his tan skin was tinged pink from the sun. He was smiling his big smile, holding up a silvery fish.

We had never caught a fish that big when we were kids, although not from lack of trying. But sitting on the dock, our lines dangling in the choppy water, listening to Tom talk about Queenscliff's marine life, that wasn't really the point. He would enlighten me with endless facts about the ocean (*Did you know that fish scales are laid down in rings each year, like tree rings, so you can use them to age the fish?*), distracting me from what was happening at home.

Those were good times, but they didn't last. We'd not spoken in at least three years, Tom and me, but we'd kept in touch via social media, messaging each other a couple of times a year. We never talked about what happened in 1992. Did it quietly haunt him the way it did me?

Downstairs, the internal door between the garage and house closed and Claire's voice drifted upstairs: 'God, it's so dark in here.' The hallway light came on, beaming soft light up to the landing outside my office.

Another light switched on downstairs and I heard her in the kitchen, opening the refrigerator and closing it again.

Claire's shoes clicked across the hardwood floor but then she must have kicked them off because the noise stopped, replaced with the soft groan of the stairs under her stockinged feet.

At the doorway to my office she said, 'I thought you were making meatballs?'

'Tom's dead.'

'What?'

'Boat wreck.'

Claire lifted her hand to her mouth. Her make-up had mostly worn away, but her hair, tied in some artistic way at the back, looked exactly as it had when she left for work at seven that morning. 'What happened? How did you hear?'

'Facebook. Tia posted. I don't know any more than that.'

Claire sat on the arm of the sofa in the corner of the room. I'd put it there in case clients visited, but in the seven years that I'd been freelancing as a writer-for-hire none ever had. Its purpose, really, was a reading chair for me.

'She must be so . . .' Claire began. 'I can't imagine . . . We'll have to send something. A gift basket maybe. Flowers at the very least.' She shook her head, still disbelieving. 'Oh, Drew. Are you okay?'

I nodded.

'I'll open a bottle of wine,' she said with conviction. 'Raise a glass to Tom.' Claire always knew what to do in a crisis.

I had planned to open a bottle tonight myself. Not wine, though; something bubbly to celebrate finishing my manuscript. It no longer seemed important.

As Claire padded down the stairs, I turned back to my laptop and touched the trackpad, illuminating the screen. I stared at it for a moment, that blinking cursor, then tapped the delete key, backspacing over the words THE END.

2

I nudged a meatball around the plate with my fork, sliding it through the cream sauce, feeling for the lure in my pocket with my free hand. I'd removed the two three-pronged hooks that once dangled from the fish's tail and mid-section, but the small ringed clasps were still there. I ran a finger over them.

Normally, Claire would be overflowing with stories from work during dinner. It was all not-enough-funding this and too-many-clients that. I would only be half-listening as she related the day's dramas. But it was fine. If we didn't talk about that, I'm not sure what we would talk about. I had no colleagues, and while other couples seemed to yak nonstop about their children, that topic wasn't available to us. I would rarely talk in any detail about what I was working on, and Claire knew not to push. When we met, in college, Claire was an insatiable reader. But now she was too tired at night. On the weekends, at the gym,

7

she'd listen to podcasts or, if she was going for a long walk, the occasional audiobook.

'Did Travers show up today?' I asked.

'No.'

'Did he call?'

'We called him.'

'And?'

'And . . . he's still not ready.'

'Not ready to process invoices?'

'It's more complicated than that. He doesn't have anyone . . . He just doesn't function well in the workplace at the moment.'

'Then he's not ready for a job,' I said. 'He's an adult. He needs to deal with whatever it is and move on.'

'We can cover the invoices for now.'

'But for how long?'

Somehow, the idealistic social worker I married had morphed into an overworked administrator. When the role of program manager opened up, no one else in her team wanted it, and, she'd said at the time, she couldn't sit by and watch the program dissolve, so she'd thrown her hat in the ring. A year later her boss resigned and history repeated itself. Now she was CEO but wasn't really sure how that had happened either.

Claire sipped her wine. 'The Hemmings have invited us over Saturday night. Wanna go?'

I skewered a meatball.

'I think Alicia wants to show us the new kitchen,' she said.

'I don't mind.'

Claire eyed me for a moment, as if trying to work something out. 'I'll tell them yes.'

'Okay.'

'We might even be treated to another impromptu piano recital from Chantelle.' Claire grinned at me. 'The perfect child.'

'It's not her fault her parents make her do all that,' I said.

'I know. I didn't mean . . .' She picked up her glass but held it at chin level. 'I'll get a nice bottle to take with us. What time does Hum's open?'

'Nine. Same as during the week. I can go.'

Claire always visited her parents on Saturday; sometimes I would join her.

We'd settled into a good routine, Claire and me. I wrote every day but broke it up with other tasks. On Mondays, I'd shop for the week. Tuesdays were laundry day. Wednesdays I wrote at a local cafe, just to change it up. Thursdays I cleaned the house. Sometimes I'd spend all morning doing that—not that it needed it, not that we made much mess the two of us, but it kept me away from my desk a little longer. Fridays I clocked off early, about 3.30 pm, and read. We'd get takeout on Fridays because by then we were low on groceries. Claire liked the pizza place on Lyndale so, on her way home from work, she would usually pick up a large margherita or the Mexicali for us to share. Depending on how late it was, I would usually be halfway through a bottle of merlot by the time she arrived.

'And don't forget I've got practice on Sunday afternoon,' Claire said.

I frowned, trying to work out what practice she meant.

'Carolling,' she said.

'I know.'

She smiled at me.

Listening to Claire talk about her full life—work, friends, choir group—my own felt quiet and small. I didn't want her job; it wasn't that. I didn't want any nine-to-five job. But I envied how her work fulfilled her. She was constantly pushed, knew what she was doing, and was well respected in her field. Looking after the house gave me a purpose and something concrete to hang my hat on each day . . . I had achieved something! Even if it was only checking off the charges on the credit card bill and having a hot dinner on the table at seven each night.

'Have you thought about flying to Australia for the funeral?' Claire asked.

I looked at her across the table. The candlelight flickered between us. 'Why would I?'

'Why not?'

'Because it's ten thousand miles away. Literally.' I took a sip of red wine. 'Besides, he's gone now. What would be the point?'

'Going to funerals isn't always about the person who died.'

I stabbed a hunk of meatball that had broken in two and glanced around the kitchen. We'd remodelled the previous year but kept the style true to the character of the house. Claire fell in love with the place the first time we saw it six years ago. She'd adored its turn-of-the-century charm—natural woodwork, box beams, built-ins and stained-glass windows. I was partial to the large back deck opening out to a private, fenced-in backyard and the room that I claimed as my office, overlooking elms and maples bordering the street, bright lime green in the summer and starkly bare in winter. With four bedrooms, two full baths and a half-bath, it was always going to be too large for a child-less couple, but we couldn't pass up the location in the heart of Lowry Hill, right near Kenwood Park, with tennis courts, Lake of the Isles, bike trails, shops and restaurants all in easy reach.

'Did you send your book to Eliot?' Claire asked.

It's not a book yet, I wanted to tell her. *It's a manuscript.*

'No.'

'But you've finished it, right? The book?'

'Depends on how you define finished.'

'It's got an ending, hasn't it? You're happy with it?'

Ending? Yes. Happy? How could I tell?

On my plate, the creamy sauce pooled around the mashed potatoes. 'I'll send it tomorrow.'

I took another sip of red wine as Claire spooned more string beans onto her plate.

'You should ask your writer friends over to celebrate.'

'No.'

'You could make your—'

'They're busy. *I'm* busy.'

'We're all *busy*, Drew, but everyone needs to make room in their lives to connect.'

I gave her a look and she held her hands up in surrender, a string bean flopping from her fork.

'You should think about going to the funeral, though,' she said. 'Since you've finished your novel.'

Manuscript.

'The timing's actually good,' she continued. 'It'll be summer over there, and I'm away at a conference next week anyway. Why don't you?'

Summer . . . I peered out the window at the glow of the porch light illuminating the snow-covered patio table. Everything was buried under a thick blanket of the stuff.

'I think my passport's out of date. I won't be able to get a new one in time *and* fly twenty-four hours to Melbourne,' I said, as though I needed another reason not to go.

She blinked at me. *Now you're just making excuses.* 'There are processes for emergencies like this.'

I didn't respond.

'I think you should go,' she said.

'Claire, I haven't seen the guy in, like—'

'That's not what I mean. You need to go back *there*. To Queenscliff.'

I shook my head. 'I've dealt with that.'

Claire took another drawn-out sip from her glass.

I knew what she was doing. Effecting the old therapist's trick of staying quiet so the patient would feel compelled to fill the silence, revealing something they might otherwise not.

She placed her fork across her plate, and I knew what was coming.

'I'm worried about you,' she said. 'You spend so much time alone. You disappear into your writing and you hide inside it. Nobody's allowed in. And you kind of get trapped there.'

I liked it there. It was easier living between the pages, in someone else's world. But Claire wouldn't have understood that.

'I have goals, Claire. I have to commit if I'm ever going to . . .'

'Succeed?'

'Yes.'

She held my gaze, not speaking.

'Claire, you don't—'

'You don't let me.'

I didn't respond so she tried again. 'Maybe you need to redefine success.'

I put my own fork on the plate with more force than I meant to and it clattered loudly, making Claire flinch. 'You mean I should give up? Is that what you're saying? Stop writing?'

She maintained her cool, even though I wasn't maintaining mine.

'All I'm saying is, it can't be good for you. Psychologically, I mean.'

'And going halfway around the world for a funeral *will* be good for my mental health?'

'It wouldn't only be for the funeral.'

I picked up my glass and took a deep sip, refusing to acknowledge the meaning in her words. 'We'll just send a gift basket.'

3

I stared at the bedside clock: 2.32. I hadn't slept yet. I'd been listening to the sounds of cars navigating our street, snow-ploughs humming somewhere in the distance, thinking about Tom, picturing the accident, wondering if I should call Tia.

I rolled over, punched my pillow into shape and tried again. My body tensed under the comforter as it pushed against the binds that held me there—grief, gloom, guilt.

I hadn't commented on Tia's post. I didn't want to add another platitude to the dozens already there. I am a writer, yes. But in the same way I don't like writing in greeting cards, I never know what to say in these moments. What would be the point in adding another 'I'm sorry for your loss' to a screen full of them? But that was better than saying nothing. *I should call her. I should get out of bed and call her.*

I calculated the time difference. Two-thirty in the morning

in Minneapolis meant it would be . . . allowing for daylight saving time . . . seven-thirty at night in Queenscliff.

I threw the blankets off, wrapped myself in my robe and headed into the den with my cell, switching on the desk lamp.

But then I realised I didn't have her number. I had Tom's, but not hers. I could call her over Messenger. No, I decided; I shouldn't intrude. We didn't even know each other that well. And she'd probably want to be left alone right now. I knew I would. I should just leave a message on Facebook like everyone else. Send a gift basket.

I stared at the vaulted ceiling. The previous owners had my office set up as a nursery, and remnants of glow-in-the-dark stars still blushed on the plaster. Sitting at my desk, trying to recast a sentence in my head, I would sometimes stare at those stars and imagine the baby sleeping in its crib—how it sounded and how it smelled. Sometimes I'd get lost in these thoughts, and others. Sitting in the armchair by the bookcase, I would get flashes— white light, a loud bang—and in a blink an hour had gone by.

I lifted the lid on my laptop and the screen came to life, the final page of my manuscript staring back at me. Here was one thing I could control.

I toggled to my email and punched out a note to Eliot, attaching the file. I hit send before I could talk myself out of it, not even reading the message back to check for typos.

I descended the stairs to the kitchen, took the carton of eggs and a head of lettuce from the refrigerator, ketchup from the pantry, and whacked a loaf of sliced bread on the countertop. I lit the stove and splashed a glug of oil into a pan. When the pan was hot enough, I cracked an egg and dropped it in, then tore a leaf from the lettuce. Taking a dinner plate from the dish rack, I slapped two slices of bread down and squirted a circle of ketchup on one half, flipped the egg, let it firm up for another thirty seconds, then laid it on the ketchup, topping it with the lettuce and then the other slice of bread.

I hadn't made an egg sandwich for years, maybe ten, or maybe even since college, but it was Tom's signature sandwich, and the first thing he ever made me.

I carried my sandwich back to the den and sat in my office chair, swivelling it around until I was facing the bookshelf. It was crammed full of books, novels mostly, turned at odd angles to fit the available space. On the bottom shelf, I caught sight of what I must have been subconsciously looking for. I rolled forward and extracted my childhood photo album. I hadn't printed a photo in a decade, but the ones from my childhood—birth to college—were all there in that album.

I flicked though the early years—infancy, day care, kinder-garten, elementary school—until the pictures suddenly got brighter during our time in Australia. Dad had died only the year before, in '91—shot dead in a robbery. My parents had been divorced for four years by then, and Mom was already married to Mark. Scarlett wasn't even born yet.

There weren't many family shots from that year. One of Mom in full sail; a few of brand-new baby Scarlett (she was born in Australia); one of Mark in his army uniform; Mom and Scarlett on the front porch of the house the Australian Defence Force rented for us; one of me clutching a fishing pole; and me and Tom at Marissa Davidoff's party. I wish I had more pictures from that time, but we didn't think of it. Neither Mom nor Mark were in the right headspace and it just didn't cross my mind—I was too busy living it.

I turned the page and Tom, twelve years old, hair bleached by the sun, tan skin, white teeth, smiled back at me. He had the controller of a remote-controlled car in his hand, and I remembered how he'd looked up when I'd called his name and I'd snapped the shot. We were supposed to be taking photos of the cars, but I was glad I'd thought to take one of him too.

Tom's car was an amalgam of various others he owned. The transmitter from this one, the circuit board from that. He put them together, pulled them apart, made them bigger, pimped them up. I still don't know how he did it. Logical brain. Creative brain. A rare combination, I guess.

I closed the photo album, returned it to the shelf and leaned back into the sofa. Something was holding me in place, but something even stronger was pulling me away. Queenscliff would never leave me, although I left it twenty-six years ago, vowing never to return.

But an ache drummed inside me, and I knew somehow that it still had room to grow.

I opened the top drawer of my filing cabinet and took out my passport. It was still valid.

I'd run out of excuses.

4

Claire dropped me off at the airport. I checked my bags and sat in the terminal nursing a paper cup of coffee, strong and gritty, staring at the Christmas decorations strung from pillar to pillar. It was four in the afternoon and I hadn't eaten since breakfast. They would feed me on the plane, I figured.

With thirty minutes to wait till the flight boarded, I shouldered my messenger bag and headed to the retail stores that lined one end of the terminal. Like a moth to a wool sweater, I took myself into the bookstore, headed straight for the fiction section and scanned the shelves for *Saving Grace*. It wouldn't be there. It had probably never been there. I mean, at the airport? The airport is peak position for any novel to catch the primed traveller market. I didn't understand why I did this to myself. It was a form of self-torture I seemed incapable of resisting.

Near the exit stood a large display made from glossy cardboard featuring the latest blockbuster all-American novel from C.J. DeBono. In grad school, he was just Christian Debono (yes, with a lower case 'b'); now he was one of the most celebrated writers in the country. His first novel was good, admittedly: a four-hundred-page tome on smalltown America told from the perspective of a fourteen-year-old boy. It wasn't young adult fiction (he wouldn't stoop that low), and the voice was too sophisticated for a fourteen-year-old, but nobody seemed to notice—or, if they did, they didn't care. His second received mixed reviews but sold well based on the popularity of the first.

Christian and I were two of twelve accepted into the graduate program at Hamline from more than four hundred applications that year. I was twenty-nine by then, but really knew nothing about the world. I was married, yes, but knew so little about relationships or the struggles of adulthood. It was really quite shocking how naive I was. But my college professors had been so encouraging. 'Keep going!' they urged, often writing words like 'Wonderful!' and 'Inspired!' in the margins of my stories.

After graduating, I took a few years off, working as a night porter in a hotel in Saint Paul and trying to make it as a writer. I submitted short stories and even got a couple published, but I really wanted to write a novel. With a few years of 'real world' experience behind me (and, if I'm honest, at a dead end with my writing), I applied for the MFA program.

I thought the praise I'd received as an undergrad would carry through to graduate school, that I would be similarly encouraged there. I imagined a collegial space where writerly types would build each other up, meet in sun-drenched quads for readings of our favourite authors, then party in the local bars until three in the morning, all the while supporting each other like brothers-in-arms, wading through the trenches, ending with nightly renditions of Queen songs and stumbling through the streets of the Twin Cities high on the promise of impending glory.

But no.

In the first workshop, my submission was lambasted in the most devastating way possible. It was a story about a man returning from World War II with undiagnosed PTSD (I fancied myself the next Hemingway), and the head of the program, Martin Pierce, called it sallow. He said I wasn't putting enough of myself into the story. He had clearly already pegged Christian as the course's literary star-in-the-making and everyone else was just there to make up the numbers.

It was bad enough having to sit there while my own work was eviscerated, but then I had to stay and watch my classmates go through it too. It was like constantly reliving that scene in *Game of Thrones* when Stannis Baratheon burns his own daughter at the stake in a misguided attempt to fulfill his ambitions of power.

When the three years ended, we all walked out of there with MFAs clutched tightly in our hands. Christian, however, left with a nice warm introduction to Martin's agent, followed by a big fat offer of publication from Little, Brown (Martin's publisher) for his still-unfinished first novel.

To one ugly part of me, Christian's success felt unfair. But of course it wasn't. He wasn't just another talentless, well-connected racketeer whom the Gods of Publishing had unjustly smiled upon. He actually could, to the envy of us all, write.

In the airport bookstore, I purchased the new short-story collection by Curtis Sittenfeld and a four-pack of Big Red cinnamon gum. If I could have smuggled a bottle of Seagram's onto the plane, I would have.

★

Waiting at the gate, gum in my mouth, I checked my email. There was a message from Eliot: *Received the MS safe and sound,* she'd written. *Love the title! I'm excited to read it.*

I typed a quick message back to let her know I was going to Australia for a week, not that this would make a difference to anything. It wasn't like I'd be needed in New York City urgently for a three-way bidding war for my book. Or would I?

Then I called Claire.

'What did you forget?' she answered. I could hear the purr of the heater blowing warm air through the car.

'Nothing. Just wanted to say goodbye . . . again.'

'Oh-kay. Everything alright, Drew?'

I was an anxious flyer; Claire knew this about me. I rarely slept on planes (not for lack of trying), and I didn't like watching movies on those little screens. A nervous energy pulsed though me the entire time until I touched down at my destination. It wasn't that I was afraid of dying as such, but that I would die with so many loose ends still untied.

I felt the urge to tell her I loved her, but I never did that, and saying it now might alarm her. It wasn't just the flight; it was where I was headed. What would it feel like to go back?

'You'll visit Mom and Scarlett while I'm gone?' I said.

'I've got the conference,' Claire reminded me.

'I know, but . . . No, it's fine.'

'Text me when you touch down, okay?'

'Sure.'

'And Drew?'

'Mmm?'

'Don't forget to breathe.'

I returned my phone to my pocket and glanced across the terminal. Stories floated all around me—the young Asian couple leaning on each other, asleep, between flights; businesspeople tapping away feverishly at their laptops; old people squinting at their phones, cautiously poking and sliding with one finger; children with their faces pressed to the tall windows overlooking the runway.

Across the row of seats from me, a mother fumbled in her carry-on, looking for something, while Dad made faces at the baby he was bouncing in his lap. He kissed her face (I assumed from the pink onesie it was a girl) and buried his nose in her soft belly, making her laugh.

I'd witnessed friends cooing at their newborns just like this, making sounds I'd never thought I'd hear coming from the mouths of men I'd got shitfaced with a hundred times in college. But they'd goo-gooed and ga-gaed without a hint of embarrassment, and it softened them in a way I would never experience.

Claire had been honest with me early in our relationship: she didn't want a child. Something inside me had flinched at that, but I recovered quickly. I was too much in love to believe it mattered. Nothing felt more important than making her my wife. This might have scared off a thirty-something Drew, but at twenty-one I'd let it sink into me and float away.

Next to me, a man in a business suit straining at the seams prepared to sit, the waft of sautéed onions and tomatoes radiating from a covered cardboard container in one hand, plastic cutlery in the other and a computer bag slung over his shoulder. He landed in the chair and the whole row shuddered. He wore too much cologne—maybe he'd been sprayed by one of the women standing idly in the gift shops wielding bottles of the stuff. He dumped the bag on the carpeted floor and levered open the lid of his container, revealing a plate of spaghetti smothered in a bold red-and-brown sauce. Something about it—the smell, probably—made my head swim.

'Enough for three,' I whispered to myself, and suddenly the terminal went black.

'Sir? Sir?'

Airport terminal noises rose gently around me, as though someone was slowly turning up the volume on a stereo.

I opened my eyes to find a young man with blond hair that had already receded halfway back over his scalp kneeling next to me. I was splayed out on the carpet, a cast of onlookers watching avidly.

'I'm Alistair,' the man said in a soft Southern accent. 'I'm a nurse. I think you fainted.' His hand was wrapped around my wrist, two fingers feeling for a pulse.

I, meanwhile, was on my side, as if someone had put me to bed. Moisture beaded my forehead.

I realised then that this Alistair was the man who'd been cooing at his baby a few moments before. Was it a few moments before? How long had I been out? *Why* had I been out?

'Just stay there,' Alistair said. 'Don't try to stand yet.'

I exhaled and planted both elbows into the carpet, trying to hoist myself up.

'Stay there,' he repeated, placing a firm hand on my shoulder. 'How's your head? Any dizziness?'

'No, I think I'm okay.'

'Does that happen often? The fainting?'

'No, it's never happened before.'

'Have you eaten?'

'Yes. It's not that,' I said with a confidence I didn't feel.

Why *would* I faint? Why now?

'Are you anxious about something? The flight?'

Just then a woman dressed as a flight attendant but who was clearly ground crew (she didn't have the immaculate make-up and gleaming hair of a woman about to start work; she'd obviously been on shift for hours) loomed over me. 'Is he okay?' she asked Alistair.

'Yeah, I think so. Panic attack, possibly. He'll be fine in a few minutes.'

A panic attack? Where did he conjure that diagnosis from?

'Sir?' she said to me in a loud voice, as if I were a geriatric who'd lost his hearing aid. 'Sir?' Are you okay to fly? Do I need to call somebody?'

'No,' I said, placing my hand on the seat of the fabric-covered chair to help me stand. I wanted to show that I was perfectly alright. 'I mean, yes, I'm fine to fly.'

'Are you sure? Because—'

I held up a hand to cut her off. 'I'm fine,' I said. 'I'll fetch something to eat and I'll be okay.' Low sugar levels or hunger were not the cause of my blackout (and I was aware that I'd just said as much to Alistair), but I had to reassure her so she'd let me board the flight.

The woman hesitated, hands on hips, considering me. 'Well, alrighty then,' she said finally. 'We're boarding in twenty. I'll check back with you before then.'

I nodded and sat in the chair. She wouldn't check back with me. She would get distracted by a hundred questions from edgy passengers and forget. And that suited me.

Having made up my mind to go, I was now determined not to miss this flight.

5

I changed planes in LA for a Qantas flight to Melbourne. I was seated next to a gin entrepreneur, Flynn, on his way back from a fact-finding trip to the States.

'It's a small distillery in Tasmania,' he told me, once we were cruising at 33,000 feet. 'Set it up five years ago—just me and my wife. We've been in Asia for two, but I've been trying to crack the American market for a while.'

I like the Australian accent. There's something warm and friendly about it. Laidback in the way people mumble through sentences, almost as if they don't want to open their mouths too wide. It feels like every interaction is an informal one. As a kid, I'd had trouble understanding Tom at first. The way he spoke was kind of nasally, like the words travelled out of his mouth via his nose. And the distinctive way he pronounced vowels—elongated, diphthongy. It's like he made a U-turn right in the middle of every a, e, i, o and u. But I got used to it.

'You were looking for a distributor?' I asked Flynn.

He flicked back wavy tendrils of long brown hair. 'Yeah.'

I offered him a stick of Big Red, which he accepted. 'How'd you do it?'

'Started at the top, with the biggest players, and worked my way down. Kept going until I got a few to take meetings with me—enough to make the trip worthwhile.'

I admired the balls on him, the determination to make it happen on his own.

'Got to put yourself out there,' he said. 'It's not just about the product anymore. They want to know about *you*. What kind of ambassador are you going to be for the brand? Are you projecting the right image—good family values—on social media? All that shit.'

It sounded familiar. Authors, too, were expected to become their own brand champions, carefully cultivating an online persona that readers would want to get on board with. The truth was, there was no evidence that being online increased book sales, and that was excuse enough for me.

'How'd the meetings go?' I asked.

Flynn ran a hand along his stubbled jawline. 'Good. A couple wanted me to change the branding.' He smiled wryly. 'They wanted me to add a bouncing kangaroo or a koala clinging to a gum tree or some other crap to the label.'

This was a constant battle for me—revising to please editors or revising to please myself. When you're desperate to get a result, you'll agree to anything in an initial meeting.

'What'd you say?' I asked.

'Told 'em to fuck off.'

I smiled, and he snorted a laugh.

'Maybe not in so many words,' he added.

I've always found it easy to talk with strangers, and it's easier when your interest is genuine. But sometimes, I knew, I took it too far, creeping into personal territory too soon. Theirs. Never mine.

'How about you?' Flynn asked. 'What do you do?'

'I'm a writer. Freelance.'

'Really? My sister's a writer. Well, she used to be. She was trying to write a—what did she call it?—a *rural romance*, but she gave up. All that rejection just got too hard. I reckon you've gotta have something big driving you to put yourself through that. What do you write?'

'Articles mainly.'

I generally avoided telling strangers that I was a novelist. When I was sober, at least. Because, of course, that led to the inevitable follow-up question: 'Anything I would have read?' I'd mentioned *Saving Grace* a few times after it was published. Not once had someone heard of it, let alone read it, so I'd stopped doing that.

'I edit too,' I said to keep the conversation going. 'For the non-profit sector mostly. Funding applications, partnership proposals and the like.'

'Interesting,' Flynn said. 'I could probably use you for my push into the US. Get a local's perspective on my marketing stuff.'

'Sure, anytime.'

Up the aisle, two flight attendants had begun to serve food on trays from a trolley. I touched my stomach, which was still swirling from the episode at the flight gate. Digestive issues were nothing new for me—bloating, cramping, bent-over-at-the-waist pain—it was all in the inventory of gassy gut grievances

I'd had since my teens. I was hungry, but I didn't want to risk an in-flight emergency.

'So, this trip. Business or pleasure?' Flynn asked. (I loved the way he pronounced 'pleasure': *plej-zhah*.)

'Neither, actually. A funeral.'

'Oh, I'm sorry. In Melbourne?'

'On the coast. Queenscliff?'

'Ah, nice place that. The Bellarine.'

'Yeah. Haven't been back in a while.'

'I doubt it would have changed much. How long?'

'Twenty-six years.'

'Jesus. What were you, a toddler?'

'Sixth grade.'

Outside, the air pressure must have changed because the plane suddenly took a sharp dip. I gripped the armrest. One of the reasons I hated flying was because I liked to be in control—in all aspects of my life. I planned my novels before I started writing and rarely deviated. Other writers had tried to convince me to let go of my fixed ideas of how the story should go and let my subconscious lead me. *Surprise is where the good stuff comes from*, they'd say, but I wouldn't have it.

'And this funeral?' Flynn asked.

'An old friend.'

They fed us (I only had a beer) then turned down the cabin lights for sleeping. It would have been 10 pm in Minneapolis and my eyelids were heavy.

Across the aisle, a woman was reading *The Brothers Esposito*, Christian's latest novel. She looked to be fifty or so pages in and I wanted to ask her what she thought. But if she gushed, told me how brilliant and captivating and transporting and immersive it was, I may have caused a mid-air incident.

Christian's first novel, *America*, came out only a couple of years after we graduated from the MFA program. Franzenesque in style, it was nominated for the National Book Award and was featured in *The New Yorker*. Critics compared him to our most celebrated dead writers and to living writers so revered they might as well have been dead. All before the age of thirty.

I was writing throughout this period as well. I had landed Eliot as my agent but hadn't sold anything. I'd married Claire years earlier and we'd bought the Craftsman where we still lived. By day, Claire would corral staff, extinguish administrative fires and brainstorm yet more ways to deliver more support to more people within the same budget. At night, she'd churn away at funding applications, donor strategies and fundraising proposals—all the stuff she'd never wanted to do but came to realise was a vital part of any senior role in the sector she loved so much. And I was grateful, because her career more or less supported my writing. (Not that I was sitting at home endlessly editing dead-end manuscripts. I was making a mediocre living selling on spec to magazines like *Men's Health* and *Field & Stream* on everything from signs that your prostate might be on the blink to the best camping spots in Minnesota.)

I should have deleted my Twitter and Instagram back then, or at least stopped following Christian. Watching him skyrocket past me when we were both in exactly the same place once (physically, at least) was a stinging lesson in humility.

I'm not sure how he knew, but he sent me a message of congratulations via Twitter when my novel came out, telling me he couldn't wait to read it. I don't know if he ever did, or if he did and he hated it, because I never heard from him again. That simmered away somewhere deep in my belly—why couldn't he throw me even the smallest bone? Use his vast literary power to increase my visibility even a little bit?

I tried to remind myself that we were different writers. We were not in competition with each other; we could happily coexist in the big, bad publishing world. But his successes rubbed against me like sandpaper.

He was not an evil person, and he was unquestionably an accomplished writer, but he seemed never to have come up against any obstacles. He didn't understand the struggle that ninety-five per cent of novelists go through to, first, write something saleable, then get noticed by an agent, then get picked up by a publisher and then to actually 'find an audience', as they liked to say in the literary world. Not that writing the kind of books he did was easy, but the road ahead of him seemed paved with glistening diamonds from the beginning.

Now, en route to Melbourne, I myself read for a while, the first story in the Curtis Sittenfeld collection, then I closed my eyes, the soft tapping of Flynn's fingers on his laptop lulling me into a shallow, fitful sleep, where I met up with Tom . . .

Tom and I are kayaking across a dark bay. We don't know where we're going. Our spindly, twelve-year-old arms are paddling madly, as if we're trying to get away from something. Tom falls overboard and slips beneath the black water.

A bump of turbulence woke me. The cabin was fully dark and Flynn was asleep. I must have dozed for longer than I thought. It reminded me of when I'd woken from my fainting episode in the terminal. Alistair, the off-duty nurse who attended to me, had advised I get checked over by a doctor once I reach my destination and I'd nodded my agreement, even though I knew I wouldn't do it.

Then the dream came back to me in a rush. These were frequent night-time visitations for me—dark bays, endless ocean, splatters of blood. And that white light. Always the damned white light.

6

A soldier was waiting for us in the terminal of Melbourne's Tullamarine Airport when we exited border control, me clutching onto Mom's hand. It was the tail end of January, the Australian school year had just begun, and I had turned twelve four days before.

The GI was younger than Mark, with buzzed army hair and an eager smile. He wore light olive khaki from head to toe and a slouch hat like a sideways beret and held a piece of paper with *Corporal Mark Boyd* printed on it—not that we could have missed him in his full uniform, when everyone else in the airport seemed to be dressed in t-shirts or summer dresses and flip-flops.

'Welcome to Australia, Corporal,' the soldier said to Mark. He saluted, then extended a hand. 'I'm Private McGinty.'

Outside, the air was dry, the sun a blinding white star in the sky that was impossible to look at directly. McGinty led us through the parking lot opposite the terminal, pushing a cart with our bags piled high, telling us that the next few days were set to be even hotter. 'Mid to high thirties,' he said, which didn't sound hot to me until I realised he wasn't working in Fahrenheit.

McGinty unlocked a white Fairlane with army plates. Inside, the air was stifling, and Mom left the door open while the men loaded our cases into the trunk.

It was a ninety-minute drive to Queenscliff. McGinty made conversation in the front seat with Mark, while Mom and I took in the scenery (lots of yellowing fields and highways lined with trees). Mom looked especially tired. Her back hurt, she said, and she'd hardly slept on the twenty-five-hour flight from Minneapolis, with brief stops in Los Angeles and Seattle. Being seven and a half months pregnant didn't help.

'Heard you were in Iraq,' McGinty said to Mark as we sped along an expressway on what, to me, was the wrong side of the road. The steering wheel was on the wrong side too. Was everything going to be the wrong way around in Australia? Maybe it had something to do with being in the southern hemisphere? It didn't look at all like an expressway at home. Where were the billboards?

'Uh-huh,' was Mark's only response. I wasn't sure if he didn't want to talk about it in front of me and Mom, or if he didn't want to talk about it all. He rarely mentioned it at home.

'How was that?' McGinty asked, flicking on his blinker and changing lanes to pass a semi.

'I was there for Desert Shield, then all through the campaign.'

'But that wasn't long, was it?'

'Six weeks in the air, four days on the ground. Most of the boys were home by spring. Hardly any casualties. On our side, at least.' Mark turned his attention to the expansive fields outside the window. 'You boys get off the base much?'

'From time to time. We might go into town for a bite or for a drink at the pub. But we've got everything we need on the island.'

'Swan Island?'

'Yeah. It's just us ASIS guys. Plus the private golf course on the western part. You play golf?'

'No. What else is there to do in town?'

'There's fishing.'

My ears pricked up at that.

'Not much of a fisherman,' said Mark.

'Swimming at the beach. Water sports. Hikes. The lighthouse. You can catch the ferry across to the Mornington Peninsula, have lunch. Takes about forty minutes. You can even take your car with you.'

Mark made a low noise of acknowledgement. He wasn't usually this short with new people. Maybe he was tired from the flight. Or maybe it was an army-rank thing.

'There's the fort, too,' McGinty went on. 'You can take a tour.'

'Is that on the base?'

The soldier shook his head. 'On the mainland. It's decommissioned now. But Queenscliff's played a big part in Australia's military history, for a little seaside town.'

He pronounced Australia like 'Ah-stray-yah'. Was that how you were supposed to say it?

We continued through a small city called Geelong and then along a two-lane road, passing a sign that read: BOROUGH OF QUEENSCLIFFE.

'This is it,' McGinty said as we coasted by a high school on the left, overlooking a sprawling green bay.

Mom and I sat up in our seats, interested to see the place where we'd be living for the next two years so Mark could fulfil his contract to the Australian Army. What he'd be doing, I didn't know, and didn't much care either. In any case, I knew better than to ask.

'How far are we from the base?' Mark asked.

McGinty dipped his head, looked through the reflection on the windshield and pointed straight ahead. 'About half a kay that way. There's a bridge on the other side of town, and a checkpoint. It's the only way onto the island by car or foot.'

We rounded a few bends and seemed to come to a main street of sorts. Entering Queenscliff was like stepping back in time. Mom stared at the wide street, lined on both sides with low-rise period buildings—the Vue Grand Hotel, a two-storey post office with a clock tower in the middle and a library that, like the post office, had probably been there since the 1800s. We stared in wonder, as if we were entering Willy Wonka's chocolate factory or some kind of promised land.

Further on, we saw modern stores—a bakery, a butcher shop, a gas station on a corner and a grocery store called Foodland.

'This is Hesse Street,' McGinty said. 'It's the main drag. I'm taking you the long way so you can get a feel for where we are.'

'Busy little town,' Mark said.

McGinty gave off a puff of laughter. 'Most of this lot are holidaymakers. Population swells from three thousand to—I don't know—fourteen, fifteen thousand in summer. It's dead here in winter.'

The storefronts thinned out and Hesse Street dipped toward the bay beyond a wide expanse of straw-coloured grass. We followed the road around to the left, continuing along the shore. Even with the car windows closed I could smell the sea.

35

'Over there's the old railway,' McGinty was saying. 'Only takes tourists to Drysdale now.'

Mom craned her head and then smiled at me, as if it were all so exciting.

'And there's Swan Island, out in the bay there.'

Across the bay sat a dark, expansive mass of land half-hidden beneath a shadowy canopy of trees. High clouds shrouded part of the island in black, even on that bright day, giving it an ominous, almost menacing presence. I couldn't imagine what went on there, but it was bound to be something important and covert.

We followed the coast for a few hundred yards, my eyes still fixed on that island, until the road wound around to the left, up a hill.

'This is Mercer Street,' McGinty said. 'Where the house is.'

We passed a stately church then McGinty pulled up in front of an old home set back from the street. Small trees in the yard concealed a squared-off clapboard house with a porch in front. It wouldn't have looked out of place in one of the older suburbs of Minneapolis, like North Loop or Linden Hills.

A long driveway ran along the left-hand side of the house, but a low metal gate barred entry.

McGinty parked the car nose first into the hem of the tree lawn. We climbed out and stood looking up at the house. It was painted white, with light-blue trim around the windows and across the crown of the porch. Two years. By the time we left, I would have a two-year-old half-brother or sister. Maybe another sibling on the way. High school.

'This is it,' McGinty said, clapping his hands together like a TV gameshow host. 'I hope you'll make some fantastic memories here.'

36

7

The house was already furnished. The army owned it, McGinty explained, using it to house people, and sometimes their families, stationed on Swan Island or at what he called the staff college. The period style of the exterior didn't match the interior decor. Inside was modern, with exposed brick walls and floor-to-ceiling wood panelling in the den.

We deposited our bags at the door and the four of us wandered through the house, McGinty pointing out its features. It smelled freshly painted and the beige-coloured carpet in the bedrooms looked as if it had never been walked on.

My bedroom was on the right-hand side of the house. It had two twin beds, the mattresses bare, and a desk in the corner. In a built-in closet, wire hangers dangled from a stainless-steel rail. I didn't have much to unpack—only the clothes in my suitcase—until the rest of our stuff arrived by ship in a week's time.

Mark had told me I should only bring clothes and a few toys. (What twelve-year-old had 'toys'? You could tell he'd never had any kids of his own.) I'd brought a few novels to tide me over—*How to Eat Fried Worms*, two *Three Investigators* novels and Stephen King's *Four Past Midnight* story collection.

The house had a large yard out back; maybe Mark would let me get a dog? I had one back in Minneapolis—a beagle named Davey—but he was on loan to my cousins until we moved back.

With the tour finished, McGinty wished us well, gave Mark a number to call if we needed anything, and confirmed Mark's pick-up time on Monday morning.

Mom spent the first hour in the kitchen—cleaning inside every cupboard and taking inventory of the pots and pans, dinnerware and glasses. Even from my bedroom I could hear her muttering to herself about things she should have brought from home or, as it turned out, didn't need to. 'Oh, shoot! I knew I shoulda packed the— Mark! There's no Mr. Coffee.'

'So, we'll buy one, Cathy,' Mark called from somewhere else in the house—probably the den. 'I'm sure Australia has coffee makers.'

'But you'll want your coffee in the morning.'

'I'll survive for one day.'

'*You* might,' she said in a quieter voice.

I sat on one of the twin beds looking at the empty space, only four books on the shelf. Mom soon emerged in the doorway holding a stack of linens, handed them to me, then left again.

I made both beds, not sure which one I would sleep in yet. Maybe I'd use them both? Maybe I'd make a friend and we could have sleepovers.

I was tucking in the last sheet when Mom appeared in the doorway again.

'All set?'

'Yeah.'

'It's a nice room you've got here.'

'I guess.'

Mom stood in the doorframe, holding herself in the way she always did now—crabwise hands pressed into her tailbone, belly protruding, leaning slightly backward from the hips.

'Hon, Mark and I are gonna run to the store. Want to come with?'

I shook my head. 'I might go for a walk.'

'Okey-dokey. But don't get lost! You know our address, right?'

I nodded.

'Do you want anything special from the store?'

'Cereal. Cinnamon Toast Crunch, if they have it.'

'Okay. Anything else?'

'Peanut butter. Jelly.'

She waved a small piece of paper I hadn't noticed she was holding. 'Top of the list!' She flinched, touching her bulging stomach.

'You okay, Mom?'

She pursed her lips together. 'Jelly Bean just gave me a kick is all. You like your room?'

'Sure. It's fine.'

'You did a super job of the beds.'

I gave her a look. I'd been making my own bed since the first grade.

She stepped into the room and sat on one of the beds, tapping the thin blanket. I sat in the space right by her so our arms were touching.

'It's a big change, I know,' she said. 'With Mark, and a

new country. But we're in it together, right? We'll look after each other. And your little brother or sister.'

'Sure, Mom.'

She patted my leg. 'It's gonna be great. You'll see.'

I set off down Mercer Street, in the same direction we'd come from. All around me was ocean, I could sense it, but I also knew it from a map I'd seen of Queenscliff.

Back in Minneapolis, I'd had to go all the way into the Central Library to find a map of Australia detailed enough to include it. I found the state of Victoria at the most south-eastern part of the country (if you didn't include the island of Tasmania), shaped kind of like a right-angled triangle. The bottom, flat part of the triangle had a small chunk nibbled out, right in the middle, and on the west of this chewed-out parcel of land, which was surrounded by a bay, was the Bellarine Peninsula. On its southernmost tip, a narrow tongue of land extended into the sea: that was Queenscliff. I'd paid ten cents for the librarian to copy the map for me.

Walking up Mercer, this map imprinted on my mind, I knew that ocean surrounded me on three sides, so almost any way I walked I would hit it. I turned the corner at the top and followed the railway line back to the main street, but this time I turned left and headed for the water.

My dad would have loved this place, I thought. He loved the water, would have loved all this ocean and good weather. He'd be in his outdoorsy element.

The ocean held a kind of mystique for me, as it had for my dad. Minnesota had lakes, thousands of them, and I'd spent countless hours on them and by them with Dad, but the ocean was different. It was endless, stretching for miles. The vastness of it both mesmerised and scared me. I'd never swum in an ocean and had only been to an actual beach a few times.

I continued along the shore, swarming with people baking under the sun. The tide came in and receded, each time leaving a sparkle on the sand. Overhead, gulls dipped and soared against a peerless blue sky.

Everything felt alive and new. I'd left a snowy Minnesota, sat on a cramped plane forever, and now I was here, in the sunshine, breathing in the sea air, soaking up the sun. It was as if I'd crossed into another dimension, where things kind of resembled the States but where the people spoke funny and drove on the wrong side of the road.

Up ahead was the patrolled bridge to Swan Island that McGinty had mentioned. It was long and narrow with low-slung steel barriers on either side. At its entrance was a guard house, and as I got closer I could see the boom gate blocking the road and strongly worded signage threatening anyone who entered without authorisation. This was where Mark would go to work each day.

Beyond the bridge was a pontoon, accessible by a smaller bridge that was more like a gangplank with white railing. Kids swam around this compact pontoon; some fished from the top of it. Many of the kids looked to be around my age and there didn't seem to be any parents watching them. What if they drowned?

I crossed the gangplank and stood at the end of the pontoon, gazing at the water, appreciating that I could have this view whenever I wanted for the next two years. Squinting, I raised my hand to block the stab of the sun's harsh rays. I couldn't imagine it ever being cold or rainy here. I already knew it didn't snow in this part of the world.

'Oi! You!'

A kid about my age, holding a fishing pole, beckoned me over with an upward tilt of his chin. 'Give us a hand, would ya? I've caught a big one.'

I stepped closer and waited for instructions, but the kid didn't give me any. Instead, I stood there watching as he worked the fish closer and closer by pulling the tip of the fishing pole up, then reeling quickly as he dropped the tip down. He took a few steps back, then quick-reeled the slack as he stepped forward again. He seemed to be fighting with the fish, keeping the line taut. 'I'm tiring him out,' he said, like it was all part of some grand plan.

I wondered again what I was doing there. This kid didn't seem to need my help at all.

He drew the line closer and I got my first sight of the fish as it thrashed on the line at the water's surface.

'What is it?' I asked, leaning in for a better look. The other anglers around us were looking now, too.

'Flathead. Grab that net, would ya?'

I found the round fishing net on the pontoon beside his bare, brown feet and picked it up by its short wooden handle. I held it out over the water and the kid kept reeling in the line until the fish was dangling at chest height. I stuck the net under and he lowered the fish in.

'It's pretty big,' he said. 'A female, I reckon.'

He placed the pole on the pontoon and took the net from me, admiring his catch for a moment. He crouched down, lay the net on the boards and worked the hook from her mouth.

'She's a beauty,' he said. 'Pretty old but still got lots of breeding in her.'

A beauty? She was nearing a foot and half long, an ugly shade of speckled brown with a head wider than her body and eyes that bulged in two squishy lumps; she looked to me like a catfish.

Satisfied, he picked up the net again, fish still inside, held it above the water and turned it upside down. The fish plopped back into the bay and swam away.

'Why'd you do that?' I asked. Maybe fishing was illegal? Maybe flatheads were poisonous?

'Big flatties are too valuable to kill. She's got lots of spawning seasons in her yet.'

He spoke with the authority of a fully grown man.

Now that the excitement was over, I got my first proper look at him, this kid sitting on the pontoon, readying to bait up again. His hair was long all over and windswept, brown, but flecked with gold from hours in the sun. His tan was so baked in, it looked like he must've been born that way. (I was suddenly aware of my pasty complexion. I'd been walking for ten minutes already and it would be another ten back. I didn't have a cap and wasn't wearing sunscreen, so I was bound to get a sunburn.)

Beside him was an open tackle box: brightly coloured lures, reels of fishing line, a set of battered pliers, a small tube of sunscreen, a plastic box of hooks and sinkers, a sodden box of bandaids, nail clippers, a blue spray can of something called Aerogard, and a tailor's measuring tape unfurled and snaking around the other contents.

'You on holidays?' he asked me as he rummaged around in it.

'No, we just moved here.'

'Where from?'

He grabbed the pliers and snipped the lure off the end of his line—a golden-scaled fish with two sets of hooks dangling from its underside.

'Minnesota.'

'Where's that?'

'America!'

He nodded. 'That's why you talk that way. What year are you in?'

Nineteen ninety-two, I thought, perplexed by the question. What year was *he* living in?

'At school,' he clarified.

'Sixth.'

'Me too! Are you going to Queenscliff Primary?'

'Start Monday.'

'Cool. What's your name?'

'Andrew.'

He placed a hand on his bare chest. 'Tom.'

When he removed his hand, I noticed that his chest dipped inward, as if his breastbone had sunken into it. It looked like the centre of his torso had been scooped out, leaving a small dent.

'You like fishing?' he asked.

'Sure.'

I'd fished a lot at home when I was younger, but hadn't been much since Dad died.

'Cool,' Tom said again.

'Do you throw everything back?'

He smiled with one corner of his mouth. 'No.'

'What are you trying to catch?'

'Whiting, trevally, leatherjackets.'

Leather jackets? Was that a euphemism for something? I must have looked confused because he explained.

'It's a kind of fish. Leatherjacket. One word.'

I wondered if he liked words as much as I did. If he did, we could be friends.

'Is this a good place to fish?' I asked.

'It's good to die.'

'What?'

'To die. It's good.'

'What?' I repeated.

'To. Day. It. Is. Good.'

'Oh . . . *today*.'

'That's what I said.'

'I thought you said—' I shook my head. 'Isn't it better to fish when the sun's down?'

'Sure. If you can be arsed getting up that early. In the daytime, it depends on the tide. Best is at high tide or on the change.'

Something burst out of the water in front of the pontoon and I jumped backward. 'What the heck was that?'

Tom was unfazed. 'Fur seal. They can be kind of annoying when you're trying to fish.'

Seals? Wow.

He handed me the golden fish-shaped lure he'd snipped from the end of his line. 'Thanks heaps for your help.'

Was he giving it to me?

I didn't take it at first so he held it up a bit higher. 'For luck.'

I took the lure, careful to avoid the hooks.

'Thanks,' I said. 'I better go.'

He touched his fingers to his brow in a salute. 'See ya round, Drew.'

8

Mom found some placemats in a drawer and asked me to lay the table for supper. In the States, Mark sat at the head, with Mom and me sitting either side of him. We'd sat the same way when Dad lived with us. I wondered how it would be when the baby was old enough to sit at the table too.

The placemats were hard, cork-backed and featured colourful paintings of Australian landmarks like the Opera House and Ayers Rock by an artist named Ken Done.

'I couldn't get Sprite,' Mom said, placing a large plastic bottle of Mello Yello on the table.

'No Mountain Dew?' I asked.

She shook her head. 'We're trying new things, right?'

Mark was already seated, with a squat brown bottle of beer at his fingertips.

Mom dished out cold cuts and coleslaw that she'd made herself.

'Andrew, what did you see on your walk?' she asked too formally. She poured pop into our glasses.

'The beach.'

Mark pointed his fork at me. 'You need to watch out for sharks here. They're everywhere. They'll swim right up to the beach and take a bite out of you.'

I'd seen *Jaws* in the fourth grade and it had put me off swimming in the open sea for life.

'I saw a seal,' I said to shift the image of the shark from my mind.

'They're okay,' Mark said with an authority I didn't think he had any right to. 'But Australia has the most dangerous sharks in the world. Ever heard of the great white?'

Back on the sharks. I shook my head.

Mark took a swig of his beer, eyeing the green-and-red label. 'Deadliest snakes in the world here, too.'

'Now, Mark, don't go scaring him,' Mom said.

I shovelled a fork load of slaw into my mouth, crunching on the cabbage.

'I'm looking out for him, Cathy.' He glanced again at me. 'And watch out for rips. They can pull you right out to sea, just like that.' He snapped his fingers.

I wished I had a dictionary on hand so I could look up the word 'rip'. I pictured a slimy green sea creature, water dripping from its fangs, its long, tentacle-like arms dragging me out to sea.

Mark rubbed his shoulder, as if he'd been lifting something heavy. 'Pass me that . . . um . . .' He squeezed his eyes closed. 'The red sauce over there.'

'The ketchup?' Mom said.

'Yeah.'

Mom handed the bottle to Mark. 'How about we all go for a walk down to the beach after supper? It's a nice night. I'm sure it's gonna be light for a few more hours.'

I trawled my mind for an excuse. It would have been okay if it was just me and Mom, but I didn't need to hear any more of Mark's chilling facts about Australia.

'Sure,' Mark said, upending the ketchup bottle over his meat and knocking the base with the heel of his hand.

Mark and my dad were opposites in every way. Mark was tall and muscular; Dad had been short and soft in the middle. Mark was strict and unrelenting in all aspects of his life—his close-cropped hair, his neat clothes, his polished shoes. Dad had a haircut every six months, wore the same clothes year after year, and only replaced his shoes when his toes started popping through the end. Mark was a soldier everywhere he went, in or out of uniform. He had a constant, watchful look about him, always surveying his surroundings. My dad moved through life as though in a dream, taking each day as it came, never sweating the small stuff like bill payments or planning a meal ahead of time.

How could Mom have loved two men that were so different?

After supper, Mom sat at the table, the newspaper spread in front of her. It was her nightly ritual after the dishes were done and the kitchen tidied—sitting with a coffee and reading the newspaper from cover to cover, sighing at the injustices, tutting over the inexplicable.

'No walk?' I said.

'No. Mark's . . . I don't know what he's doing. Got distracted with some darn thing.'

'What's news?' I asked, placing a hand on each of her shoulders.

'Sounds like Russia and the US are gonna be friends now. The Cold War's over apparently.'

She turned the page and I rested my chin on the crown of her head, smelling her shampoo. 'You don't believe it?'

'I don't trust that Boris Yeltsin, hon. Had his personal problems, I know that, and the people seem to love him, but he's still got all those nuclear weapons at his beck and call.'

'How 'bout just you and me go for a walk?' I suggested.

Mom twisted her head, searching for Mark. 'Well . . . okay. Better go find him, though. Tell him where we're going.'

I found Mark in the garage at the side of the house, the smell of trapped moisture and grass clippings in the air. The concrete floor was badly oil-stained and crumbling in sections, and it only had enough space for one car. Thin rods of light shone at an angle through three small multipaned windows set in the garage door, illuminating the contents: a manual reel lawnmower, an ancient spade and an outdoor broom. A freestanding cabinet stood in one corner, no doubt holding more garden tools.

Mark stood at the built-in workbench, his back to me, holding a pistol to the light, studying it.

'Mark?'

His body spasmed. 'Jesus Christ, boy. Don't sneak up on a man like that. Almost gave me a heart attack.'

'Sorry.'

I eyeballed the gun and Mark returned it to an open case on the timber workbench, furry with dust. 'Just looking for a safe place to store this.' He slammed the lid shut, making both me and the dust flinch.

'Mom and I are going to the beach.' Grudgingly, I added a couple more words: 'Wanna come?'

He ran a palm over his buzz cut, showing wet patches in the pits of his white undershirt. 'Nah, you two go. I'll finish up here.'

I turned to leave, but then he spoke again.

'Hey, Andrew? Watch out for sharks.'

Mom and I headed to a different beach from the one where I'd been that afternoon. It was 7 pm now, but the sand was still crowded with people: lying in the sun, tossing tennis balls and splashing in the shallows.

We traced the tideline barefoot, one of Mom's hands holding mine, the other supporting her belly. She walked with a constant arch in her back these days, toes pointing outward.

'Boy, it's still hot, right?' she said, narrowing her eyes against the sun. Then, anchoring a hand on one knee for support, she bent down, scooped up a handful of sea water and spilled it down her face, droplets falling onto her cotton dress.

'You okay, Mom?'

'Sure.'

I glanced at her stomach, swollen with the life growing inside it. 'Mom, how will Jelly Bean know when to come out?'

'It just will, hon. I guess when the baby outgrows me it'll know it's time to leave.' She squeezed my hand. 'You'll outgrow me again too one day, and you'll want to leave me for the next chapter of your life. College, girlfriends, what have you.'

I squeezed back. I couldn't imagine a world away from my mom, especially now that Dad was gone.

'Mom?'

'What, hon?'

'Mark . . . he seems different.'

She rolled her lips together. 'I know. The war, it . . .' She didn't finish the sentence.

I hadn't been Mark's biggest fan before he left for the Gulf, but at least back then he had a sense of humour. Now his moods were unpredictable, and the switch could flick at any moment.

'Be patient with him, okay? For me? With everything else going on, I don't need my two best guys not getting along.'

I nodded, looking across the bay at a container ship in the distance.

Mom exhaled. Then, with what looked like agonising difficulty, she leaned down to scoop up more water. This time she flung it at me.

'Hey!' I protested. Despite the heat, the water was still icy as it hit my skinny chest.

'Hey, yourself.' She kicked up water this time, dousing my t-shirt.

I quickly mobilised, kicking water straight back at her. She laughed and tried to move away but I had an advantage—I could duck and weave in a way she couldn't. I scooped up water with both hands and hurled it at her, soaking the front of her dress. She shrieked with the shock of it and then let out a peal of laughter, seeming not at all embarrassed by how her dress clung to her boobs and belly.

She held up both hands. 'Okay, okay. I surrender!'

I gave her my best villainous smile and planted dripping hands on my hips, stirring the sea water with one foot, teasing her.

She braved a step closer and grabbed my head in both her hands, kissing my wet hair repeatedly.

I was lucky to have her. But with Mark as the only other person in her life, she was just as lucky to have me.

9

The white light hit me first, just as it had the day I'd arrived in Melbourne with Mom and Mark twenty-six years ago. It was summer then, too. But January. Hot and dry.

I exchanged two hundred dollars at the airport, collected my rental car and took off along the expressway to the Bellarine Peninsula, twice having to consciously remind myself to drive on the left-hand side of the road.

I sped along the well-made road, flitting under the visor of soaring gumtrees, the sun blazing overhead and the AC on full. Fifteen minutes in, the glare having become unbearable, I pulled into a gas station for a pair of cheap sunglasses.

At the register, I fumbled with the bank notes. The currency had changed since '92. It was no longer made of paper but instead a kind of silky plastic.

Outside, I walked around to the wrong side of the car,

corrected, and climbed into the driver's seat. Back on the road, I continued south toward the coast, following the directions of the GPS. Nothing in particular ignited a memory, but the roads had a familiar feel about them—the same green road signs and distinct lack of billboards bordering the highways.

An hour and a half after leaving the airport, I drove into Queenscliff. I hadn't heard much about the town since leaving. Aside from the occasional social media post from Tia (Tom was also on Facebook but rarely posted), I had not seen the place in all that time. I'd never had the urge to look at it via Google Earth.

Switching off the distraction of the GPS voicing directions, I drove along a thin strip of land bordered by ocean on either side, the road dappled in the shade of tall cypress trees, past a large triangular patch of land where the high school once stood. I wound my way around a few bends, passing the majestic Royal Hotel (now called Hotel Q, and looking a lot fresher than it did in my memory), and glimpsing the black lighthouse at the far end of the street.

I turned left at the first roundabout then slowed at the second, the unchanged Uniting Church on my right, then continued down the single-lane main street, cars parked at forty-five-degree angles on either side of the road. At first glance, Queenscliff had not changed much, just as my seatmate on the plane had predicted. But something clenched in my stomach at the sight of it.

On the outside, it was still small, still rich with history. It was easy to look at parts of it and imagine the gold rush era we'd learned about in elementary school here—substitute the asphalt for a fine gravel and the cars for horse-drawn vehicles, maybe add the smell of horse manure and swarms of flies feasting on it—and you'd be easily transported back in time a hundred and fifty years.

I switched off the AC and powered down the window, hoping to catch a whiff of salty air. It was faint but there, and pieces of my life from '92 began to coalesce around me. I passed the old ice creamery, the fish-and-chip shop, the drugstore, the library where I'd spent many hours, the grand old post office—all seemingly untouched. It was as if the world here had stood still for twenty-six years, awaiting my return.

Passing the Vue Grand, as Hesse Street began its gentle slope toward the ocean, I started to clock small differences—the gas station on the corner was gone, so too the old grocery store, replaced with what looked like a clothing boutique. The faded marquee for Eddie's Emporium still hung over the sidewalk, but the store itself no longer existed in its previous dollar-store form.

I slowed the car as a tightness formed in my chest, but it passed, and I continued to the bottom of the street, turning right before it intersected with the ocean, and followed the road around, driving past the old Esplanade Hotel (now a brewhouse) and up Hobson Street to my accommodation, parking the Corolla at an angle in the street outside.

I vaguely remembered the building from my childhood. I'd never stayed there, of course, but it was hard to miss the two-storey, square structure with a pitched roof and large wraparound porches on both floors. Looking at it now, it called to mind a Southern plantation-style house you might find in Mississippi or Louisiana, with its narrow, white columns and slender wooden gallery posts.

I grabbed my bags from the trunk and climbed the four steps to the front door, entering a small reception area, heavy with warm colours and a miniature Christmas tree on the countertop.

The man behind the desk, about fifty and of Asian descent, wearing a name tag that said *Leon* along with the hotel's logo, looked up when I entered.

'Hi,' I said. 'Drew Iverson. Checking in.'

'Hi, Drew. Welcome.'

Leon tapped his keyboard, eyeing the screen. 'Still just the five nights?'

'Yeah.'

Leon had a full head of thick hair that swept up from his forehead and wore glasses with rims the colour of a summer sky. Flabby skin hung over the collar of a crisp blue button-down.

I looked to my left to a cosy lounge area with two couches, a fireplace and bookshelves lining the walls. A life-sized Santa mannequin stood in the corner. To my right was a small, casual restaurant, empty of people at this time of day.

'Let me just print this for you to check and sign,' Leon said. 'Is it just you?'

'Just me.'

I wondered what he made of me travelling alone. It was unlikely I'd be in Queenscliff—a seaside vacation town—on business.

The printer whirred and he handed me an A4 page with my contact information and the terms and conditions of my stay. I glanced at the contact details but didn't read the rest, and signed at the bottom. After dating it 12/11/18, I remembered that Australians write the day first, then the month and year. Never mind; they'd work it out.

'First time in Queenscliff?' Leon asked.

'No, but it's been a minute.'

He reviewed the page I'd just signed. 'You've come a long way. I hope we deliver for you. The weather's good, at least.'

I gave him a tight smile.

'I've popped you in room two-twelve.' Leon handed me a swipe card and pointed to a carpeted staircase to my left. 'Up the stairs, take a right. Give me a yell if you need anything.'

Room 212 was large, with an open fireplace that looked as if it had never been used. The walls were mid-grey with white trim, and a queen-size bed with white linen sat on carpet in a darker, hard-wearing grey.

A silver lamp with a long arm hung over a club chair and in the corner stood a clothing rack on casters, wrapped in white canvas—the closet, I guessed.

I opened a set of glass double doors and stepped onto the porch. It was ten or twelve feet deep and, although it ran the length of the building, large planters demarcated the sections reserved for each room. In my section were four white Adirondack chairs with orange-and-white striped pillows, and a wooden table painted white to match. I could see the ocean, although barely, through the pines lining the foreshore.

Back inside, I stripped out of my clothes, heavy with the stink of dry sweat from the long hours on the plane, the blast of heat as I stepped out of the airport and the drive to Queenscliff. I sat on the edge of the bed in my underwear and socks, making fists with my toes. The long flights had taken a toll on me, only some of which was due to lack of sleep.

Over the bed hung an artwork—a school of bright orange koi in a pond of azure blue, reminding me that I'd packed Tom's lure in my carry-on. For no reason I could think of; I'd never travelled with it before.

I took a quick shower and changed into shorts, a t-shirt and running shoes. Then, grabbing my sunglasses, I headed down the street on foot.

As I walked down Hesse, I took in the faces. It occurred to me that I could, conceivably, run into someone I knew from back then—a classmate, a teacher, a shopkeeper, a friend's parents. Would I even recognise them? Would they recognise me? How would they treat me if they did?

Although Queenscliff hadn't altered much, it did look different through adult eyes. I could appreciate the historic architecture in a way I couldn't as a child; as a kid the quaintness of the town had just seemed old-fashioned. Back then, I'd perceived Queenscliff as a place separate from the rest of the world, an untouched corner suspended in time. Seeing it now, it was as if that fantasy had come true. What had existed in my mind for the past twenty-six years as a diorama was now a real, in-living-colour place. If circumstances were different, I might have taken some pictures, posted them on Instagram, but I wasn't on vacation; I was here for a funeral.

I walked to the bottom of the street and continued through the roundabout, headed toward the water, past the bridge to Swan Island, where I expected to see the pontoon where I'd first met Tom. Instead, I was met with a part of town that time had forgotten—a crumbling sea wall and a bare gravel pavement now choked with weeds. The pontoon was gone.

I continued along the water, through a parking lot, to a modern marina housing boats that probably cost more than my house.

A tall observation tower overlooked a chic harbour. In the water, two stingrays glided between the boats—dive charters, deck boats and catamarans. Gone was the fishing trawler that sold fresh fish on weekends. Nobody was fishing off the timbered walkways. Maybe it was banned now?

I liked progress, but the development felt out of step with the

Queenscliff I remembered—a quiet, Victorian-era town known for its historic pubs and proud military history.

I followed the shoreline east, stopping to look across the bay to Swan Island. It was exactly the same. I don't know what I'd expected to see or feel. It held such power in my mind. That island was the reason we'd come to Queenscliff. Had it not existed, who knew how my life might have turned out?

10

I hadn't let Tom's family know I was coming. I'd met his wife, Tia, only once before. When they were honeymooning in the US they'd stopped in Minneapolis and stayed with me and Claire for two nights. I hadn't seen his parents since I was twelve, but I assumed they were still alive—at least, I hadn't seen anything to the contrary on Facebook—and still lived in Queenscliff. I'd never met his kids but had tracked their growth online. Adam must be twelve or thirteen now, Missy maybe nine or ten.

My plan was just to show up at the church, spend another four nights in Queenscliff, then two in Melbourne to justify the distance I'd travelled. I'd packed the one suit I owned—dark grey with a faint pinstripe. The pants were too wide at the ankle to be fashionable anymore and the jacket was slightly big (I'd lost weight since I'd bought it ten years earlier); the shirt and necktie were relatively new. But it turned out I needn't have bothered, because when I got to the church the next morning, I discovered that few men wore suits. Pants, yes. Shirts, yes, but hardly any neckties. It was, after all, thirty-two degrees on the local Celsius scale.

I'd never had much reason to pass the Catholic church in '92. Hardly even registered it was there. It was located in the high part of the town, where anyone who had money lived. The houses were much nicer there, the views more picturesque and the gardens more carefully tended.

Thankfully, the church was cool inside. I found a seat midway along the rows of timber pews, Bibles poking out of small slots at each end. Tia sat in the first row, her children on either side, but I couldn't get a good view of them. Adam, from the back, sat nearly as tall as his mother, and Missy clung onto Tia's arm, her face buried in her mother's shoulder. In the row behind, I recognised Tom's parents, Gavin and Gillian. They'd always insisted I call them by their first names, as did all the adults I met in Australia that year, aside from my teachers. Next to them was Tom's older brother, Henry.

The priest delivered a short eulogy about Tom's life—how he grew up in Queenscliff, started a successful fishing charter business and was raising young children. He spoke of a man devoted to his neighbours, to the town, to his work and his family. It was strange to think of him in this way—as a grown man with family responsibilities and a business to run. That was ridiculous, of course. I, too, was fully grown with (some) responsibilities, but I still pictured Tom as that twelve-year-old, even though I had seen him in person in the intervening years, and stayed in touch online.

Henry spoke on behalf of the family. 'As a kid,' Henry said, 'Tom was always building something. He tinkered in Dad's shed constructing everything from billycarts to jewellery boxes. He spent a lot of time in the shed as an adult, too, but ever since installing a fridge and wiring up a TV in there, I don't think he was building much. Maybe his belly.'

This met with a rustle of laughter.

Henry was three years older than Tom and me, and I didn't see him much during the period I lived in Queenscliff. He was always in his room listening to music, devising dance routines, tailoring his own clothes. He treated us, and everyone else, with a kind of contempt, as if he just knew that everyone was against him and so he might as well erect the wall himself.

'Tom loved his boat,' Henry went on. 'He loved the water. He spent more of his waking hours out there than anywhere else.'

I looked again at the front page of the order-of-service booklet. *Thomas Adam Howell. 16.9.1979–6.12.2018.* I looked for a long time at the dash between his birth and death dates. Florence Nightingale had talked about the dash and what that little line represented—a whole life; everything that person achieved between birth and death. Tom's dash should have been longer. It should have kept going.

When Henry returned to his seat, a photo montage began to play on a screen above the altar. It traced Tom's life from birth, through elementary school, adolescence, young adulthood, marriage, fatherhood and work.

I'd held on to my tears until that point, but now they came in a flood. I cried for my lost friend, for the husband and father in that casket. But more than that, I was crying for how loyal Tom had been; how he'd proved himself to be the kind of friend you are lucky to get once in a lifetime. How we'd shared a life-changing experience together but could never talk about it.

And how talking about it might have changed things.

With the service over, the casket, draped in flowers, was carried up the aisle by six pallbearers—Tom's brother, his dad, his son and three other men I didn't recognise. This was when I got my first good look at Adam in the flesh. He had Tom's eyes, and maybe the same mouth, but that's where the similarities ended. He was more like a male version of Tia—the dark skin tone, her nose, the same triangular face.

Tia and Missy followed the pallbearers, and the other guests filed out behind them.

Outside, they loaded the casket into the back of a waiting hearse parked in the church's forecourt.

Tia, Adam and Missy huddled together near the back of the funeral car and, one by one, people coasted past them offering condolences.

With the sun belting down on us, I shrugged off my jacket, flung it over my shoulder and loosened my tie. I slid on my sunglasses, but they could not fully diffuse the glare radiating off the white concrete under our feet.

'Drew?'

Henry was at my side.

'Henry.'

'My God, Drew.' He studied my face for a moment then gripped my hand between both of his, shaking it enthusiastically. 'How are you?'

'Fine. Fine. Thank you.'

He looked younger than Tom had in the pictures I'd seen recently, his skin clear and unblemished, and his eyes bright—healthy living, probably. Maybe a good skincare regimen.

'I didn't know you lived in Australia,' Henry said.

'I don't.'

'You came all the way from America?'

'Yeah.'

'For this?'

'Yes.'

'Wow. Tom would be . . . he would . . .' The words caught in his throat.

I squeezed Henry's shoulder, feeling muscle under his jacket. 'I'm so sorry about Tom.'

'Thank you. It's all a bit hard to believe. He was the youngest. He was meant to outlive us all.'

'How are your folks doing?'

Henry took a breath. 'Mum doesn't know what to do with herself. But it's made me realise that people go through this all the time. You hear about deaths on the roads every day. But you don't stop to think of the effects. How the pain ripples out. Makes you appreciate what you've got just that little bit more.'

I had not stopped to think of that. Until today, Tom's death had not seemed real; it was like some story you hear on the news but which is happening so far away that its tentacles don't reach you. That's exactly what Henry was talking about.

Then Henry said, 'I just wish maybe he'd . . . I don't know . . . talked to someone.'

I wasn't sure what he meant by this and tried to read his face for a clue, but his expression gave nothing away as he stared at the crowd milling about in front of the church. So I asked him point-blank: 'What do you mean?'

Something flashed behind Henry's eyes—a fleeting look of apprehension—but then it was gone. 'How long are you staying?' he asked, as if he hadn't heard my question.

'Oh. A few nights here in Queenscliff then Melbourne for a couple more. Then home.'

'Well, we've certainly turned on the weather for you.'

'It's snowing in Minneapolis.'

'Oh, yes, of course it would be. I was in New York two Christmases ago. It was spectacular.'

'Work or vacation?'

'Bit of both. I'm the director of a theatre company. So . . . Broadway.'

'Fabulous.'

Fabulous? I couldn't recall ever using the word before. But it felt right. And his occupation didn't surprise me. Henry had always had a deep vein of creativity coursing through him, like a low, stifled hum waiting to burst into song. I'd always found it easier to bond with creative people—they understand the hustle and the struggle that burbles beneath the launches and the lights and the red carpets.

I should talk to Henry more while we were both in town, I thought. The lead character in the manuscript I'd just sent Eliot was in the theatre. Maybe I could get some useful insights from him?

'I don't need to ask what you're doing,' Henry said, leaning in. 'I read your book.'

'Really?'

'Of course. Borrowed it from Tom.'

I'd learned to not ask what people thought of my novel in these situations. If they wanted to say, they would. Otherwise, they might say something generic (*It was great!*), in which case you knew they weren't that enamoured with it, or *I enjoyed it.* It was only when people's faces really lit up, or when they told you exactly what they liked about it (*I loved the tension between Grace and Joby, and how the mechanical problems with the car symbolised the deep fractures in their relationship*), that you knew they were the real deal.

'Have you seen Mum and Dad yet?' he asked.

'Not yet.'

'They'll be rapt to see you. Wow.' He shook his head, a smile pulling at the sides of his mouth. 'I still can't believe you came all this way. I'm heading back to Melbourne first thing in the morning, but we can catch up more at the wake, okay?'

'Sure.'

He shook my hand again. 'Good to see you, Drew.'

I felt ridiculous standing there on my own, the sun bearing down on me, and it was too early to head to the house for the wake. Maybe I could duck back to the hotel and change into something cooler? I thought about approaching Tom's parents but they were surrounded by a circle of people. Instead, I joined the line to offer my condolences to Tia and the kids.

The line moved at a glacial pace, rivulets of sweat dripping down the sides of my body from my armpits. I wasn't wearing sunscreen and imagined the skin on my thinning crown reddening.

When I reached Tia, she at first looked at me with a question, seemed to decide she didn't know me, then gave me a small smile. 'Thank you for coming.'

I removed my sunglasses. 'Tia, it's Drew.'

'Drew?' She flung her arms around me. 'Oh, Drew,' she said into my hair. She stepped back. 'Drew.' She put a hand to her mouth and started crying. 'Kids, this is Drew.' They clearly didn't know who I was but smiled politely. 'Tom would have been so touched that you came.' She lay a flat palm over her chest. 'Wow, you came. Were you already in Australia?'

'No.'

She turned to her children. 'Drew was one of Dad's best friends. He lives in America. He came all the way here.' She turned back to me. 'He would have loved to have seen you.'

Tia hadn't lost any of her New Zealand accent—Dad's *bist* friends; he *luvs* in America.

'Me too. Tia, I'm so sorry.'

I wanted to look more closely at the kids, searching for traces of Tom, but didn't want to appear creepy. Missy had long dark hair like her mother, woven into braids close to her head, and a heart-shaped face. Adam had turned away to talk to a boy his age standing beside him.

Tia clasped my hand. 'Thank you. You're coming back to the house, of course?'

'Yes. Yes.'

'Good. Where are you staying? You can stay with us.'

'Thank you, but I've got a hotel.'

'You should have let me know.'

'I didn't want to . . .'

I sensed that I was holding up the line of people waiting to offer their condolences. I squeezed Tia's hand. 'I'll see you back at the house.'

Ten minutes later, two funeral directors slid the casket into the hearse and, ever so gently, closed the large rear door.

I slotted my sunglasses back on and walked in the direction of my rental car, plagued by a disturbing sense that another door, somewhere, was still open.

11

Tom and Tia lived on Richards Street, on the west side of town, near the water. *Near the water.* Everything was near the water in Queenscliff.

Cars lined the street outside the house. I parked, then undid my necktie and flung it across the passenger seat, on top of my jacket.

The house was a double-fronted clapboard on a corner with a basic garden out front. Lines of easy-care shrubs poked through generously spaced pickets, and small parcels of thick grass bordered a brick path, set in a basket-weave pattern, curling from the gate to the porch.

The front door was already open and I followed an older couple down a narrow corridor, lightly varnished boards underfoot, taking in the framed photographs lining the walls as I went: Adam and Missy at various ages; Tom and Tia on their wedding day; the kids with a golden retriever; Tia sitting on the bow of a ship with wind blowing hair across her face.

I helped myself to a pre-poured glass of beer from a table in the living room and wandered back into the kitchen area. Large windows opened to a paved backyard that overlooked the bay and Swan Island. A faux Christmas tree, inappropriately festive, stood in the corner but without presents underneath.

Someone came to stand in front of me—a woman in her sixties, long white hair with a red streak in the front. 'Are you Drew Iverson?'

'Yes,' I answered. I mined my mental files for an image of this woman. Had she been one of my teachers? A classmate's parent? Nothing nudged a memory loose.

'I'm Margot,' she said. 'Margot Mackenzie-Maris. I was so excited to hear we have a famous author in our midst—and all the way from America!'

Something inside me twitched.

'Tia told me,' Margot said. 'She knew I'd be interested, because I'm a writer myself.'

Margot spoke with the *other* kind of Australian accent—a more cultivated, private school inflection with rounded vowels that were an unmistakable reminder of Australia's modern British heritage.

'Oh, wonderful,' I said. 'What do you write?'

She adjusted the multicoloured chiffon scarf around her neck. 'Published my first collection last year.'

'Collection?'

'Short stories. They examine the intersection between gender and food.'

'Those things intersect?'

'My word, they do.'

'Interesting.'

'Copies are available from my website: Margot-Mackenzie-Maris-dot-com.'

'I'll check it out.'

That was a lie. I would not check it out. But that's what writers say to other writers all the time: *Can't wait to read your book!* They never do.

'What are you working on now?' she asked me. 'Another *blockbuster*, I hope.'

I didn't know what Tia had told her, but the words 'blockbuster' and 'Drew Iverson' had no right sharing a sentence. But I wasn't about to correct her. No one knew how successful *Saving Grace* was—or wasn't. Even if I had admitted it only sold two thousand copies, she wouldn't know if that was good or bad in the American market.

'A new novel,' I said. 'Just finished it, actually.'

'What's this one about?'

When people ask what a book is about, they don't actually want to know what it's about, they want to know what happens. Still, I hadn't yet come up with a short form of words to describe it—my 'elevator pitch'—so found myself flailing.

'It's about a twenty-something actor named Grady who moves from Memphis to LA to pursue his acting dream. He gets an agent, starts auditioning, and then a pilot he stars in gets picked up. Meanwhile, he meets a Warner Bros tour guide named Skylar, also a struggling actor, and they fall hopelessly in love. But then his TV show bombs and he and Skylar discover they want different things.'

I sipped my beer and Margot stood there in silence with an expectant look on her face, as though waiting for the punchline.

When she realised I was done, she said, 'Oh, that's it? Great. Sounds . . . great. So, how's it end?'

'He goes back to Memphis and joins a local theatre company.'

'Oh.'

'But it's good. He loves the stage. It's his first love, really. And he's fine. He's happy. He finds his place.'

I really needed to work on my pitch.

'Well, that's good then. What's its title?'

'*Woodland.* It's a play on Hollywoodland. That's what Hollywood used to be called back in the day. And I love the idea of Grady being lost—you know: in the woods.'

She made a hmm sound. Was she impressed or confused? 'And when can we expect to see *Woodland* on our shelves?'

I exhaled deeply. 'Next year, hopefully. It's with my agent now.' I held up crossed fingers, completely aware of how dickish I must have looked but unable to stop myself.

'Excuse me, Margot. I'm going to say hello to Gillian.'

'Lovely to meet you!'

I found Tom's mom weaving through the living room with a platter of sandwich triangles, people telling her repeatedly to stop—that they would take over—but nobody did. Maybe she appreciated the excuse to keep moving, not having to pretend she could think of anything other than her dead son and not wanting to have to try.

I moved into her path and she looked up. 'Hello, Gillian. It's Drew Iverson.'

'Drew!' She handed the platter to a woman standing nearby then she hugged me, smelling of citrus. 'How are you, my darling? Henry told me you'd come.'

'I'm good. I'm so sorry about Tom.'

Her eyes filled with tears and she nodded to acknowledge my condolences. She placed her hand on the arm of the woman who had taken the platter.

'You okay, Gillian?' the woman asked. She was younger than me, probably around thirty, and wore a ridiculously bright dress—too bright for a funeral. I liked her straightaway; she gave zero fucks.

'Yes, darling, I'm . . .' She looked at me. 'This is Meryn,' she said. 'She works at one of the ice-cream shops in town.' Gillian turned back to Meryn. 'This is Drew. He lived here for—what, six months?—when the boys were in primary school.'

'Only six months?' Meryn asked.

'Less,' I said.

'I guess six months can feel like years when you're a kid,' she said. 'I remember summer holidays lasting forever.'

'It felt like a lot longer to me too,' I said. 'But we had to go back to the States.'

'Oh.' She regarded me quizzically for a moment before something clicked into place. '*Now* I know who you are.' She tipped her head to the side, understanding dawning, but then confusion creased her brow. 'You came back?'

I nodded.

'I never walk down your old street,' Gillian said. 'I can't pass that house without thinking about what happened there.'

I took another sip of beer, not knowing what to say.

Meryn restitched the thread of the conversation. 'We always said it was haunted as kids. I think the defence force eventually sold it to some sea-changers from Melbourne. I don't know who they are, but no doubt they've heard about its history.'

I hadn't considered the legacy my family had left behind

when we departed Queenscliff so suddenly. How the incident might have affected the town, taken away its innocence for a time. The house on Mercer Street was now the subject of local legend. I imagined kids daring other kids to break in or sneak into the backyard looking for ghosts. Boo Radley, perhaps.

'You're married, I think Tom told me?' Gillian said, probably to change the subject more than anything.

'I am. Her name is Claire.'

'Is Claire a writer too?'

'God, no. She's the CEO of a non-profit.'

'No kiddies?'

I shook my head. 'We decided against it.'

'Oh,' Gillian said. 'Some people do. Gavin's around here somewhere. He'd love to see you.'

'I'll find him later.'

Outside, a basketball vibrated off a ring and I peered out the window. Adam was there, still in his black dress pants but with the sleeves of his shirt pushed to the elbows, perspiration glazing his face. Something about the way he held himself, the way he moved, reminded me of Tom.

Instead of seeking out Tom's dad, I wound my way through the rear section of the house—a living room with a beaten-up dining table and two couches in an L shape around a wall-mounted TV—to the backyard. The yard was a decent size but without a lawn. The half closest to the house was paved in brick, and an aluminium garage filled the back half. Two older men puffed on cigarettes and Adam shot baskets from close to the ring, landing most of them.

I watched Adam for a moment. The downcast look on his face was hard to interpret. Sadness? Teenage petulance?

I moved closer and raised my hands, showing Adam my

palms. He passed me the ball and I took a shot, missing. Adam caught the rebound and threw it back. I tried again, the pressure greater this time, but missed a second time. A sportsman, I was not.

'You like basketball?' I asked.

'S'okay.'

Over the top railing of the timber fence I could see Swan Bay, Swan Island looming in the distance.

'Do you follow the NBA?' I asked.

'Nuh.' He took a shot. The basket looked lower than regulation height, and the red, white and blue net, faded by the sun, hung unevenly around the ring.

'I'm Drew.'

'I know.'

'You in high school now, Adam?'

I remembered that Australians don't have middle school. They go straight from what they call primary school to high school.

'Year 7.' He took another shot, the ball swishing through the net.

'You're about the same age as I was when I met your dad. We were in sixth grade together. At the school just around the corner.'

He gave a small nod of acknowledgement then passed me the ball.

'You like school?'

An indifferent shrug.

I searched my mind for a follow-up question. 'Where's the high school now? I noticed on my way in that the old one's been torn down.' I shot and made the basket, my dignity somewhat restored.

'Ocean Grove.'

'Bit too far to ride your bike, huh?'

I'd bypassed Ocean Grove on the way into Queenscliff the day before. From memory, it was another seaside town, a fraction bigger than Queenscliff, and around fifteen minutes away by car.

'Yeah,' he said. 'Basketball was originally played with soccer balls. Did you know that?'

'Really?'

'And there was no dribbling.'

'Is that so?'

Adam was morphing into twelve-year-old Tom before my eyes—the same fascination with random facts. Tom would only need to hear something once and, if it interested him, he wouldn't forget it.

'The rings were peach baskets,' Adam went on without making eye contact, 'and the first backboards were made from chicken wire.'

'You're a sports history buff?'

He shook his head no. 'Don't really like basketball anyway.'

'Me neither. Do you like words?'

He gave me a strange look, as if words were an odd thing to like.

'I like words,' I said. 'Always have. Did you know that the word "gym" comes from an Ancient Greek word meaning "naked"?'

Adam blinked. 'That's . . . creepy.' He held the ball to his chest, like a shield. 'Am I going to have to find my taser?' He said it so blankly that I couldn't tell if he was joking.

'No. Shit. God, no. Sorry.' I had no idea how to talk to teenagers. 'Ah . . . What about this one? "Arena" comes from the Latin word *harena*, which is a kind of fine-grained sand that covered the floor of ancient stadiums like the Colosseum in Rome to absorb all the blood and stuff.'

He raised his eyebrows. Slightly. It would have been easy to miss. He passed me the ball.

I was running out of interesting sporting etymologies. 'Got any plans for the summer?'

'I don't know.'

Bad question. Any plans they'd had for a family vacation had no doubt flown out the window.

'When you live somewhere like Queenscliff, why do you need to go anywhere else?' I tried.

He didn't respond.

'I mean, you've got the weather and the beach. It's paradise, right?'

No kid thought they lived in paradise; I know I didn't in my teens in Ely, in northern Minnesota, although it was a beautiful place. Adam probably thought he lived a million miles from the action. He was undoubtedly bored living in a small town, as I had been in Ely. Also, it's probably hard to appreciate the scenery when you've never known any different. Problems are the same wherever you go.

A bead of sweat dripped down my forehead. I wanted to offer some kernel of advice that Adam might need to hear right now. That might help him in some way. But who was I to him? Just another adult full of bromides who didn't really understand what he was going through. Except I kind of did.

He gestured to the ball in my hands and gave a sort of upward nod toward the basket.

I took a shot and it bounced off the ring. Adam stepped forward and caught the rebound.

Maybe I should tell him something about Tom as a kid? Share a memory? Try to coax a smile out of him? But suddenly I couldn't think of one thing to share.

'You know, Adam, it's going to be okay. Some things we can change; some things we can't. Try to focus on the things you can.'

Jesus Christ. I should have rehearsed that in my head first.

He handed me the ball. 'I'm going inside.'

12

Later, in the kitchen, with most people gone, I dunked my hands wrist deep into a sink foaming with soapsuds.

'You don't have to do that,' Tia said from the doorway.

'Most of it was already done.'

'Really, you don't—'

'I like to feel useful.'

Tia's entire body looked weighed down—her eyes downcast, her chin dipped. She rounded the counter and scooped up a dish towel. 'I'm glad *that's* over.'

'I bet. It went well, I think.'

'I don't know what possessed me to have it at home. Country hospitality, maybe. Tom would have liked it.'

It only occurred to me now that I didn't see anyone from Tia's family at the funeral or wake. New Zealand wasn't that far away. And I'd flown all the way from the States! Probably not the time to ask about it.

'I saw you talking to Margot,' she said. She chose a dripping glass from the dish rack and pushed one end of the towel inside it. 'She fancies herself as Queenscliff's resident author.'

'She was friendly enough.'

'She's involved with the local writers' festival we have here every May. Do you go to festivals? Book tours?'

I rinsed another glass clean of suds. 'Not lately. I've been trying to finish off a manuscript. Plus it's winter in the US and, in Minnesota especially, it's freezing this time of year.'

That wasn't really a reason not to travel around promoting a book, I thought, but Tia didn't question it.

'How's Claire? Still out there saving the world?'

'Yeah. Nothing changed there. Works too hard. Loves it too much.'

She returned the dried glass to the cupboard. 'How can you love work too much?'

What *did* I mean by that? That she'd prefer to be there rather than home?

'I don't know,' was all I could come up with.

'You must spend a lot of time on your own.'

'I do, but I don't mind. I like it actually. I'm happy escaping to other worlds.'

She picked up the platter I'd just rinsed, warm water falling from the edges. 'Are you still freelancing?'

'Yeah. Probably spend half my time doing that and half my time on my own stuff. I should probably write a piece on Queenscliff while I'm here and try to sell it to a travel magazine. Pretend to work, at least.'

'Maybe you could make the whole trip tax-deductible?'

'Yeah.'

She returned coffee mugs to a wide drawer. 'Why don't you stay for dinner? There's plenty of food left.'

I didn't have any other plans; nobody else to see.

'Yeah, okay. Thanks.'

Dinner was leftover appetisers reheated in the oven and desserts that you could pinch between two fingers. The four of us—me, Tia, Adam and Missy—sat at the kitchen table. Adam ate. The rest of us grazed. Tia and I sipped red wine from large, bowl-like glasses with long stems.

'How come you've never visited before?' Missy asked me.

'It's a long way,' I said.

'How long?'

'About twenty-five hours when you add in the layover.'

'Just imagine,' Tia said, 'waking up in the morning, going to school, coming home, having the whole night at home, going to sleep and waking up again in the morning—only spending that whole time sitting in one place.'

'Boring.'

'Get this,' I said. 'When I go back, I leave here on a Tuesday and arrive home on the Monday—the day before I left. How weird is that?'

'It's like a time machine,' Missy said.

'Kind of.'

'You're going back on Tuesday?' Tia asked.

I nodded. 'But I'm spending a couple of days in Melbourne first. Leaving Queenscliff on Sunday.'

'You should go to Adventure Park,' Missy suggested.

'What's Adventure Park?' I asked her.

'You don't know what Adventure Park is?' She sounded incredulous. 'Didn't you used to live here?'

'It wasn't there in the eighties,' Adam said, deadpan.

'Settle down,' I said. 'How old do you think I am?'

'The nineties, then. Same diff.'

I hadn't heard that expression for a long time. *Same difference.*

'So, what's this Adventure Park?' I asked Missy, trying really hard not to use a kindergarten-teacher voice.

'It's a water park. Pools and slides and stuff.'

'I don't have anyone to go with. And I didn't bring my bathing suit anyway.'

'You wear a *suit* to go swimming?'

I looked at Tia for help.

'He means bathers, darling.'

It occurred to me then that I hadn't in fact packed a bathing suit. I guess I equated beach swimming with a vacation, which this most certainly was not.

'You could borrow Dad's,' Missy said. 'He won't mind.'

I kept my eyes on her, looking for a crack in her composure. It didn't come—she carried on picking at her curry puff.

'We'll see,' said Tia.

I couldn't help but stare at those kids—Missy with Tom's nose and high hairline, and Adam with something of Tom's spirit that I couldn't yet pin down. I wanted to reach over and hug them both, maybe to feel closer to Tom, maybe to offer comfort that would only have unnerved them.

After dinner, I helped Tia load the dishwasher and then we took our glasses to the sofa in the living room. The sofas had been pushed back into place after the wake, erasing any sign that an event had taken place there that afternoon.

Tom was on my mind. What Henry had said to me at the church was at the forefront of it.

'What do they think happened out there on the water?' I asked once we'd settled in.

Tia hesitated.

'I'm sorry. If it's too soon . . .'

'No, it's . . . it's fine.' Tia blinked rapidly. Maybe it wasn't fine. But she continued. 'They're writing a report. I don't know. They seem to think it had something to do with petrol vapours igniting.'

Wouldn't he have been able to smell that? Or have had some kind of gas-detection device on board?

I didn't ask any of this, of course, nodding and taking another sip of wine instead.

'Did he have insurance?'

Tia nodded. 'But they'll want to do their own investigations, I guess.'

'Investigations? Plural?'

'There's the insurance on the boat and his life insurance. But getting money out of insurance companies is like— well, they're tighter than a clam's arse at high tide.' She sipped her wine. 'We'll be okay, though. We own the house. And we've got enough to see us through.'

'Are you working?'

Tia kicked off her pumps and folded her legs under her butt on the sofa. 'At the Catholic primary school in Drysdale. It's perfect—I get all the school holidays off.'

'You're a teacher?'

She shook her head. 'Admin. Three and half days a week. The kids walk home. Or they go to GGs'—Gavin and Gillian's. I'm home by four anyway.'

I hoped they'd be getting a big insurance payout. If the Australian education sector was anything like the US, Tia wouldn't be bringing home buckets of money. Maybe the Catholics were more generous.

'Do you have time off?'

'Yeah, I'm not going back this year. We were due to finish on the twenty-first anyway. I might go in to help wrap a few things up. The kids won't go back, though—it's not worth it.'

Tia fell silent, then began to cry. 'I can't believe he's gone.'

I reached out and touched her hand.

'I don't think it's really sunk in yet,' she said. 'That he's not coming back. It seems so unbelievable. I mean, you plan for all these contingencies—what if the business fails, what if I lose my job, what if one of our parents get sick—but you never consider *this*, because it's not supposed to happen. You're not supposed to die at thirty-nine. Here one day, gone the next. No warning.'

I didn't know what to say to that. I hated this about myself. Give me a few hours to come up with dialogue in a book and I can work it out, but put me on the spot and I'm useless.

Tia looked up from her glass. 'I'll tell you what, though, Drew—it does teach you perspective. Some things are just not worth the time and energy.'

13

I'd drunk too much of Tia's wine to drive even the short distance back to my hotel, so I started walking. It was a warm night, the moon hanging in the darkened sky above me, stars shimmering, and I found myself on the road alongside Swan Bay, heading in the opposite direction from the one I should have been going. Some in-built navigational tool that had lain dormant for twenty-six years guided me down Stevens Street to the elementary school.

The school had changed little from the picture in my mind, although a few small differences caught my eye—colourful shade sails now protected a new-looking construction of play equipment, and large rainwater tanks fed a community garden. The main building was the same: squat, cinder block, surrounded by shrubbery, albeit more established now.

I ran my hand along the top of the low, steel-mesh fence, hearing the faint honking of swans in the distance.

I headed up Stokes Street, the way I had every afternoon after school, thinking about what Tia had said about perspective and how we spend our time. Was there something, or *someone*, she'd wasted her time and energy on? Maybe she just meant that, in times like these, you realise the value of being with the ones you love rather than wasting energy with people who bring you down.

Streetlights were intermittent, but yellow glows from house windows and the occasional porch light guided my way.

At the first roundabout I hesitated but then turned down Mercer—the street where we'd lived all those years ago. The street had changed little, as far as I could tell, and for a moment I slipped into the past as if through a tear in the space–time continuum. It was still a wide street, the bitumen butting against broad grass strips lined with ornamental trees where the odd car was parked with its nose into the kerb. An unnecessarily wide ribbon of path and lawn bisected the road and the rows of houses, as if the town planners had thought that it might one day be a bustling thoroughfare necessitating two lanes of traffic in both directions.

The houses were all old-timey back then and most still stood. (That was a blessing in some cases; a tragedy in others.) Many had been updated, painted in more modern colours—greys and whites. Christmas trees lit windows, and strings of miniature lights dangled from pillars and spindlework.

It was after 11 pm now and the street was quiet. In the still moonlight I stopped halfway between Stokes and Hobson, outside our old place, but on the opposite side of the road. The thick canopy of a large tree obscured virtually the whole house.

I'd pictured this moment, in a part of my mind of which I was not fully aware, a thousand times. How I would feel seeing that house again; whether I would experience the kind of visceral reaction I expected. I crossed the road to take a closer look.

I wondered if it was still owned by the military. *No, the woman at the wake said she thought a couple from Melbourne had bought it. Did they know what happened there?* Given that most of the townspeople knew, it was probably not a secret. By law, the selling agent probably had to declare it.

The garage was still there, off to the side, but they'd replaced the sectional garage door with something more in keeping with the architecture of the house.

A thick thread of red tinsel drooped from branch to branch over the weeping cherry tree on the front lawn, a few oversized ornaments dangling from the sagging boughs. The outline of a light-up Santa glowed in the front window. It looked friendly enough. Perhaps a young family lived there. Perhaps they were happy.

Memories long buried in my subconscious ignited and crystallised. I pictured the inside as clearly as if I'd walked through it yesterday. I would have liked to have gone in, seen my old room, Scarlett's nursery, the backyard. Maybe not the kitchen. It would have been updated by now, the layout no doubt redesigned to be more functional for a modern family.

Maybe seeing it now would replace the images that had haunted me for so long?

Or maybe it was better that I couldn't. Maybe seeing it again would unlock something I'd squared away long ago.

14

My schoolteacher's name was Mrs Lennon. She told the class I'd come 'all the way from America' and assigned me a buddy named Jarod to 'show me the ropes'.

Jarod obviously hadn't interpreted the buddy arrangement to extend to playtimes, so at recess I stood at a low, chain-link fence overlooking the heavy brown waters of the bay.

I couldn't believe I went to a school that practically backed onto a bay, only a patch of sloping grass and a few trees between us. Did every school in Australia have views like this?

I'd already eaten the snack Mom had packed for me in a plastic container she'd found in the kitchen. I was tempted to eat my sandwich too, just because I was bored and wanted to look like I had something to do.

'That's Swan Bay,' a voice said behind me.

I turned to find Tom standing there, the kid from the pontoon, dressed like me in the red school polo shirt with the school logo, a black swan encircled by the words *Queenscliff Primary School*. The only difference was that my shirt was brand-new and his was faded and stretched at the waist. 'And see that big bit of land out there? That's Swan Island. No one knows what goes on there. It's some secret military base where they train assassins and sharpshooters and all that.'

Tom flicked his wrist over and a Coca-Cola yo-yo spun to ground level and hovered there a few seconds until he snapped his wrist again and it rocketed back up the string.

'That's where Mark works.'

'Who?' Tom climbed onto the fence so his legs were dangling over the other side. The thought that he was technically out of the school grounds felt dangerous and exciting to me.

'My stepdad.'

'What's he do?'

I shrugged. 'He's in the military. He was at Desert Storm.'

'The Gulf War?'

'Uh-huh.'

'Cool. I bet he's a sniper. Or maybe a bomb expert. There were booby traps and IEDs everywhere in Iraq.'

I had no idea what an IED was.

'Does he have a gun?' Tom wanted to know, spinning out the yo-yo.

'Yeah.'

He held the toy in his hand. 'Have you touched it?'

'No.'

Tom looked disappointed.

'But I could if I wanted.'

'Cool.'

I had no interest in touching Mark's gun, but I didn't want to lose the chance to make a friend.

Below, between the sloping grass and the water, a train whistled past. I hadn't realised the track wound through there.

Train tracks had always scared me for some reason—something to do with a big, strong, unstoppable force that could come around the corner at any moment.

'Australia has the longest stretch of straight train track in the world,' Tom informed me. 'It goes through the desert to Perth. And you can see it from space.'

'Cool.'

I shifted uncomfortably in my stiff school polo. My shoulders were deep pink with sunburn from a shirtless walk along the beach on the weekend.

On the field behind us, almost at the perimeter of the schoolyard, a group of boys were kicking what looked like a football to each other. Among them was Jarod.

At the far end of the field were four white posts lined in a row about eight feet apart. The two in the centre were taller than the outside ones. The aim of the game quickly became apparent—kick the ball between the posts. Based on their reaction, it was much better to get it through the centre two. Getting it through the outside ones only generated groans of disappointment.

'You like footy?' Tom asked.

'Footy?'

'Football.' He gestured to the boys on the field.

'It doesn't look like football.'

'It's not like yours.'

How could he know so much about my country when I knew nothing about his?

'All the boys play footy in winter,' he said. 'Cricket in summer. The girls play netball. Everyone plays tennis.'

'Including you?'

'Not me.'

'What do you do?'

'I fish,' he said, as though it were obvious. 'I did do tennis for a bit, but I stopped.'

I wondered where Tom's other friends were. I suddenly felt awkward, wondering if I was keeping him from them. By sixth grade, friendships were well and truly established. Most of the kids had probably grown up in Queenscliff, had known each other since kindergarten or before, and an outsider, especially one who spoke with an accent, stood out like dog's balls. Though maybe the military brought some transient families.

'I saw you in class,' Tom said. 'Sitting up the front.'

I hadn't noticed him.

'Hey, do you want to go for a swim after school?'

'Where?'

'The beach!'

'I don't have a bathing suit with me.'

'I'll lend you a pair of boardies.'

Swimming. The ocean. I hesitated. Then Mom's words came back to me: *We're trying new things, right?*

'Okay. Sure.'

The bell sounded, donging five times across the field.

'I'll meet you at the double gates after school.'

It was a small school; I could find the double gates.

'See ya later, Drew.'

I wondered where he'd got the idea to call me Drew when I'd introduced myself as Andrew. Maybe it was an Aussie thing. I didn't correct him.

15

After school, I met Mom at the school gate as arranged. She was leaning against the fence, one hand cupped under her belly as if the baby might fall out without warning. For all I knew it could. I told her I was going to hang out with Tom.

'You made a friend? That's great, hon.'

'This is him,' I said as Tom approached, backpack slung over his shoulder.

'Hi . . .' Tom said, hesitating, as though there should have been more to come afterward. He probably wanted to call her by a name but didn't know what. He didn't know my last name so he couldn't say 'Mrs Iverson'. He would have been wrong there anyway. She became Mrs Boyd when she married Mark two months before he shipped out to Kuwait.

'What are you boys gonna do?'

'Beach,' Tom said. 'Probably.'

'Oh, for fun!' Mom said. 'But you don't have a bathing suit, hon.'

'It's okay,' Tom said. 'He can borrow one of mine.'

I admired the way Tom spoke to my mom as if he'd known her for years. It was hard to imagine a situation where Tom wouldn't find some level of comfort.

'Okay then. You boys have fun.'

That was an easy sell, I thought. I wasn't even allowed to walk home from school by myself in Minneapolis.

Tom and I walked out of the school gates and headed west along the water.

Tom said: 'You can borrow a pushie so we don't have to walk to the beach.'

I had no idea what a pushie was but trusted it would become clear. 'Okay.'

'You can ride my old one. Or you can take Henry's. He never uses it anyway.' Tom gave me the once-over. 'It might be too big for you, but.'

We continued along Nankervis. I'd lost my bearings and hoped that he would walk me home after, because I would just get lost. I didn't even know our phone number yet.

We followed the shore of Swan Bay, passing under the dappled shade of trees. A lawnmower hummed in the distance.

'Do you like sport?' Tom asked.

'Do you?'

'Nah, not really. Dad's a bit disappointed, I reckon. He's footy mad. He doesn't say anything, but I can tell. Henry doesn't like sport either. Did you play any sport in America?'

I shook my head. 'Hockey's a real big deal in Minnesota.'

'We should go one day anyway. To the footy. Just so you can see it. It used to be called VFL because it was really only a

Victorian sport, but it changed a couple of years ago to AFL, so now it's all over Australia.'

'Are your parents gonna be home?' I asked, as we turned from Nankervis into King Street.

'Nah. Dad works in Geelong and Mum volunteers at the maritime museum on Mondays.'

Tom's house overlooked Swan Bay. He dropped his school bag just inside the front door and kicked off his shoes, prying the first off with the heel of the other and then with his socked foot. I copied, then followed him down a short hallway tiled in some kind of shiny dark-grey stone to an open-plan kitchen, dining and living area. The place was kind of a mess. When you grow up with a mother who is obsessive about cleanliness, you notice these things. The sink was piled high with dirty dishes, the counter a jumble of food-stained cutting boards, coffee cups with dregs at the bottom and discarded food packaging. The dinner table was hidden under newspapers, unopened mail, typed letters and bills. Where did they eat?

'You hungry?' he asked.

I nodded.

'Me too. I'm gonna make you the best sandwich.'

He sat me at the table and I watched as he pulled two eggs, butter and a ball of lettuce from the refrigerator.

He grabbed a frying pan, upturned in the sink, and turned a knob on the stove so it made a clicking noise. A round flame, blue and orange, ignited, and he placed the pan over it.

'This is my specialty. You're gonna love it.'

I looked around the room. A tall, narrow table sat beneath a window that looked out over the backyard. Family photos crowded the glassed top. Tom, maybe kindergarten-aged, holding a long silver fish from a fishing line. Another boy, about the age we were now, his butt wedged into the centre of an inflated doughnut at a water park, waving. And a couple of people who must have been Tom's parents at various ages—leaning against the hood of an old car in one; toasting each other with glasses of champagne in another, rows of grapevines in the background.

In the kitchen, Tom grabbed a loaf of bread from the pantry and slid it across the lime-green counter, pulling two plates from the draining board. Back at the stove, he dug a knife into the butter, carved out a small chunk and tossed it into the hot pan, where it sizzled. Holding the handle, he shook the pan to spread the melting butter then cracked the two eggs in. At the counter, he drew four slices of bread from the clear plastic bag and distributed them between the two plates. He tore off two whole lettuce leaves and left them on the countertop.

I was impressed by Tom's command of the kitchen. I couldn't cook a thing. I could put together a basic sandwich. Prepare cereal. Make toast. That was about it.

Tom turned the eggs with a spatula. 'Almost finished.'

He grabbed a bottle of ketchup from the pantry and put it on the counter, then went back to the stove, grabbed the pan, and flipped the eggs onto the waiting bread. He shook the ketchup bottle over the first egg until a globule blobbed out then did the same over the other sandwich before topping them both with the lettuce leaves and the remaining slices of bread.

He pushed one of the plates in my direction. 'My famous egg sandwich. Dig in.'

He took a massive bite of his sandwich while I investigated mine. We usually ate eggs scrambled in my house.

'Come on,' he said through a mouthful of food. 'Two, four, six, eight.'

I raised it to my mouth and took a bite, a dollop of ketchup smearing my face.

'Yum, yeah?'

I nodded, and I wasn't just being polite. The freshness of the bread, the crispness of the full lettuce leaf, the sweetness of the ketchup and the depth of the egg were a winning combination.

The hum of a motor sounded outside and I peered through the front window. A motorbike was pulling into the driveway.

'Here's Mum now,' Tom said.

His mom stepped off the bike. She was short, and dressed head to toe in black leather despite the heat. She removed her helmet and finger-combed her short brown hair.

My stomach clenched at the thought of her finding me like this, sitting in her kitchen eating her food. *What would she think of me?*

'This is Drew,' Tom said, shoving the last of his sandwich into his mouth as she entered. I was only halfway through mine.

'Hello, Drew.'

It was weird, people calling me Drew, but I kind of liked it.

'You new at school?' she asked.

I nodded.

'The pristine school uniform gave you away.' She placed her helmet on the counter and unzipped her jacket. 'Where'd you move from?'

'Minneapolis.'

'America?'

'Yeah. I mean, yes, ma'am.'

Tom's mom smiled as if I'd said something funny. 'Call me Gillian. What are you boys up to this afternoon?'

'Beach,' Tom said.

'Great. It's beautiful out there. Sunscreen, Tom.'

'Yes, Mum.'

'Do you need a towel, Drew?'

'Mum, it's fine,' Tom told her. 'We know what to take to the beach.'

She bowed her head. 'My sincerest apologies to you, Thomas.' She turned to me. 'Do you want to stay for tea?'

I imagined sitting around the table with Tom's family drinking hot tea from dainty cups.

'I don't really drink tea, but thanks anyway.'

She smiled. 'I meant dinner.'

'Oh.'

'Nothing fancy, just a barbie.'

I must have looked puzzled because she clarified: 'A barbecue.'

'I'll have to ask my mom.'

'Come on, Drew,' Tom said, grabbing me by the arm. 'I'll get you some bathers.'

I left my sandwich and followed Tom along a thick-carpeted hallway. He pointed out his brother's room as we passed. 'Henry goes to the high school down the street. That's where I'm going next year. Are you going there too?'

'Not sure. I guess.'

'You probably will. Everyone goes there.'

In Tom's room, I took in the details: an unmade bed, the comforter patterned with the Australian flag, and a small desk covered in hobby magazines, pens and binder books. Posters of marine life were thumbtacked to the walls.

Tom trawled through scrunched piles of clothes shoved into shelves in his closet, eventually pulling out a pair of colourful board shorts. He tossed them at me. 'Here. These should fit.'

I caught the shorts while Tom pulled his school shirt over his head and yanked both his shorts and jocks down to the floor, flicking them off with his foot. The middle quarter of him was white. Not pasty white like me, but ten shades lighter than the rest of him, from waist to just above the knee where his shorts must have stopped.

I hadn't moved, taking in the shock of his uncircumcised penis. I'd never seen one in the flesh before. Every boy I'd ever seen looked just like me down there—full helmet. Tom was full slug.

'Just chuck your clothes on the bed,' he said, unperturbed.

He'd misread my hesitation.

I turned on an angle and took my time unbuttoning my polo while Tom stripped off his socks.

'Here.' He threw a tank top in my direction.

I peeled off my sweaty socks, then slid my shorts down my legs. I was still wearing my tighty-whities.

I watched as he pulled a t-shirt over his head, cocooning his torso in it, then popping his hands out through the sleeves. I'd never seen anyone put on a shirt that way.

'Hurry up,' Tom said. 'I'll get towels.' And he left.

Once I'd changed, I folded my school clothes and put them in a neat stack on his chaotic bed then ventured back out to the living area.

In the kitchen, Tom was bundling the towels into a rucksack. Sliding his arms through the straps, he flicked his head toward a glass sliding door that led to the backyard. 'Let's get the bikes.'

The bikes were in a large garage that Tom called 'the shed'. I guess he called it that because there were no cars in there—there wasn't any room. Instead, a massive workbench overflowing with miscellaneous tools and woodworking projects filled one end. Odd lengths of timber cluttered the floor, along with displaced motors, wheels of various shapes and sizes, bikes seats, rope, chain and wire. It was like an indoor junkyard.

The only clear space was the couch—a tattered old three-seater near the door.

'Pretty cool, huh?' Tom said.

If you could call junk cool. 'Yeah. Cool.'

'Check this out.' He picked up what looked to be a motor of some kind. 'I'm building an engine for my billycart.' He motioned to a timber cart with a T-bar at the front and a long timber shaft, a rope tied to either side of the T for steering. Its wheels looked like they might have been recycled from a golf buggy. The seat was made from hard plastic and looked exactly like the ones we sat on at school.

'You made that?' I said. 'From scratch?'

'Sure. And look here.' He pointed to a large silver drum pocked with holes. 'This came out of our old washing machine. I'm turning it into a fire pit for the backyard.'

'Where'd you learn to do that? Your dad?'

'Nah. He never comes out here. Magazines mainly. Or I just make it up.'

He gestured to two pushbikes leaning against a wall in front of a ladder hanging on two hooks. 'Take your pick.'

'Which one's yours?'

'Mine's outside.'

I chose the smaller of the two.

'The BMX—good choice,' Tom said. 'Mine's a Mongoose.'

'Do we need helmets?'

'Nah.'

Tom pressed a thumb into the tyres of the BMX and wiggled the chain. 'Good to go.'

He gave me a spare pair of flip-flops and then we pedalled

back down King Street, veering to the right and heading straight, the black lighthouse in full view. We passed the Royal Hotel and took a right after the bowling club, continuing toward the glistening water until we reached a sporting field.

'That's where the Coutas play,' Tom said.

Beyond the oval we came out at a parking lot overlooking the ocean. We dumped our bikes on the grass shoulder and made our way down the steps to the sand.

Before us was a large expanse of ocean. The land curled on both sides, lighthouses poking out at each point.

That's Point Lonsdale,' Tom said, jutting his chin to the right. 'Over there is Point Nepean and Portsea.' He pointed across the bay. 'And that's Sorrento, where the ferry goes.'

Along the beach, people sat on towels, sipping from cans of pop and reading magazines. Two girls batted a tennis ball strung to the top of a vertical pole. In the water, swimmers duck-dived under the waves.

'Oh, look,' Tom said. 'Bottlenoses.'

A pair of dolphins jumped through the air together then disappeared into the deep green of the ocean. I was reminded that other creatures lurked under those waters. Sharks, for example.

'Ever heard of "echolocation"?' Tom asked me.

I shook my head as Tom dumped the rucksack on the soft sand and peeled off his t-shirt, throwing it down. I was still looking at the sea.

'It's what dolphins use to find prey. They make this sort of clicking sound and wait for the echo to bounce back to them. Cool, huh?' He planted his hands on his hips. 'Ready?'

I didn't move. There were plenty of other people swimming, I told myself. That must mean it was safe.

'You *can* swim, right?'

''Course.'

'Then let's go.'

I held back a moment. 'Did you know that *swims* will still be *swims* even when you turn it upside down?'

'What?'

I bent over and wrote SWIMS in the sand with my index finger. 'Now go stand over there.'

He repositioned himself so he could read it from the other angle. 'That's very cool.'

I felt myself grow taller.

'So, ready?'

I hesitated. 'Is it . . . I mean, what about sharks?'

'What *about* sharks?' Tom waved away my concern. 'They might take a bite, but once they taste you, they'll move on.'

That didn't help.

'Most of them are easy-going. Like a pet cat.'

'A cat?'

'We're not prey; we're just in their way. That's why they bite. They're curious. They haven't come across too many humans in their four hundred million years on Earth. They'd rather munch on whale or seal blubber than your pasty arse, anyway. The odds of dying are low. Like, *really* low.'

He ran toward the water, kicking up sand as he went.

New experiences, right? I ran after him.

Tom let me ride Henry's bike back to my place and said I could keep it for a while. All the way home I could still taste sea water in my mouth and felt it clinging to my skin. But I loved it. You feel clean after a swim in a lake, but dirty after a dip in the ocean.

I didn't care. I felt as if I'd conquered something. As if I'd crossed some vast threshold.

I parked the bike on the front porch and came through the door. Mark was home already—I could hear him and Mom talking in the kitchen.

'Maybe it's the laundry detergent I'm using?' Mom suggested.

Mark must have shaken his head because Mom said, 'How do you know?'

'Some of the other vets have the same thing. The pins and needles too. They say they're leaking.'

'*Leaking?*'

'Green stuff coming out of their eyes. Shit and piss mixed with blood. One guy says his upchuck glows in the dark.'

'Jesus, Mary and Joseph,' Mom said. 'What do their doctors say?'

'Nothing. No reason.'

'What the heck?'

'Don't know what to tell ya, Cathy.'

I stepped through the doorway.

'Here's my beach baby!' Mom exclaimed. She kissed me on the forehead. 'How was it?'

'Great.'

She beamed. 'Go take a shower. Supper will be ready soon. Where's your school uniform?'

'Oh, shoot! I left it at Tom's.'

She frowned, but not in a mean way. 'Lucky you have another one then, isn't it? Go on—shower. Scoot!'

Mom served hotdish for dinner, but Mark picked at it then pushed his plate away, the meal only half-eaten. 'This Aussie food doesn't agree with me.'

'I know,' Mom said. 'I wash your underwear.' She looked at me.

'Why don't you invite your new friend for a sleepover? I can make meatballs and a cookie salad.'

'Okay. Maybe.'

'You could rent a movie.'

Mark scratched under his arm, then across his chest. 'That deodorant you bought is giving me a rash,' he said to Mom. 'Couldn't you get Right Guard?'

'Sorry, hon. No Right Guard. You're not eating?'

'I just said I was done!'

Mom made a show of reeling back. 'Alrighty. No need to get snippy.'

'Sorry. I'm just not sleeping well here. It's so hot!'

Mom rubbed the tip of her nose, pink from the sun. 'Are you sure it's Australia? You weren't sleeping well at home, either.'

He pushed back his chair and carried his plate to the sink. 'I'm going out back.'

With Mark gone, Mom put on a cheery face. 'I'm loving these long days of sunshine. Aren't you?'

With daylight saving, it was light until after nine some nights.

'I just want to kick off my shoes and run along the hot sand into that gorgeous, cooling water,' she said. 'Don't you?'

'I guess.'

'Let's go for a walk after the dishes are done. I can read the newspaper later.'

'Sure. Okay. I'll show you where I swam today.'

She grabbed my hand and squeezed. 'Remember to go slowly, hon.' She rested a hand on her stomach. 'I'm carrying a heavy load.'

★

Tom and I hung out at school the next day. And the day after that. I found out that he usually played a game called downball at recess—four large squares divided by painted lines on the pavement and a tennis ball batted back and forth between them with an open palm.

He and I played sometimes, and I was getting the hang of it, but other times we would sit on a wall and talk.

'What's Minnesota like?' he asked on my fourth day at Queenscliff Primary.

'Snowy. But hot too. Lots of lakes.'

'How many?'

'Ten thousand. That's what people say.'

'There must be good fishing.'

'Yeah. Walleye. That's our best fish.'

'What's *walleye*?'

'I don't know. It's white. It tastes good. Everybody eats it.'

'Did you ever catch one?'

'Lots of times. With my dad. Mark doesn't like to camp. Says he did enough rough living in the army. Dad always made a fire. It was to keep the mosquitoes away but we used to roast hot dogs and marshmallows. Make s'mores. In the morning Dad would make pancakes.' I turned to Tom. 'We had to bundle all the food up in a tree so the bears wouldn't come at night.'

'Really?'

'Really.'

Considering this, a corner of his mouth lifted. 'Cool.'

Most kids would have been scared to death at the thought of a five-hundred-pound black bear prowling around while they slept. Not Tom.

'Maybe we could camp one night,' Tom suggested. 'In the backyard or on the beach.'

'Yeah, okay. Do you have a tent?'

'No. Do you?'

'No.'

Our shoulders seemed to slump at the same time.

'We could borrow one,' Tom said. 'Do you know how to put it up?'

'Yeah.'

I beamed at the discovery that there was something I knew how to do but Tom didn't. In Minnesota being outdoors was a way of life in the summer. Everybody vacationed in a cabin, and all my friends grew up fishing and waterskiing and tubing. Maybe I did have something to teach him. He probably didn't even know how to keep a campfire going.

Tom opened his lunchbox and held it out. 'Bickie?'

'What?'

He pointed to two cookies with white frosting.

I took one, examined it, then had a bite. It wasn't like anything I'd tasted before, but it was good. Coconuts, currants, white chocolate icing.

'What *are* these?' I asked.

'Venetians. Want to come over after school? We could race remote-controlled cars.'

'Sure.'

Tom bit into his cookie.

Finally, I had a friend in Australia who wasn't between the pages of a book.

16

I sat on the front porch, in the warmth, reading *Where the Red Fern Grows*, as the rain fell around me. Our boxes from home had arrived, and along with them half of my novels. The other half were in storage back in Minneapolis.

I'd inherited Dad's collection—Jeffrey Archer, Tom Clancy, Robert Ludlum. I liked them well enough, but read them mostly to be close to him: to touch the pages he had touched, to absorb the words he had. The rest of my collection was mostly Stephen King, Ray Bradbury and R.L. Stine.

Every time I heard the rev of an engine turning into our street, I craned my neck to see if it was Mark's car, a dark green Falcon.

I sat there for what felt like hours. Finally, just as I'd reached the part in the book where Billy sneaks off in the middle of the night to get his dogs, I looked up to see the Falcon inching down Mercer Street. It was slower than I'd ever seen Mark drive, and I knew that was because of the baby in the back of the car.

I had met Scarlett already, of course. Mark had driven me to the hospital in Geelong the day before to see her, all pink, face squished in a cry, eyes closed. We'd only been in Australia for about four weeks and Scarlett had come two weeks early.

Mom didn't know she was having a girl, and when Scarlett came I thought they might call her something to do with where she was born, like Victoria, but no. I guessed Scarlett suited her, though; she was kind of red.

By the time Mark came to a stop in our driveway I was on my feet at the edge of the porch, *Where the Red Fern Grows* abandoned on the wicker chair.

Mom waved at me frantically from the passenger seat. She looked more rested than I'd expected (I'd heard that babies cried all night), and it occurred to me that I'd never seen her look so happy. My first thought was that she was happy to see me after a few nights apart, but it may not have been that at all. Maybe she was just happy to be home, or happy that she was no longer pregnant in the Australian heat, or happy that she had a daughter now. Maybe it was all of those things.

Mark wanted to be the one to introduce Scarlett to her first home, so he unclipped the straps that secured her into the small capsule in the back seat, while Mom was left to fetch her bag from the trunk.

Pausing at the top of the two porch steps, Mark presented her for me to marvel at. 'Isn't she amazing?' he said. It wasn't a question but a statement. A fact. As if he'd never been surer of anything in his life.

'She's real cute,' I said.

Inside, Mark walked her around the house, showing her each room and describing its function in his Texan drawl. 'This is the kitchen where Mommy is gonna cook all your delicious food . . . This is the bathroom where you're gonna get all cleaned up . . . This is your big brother's room . . . This is the laundry room where Mommy's gonna wash all your itty-bitty clothes . . .'

It was kind of sweet, I had to admit, though I noticed he didn't seem to be assigning many jobs to himself.

At the end of the tour, he sat on the couch by the window and rested Scarlett between his thighs so he could take in her features. 'I think she has my dad's eyes,' he said. 'But I'm not sure where this black hair comes from.'

'That'll probably fall out,' Mom told him. She was standing at the kitchen table, separating the dirty clothes from the clean out of her hospital bag.

Scarlett was Mark's first child. He'd always said he was too busy with his career in the military to get married. He was younger than my mom, only twenty-eight, and he'd gone straight from high school into the service and then over to Kuwait when he was twenty-six. It sounded too young to be fighting in a war, but there were soldiers much younger than him apparently.

'Okay, hon,' Mom said to Mark. 'It's time for this little honeybee to have some milk and a nap.'

'But we just got her home.'

'There'll be plenty of time for that.'

Mark lifted Scarlett into the air, holding her out to Mom.

Mom took her and nuzzled the baby's face. 'You're gonna have such a beautiful life.'

17

One afternoon a week or so later, I was stretched out on my bed reading *The Prodigal Daughter* from Dad's collection while Mom pinned laundry to the clothes line out back and Scarlett cried in another room. She'd been crying all afternoon, and Mom had at first paced around the house with Scarlett in her arms, humming, then taken her for a walk in the carriage.

The screen door slammed and then Mom was again walking up and down the hallway. 'You can't be hungry because I already fed you, and your diaper's clean,' she was saying. 'Come on, honeybee, you must be tired. Just go to sleep for Mommy, would you?'

The phone rang, and thirty seconds later Mom was in my doorway. 'It's Tom for you.'

'Hello?' I said down the phone line.

'What are you doing?' Tom asked.

'Reading.'

'Let's do something.'

I hesitated. I only had three chapters to go in my book so could easily finish it before dinnertime.

'Drew?'

'Ah . . .'

'You can read whenever. These great days won't last.'

So Tom swung by my house and we walked for ten minutes to the black lighthouse, which was right by the fort. Queenscliff had two lighthouses, Tom explained. The white lighthouse gave off the low light, while the black lighthouse provided the high light. They worked together to guide ships through the bay. I never thought I'd be interested in how lighthouses work, but listening to Tom describe it gave me a new appreciation.

We stood looking up at the black-stoned lighthouse, surrounded by a large brick wall, cannons and a maze of tunnels, which were all part of the fort, whose job it was to protect Melbourne and ships carrying gold in the 1800s.

The gold rush. It sounded so exciting. I'd learned about the California gold rush in history class back home, imprinting on my brain images of hundreds of thousands of people descending on the west coast from around the US and overseas, hoping to strike it rich. The two words—'gold' and 'rush'—gave it a sense of glittering urgency. Then Australia got its turn.

We sat on a bench beneath the lighthouse and peered across the bay. The sun warmed us, but the wind whirled, curtaining my eyes with my hair.

'What are those orange boats I see all the time?' I asked Tom.

'They're the pilot boats. The rip out there? It's one of the most dangerous sections of sea in the world for ships.'

'Why?'

'Because it's really narrow. And the ships are really big. If they go off course even a little bit, they can run into trouble. So the guys on those boats—they're called pilots—they go out there, board the ships and steer them through the channel.'

'What *is* the rip?' I asked.

'It's where the tide meets the ocean. They collide—I don't know, something to do with the wind and the tide—but it's really dangerous. Last year, they lost a boat and two pilots in, like, thirty-metre waves. Not a job for the chickenshit.'

The word 'rip' still fascinated me because I couldn't grasp its meaning. I pictured it like a strong current that dragged swimmers out to sea, but it seemed unlikely that it would affect the massive ships that passed through the bay. Still, I'd never known Tom to be wrong about anything.

There were stories everywhere, I thought. The gold rush, the fort, Swan Island, the pilot boats, the rip. You just had to be interested enough to find them.

We sat on that bench for an hour, watching swimmers, the pilot boats zipping out to meet ships and the ferry inching its way across the bay to Sorrento. I asked questions and Tom answered them. We made a good pair—me wanting to learn and him wanting to teach. He explained things in a way I could understand, and if he didn't know the answer, he wouldn't bullshit to save face. *Maybe we could look that up in the library,* he'd say, or *ask a teacher at school?* His mom, too, knew a lot about ships—she had to, being a volunteer at the maritime museum.

We descended the wooden steps to the beach and followed the shoreline, kicking up seaweed the tide had deposited on the sand.

'So, you really like reading, huh?' Tom said.

'Yeah, kinda.'

'You do or you don't.'

I didn't respond for a moment. Then I said, 'Kids who read books are nerds. Everyone knows that.' I couldn't work out why I'd reveal that lifelong anxiety to him.

'You like it, don't you?'

'You know I do.'

'So, who cares? You like it, you do it. And don't apologise to anyone for it.'

I nodded.

'Race you to the pier?' he said.

Before I could answer, Tom broke into a run, and I took off after him. He was eight feet ahead of me the whole fifty-yard distance, despite me pumping my arms as hard as I could all the way and moving my legs as fast as they would go. He beat me. Easily. We were both exhausted afterward, collapsing onto the sand and panting like mad.

'You're slow,' he said.

'You had a head start. Next time, I'll call go.'

'Whatever you need to tell yourself.'

We lay there talking until the day started to fade then headed home via the store, where he bought me an ice cream on a stick called a Gaytime. Weird name. Great taste.

On the street outside our house, a white van, EAP SECURITY printed on the side, pointed its nose into the kerb. Even from the street, I could hear Scarlett crying.

Tom and I slipped through the front door and walked down the hallway past my room. He extended a finger toward my bedroom door. 'Nice sign.'

In our boxes from America was a sign that had hung on my bedroom door since I was a baby—ANDREW'S ROOM—with a picture of a sleeping lamb. My face reddened.

I peered around the corner and saw Mom bounce-walking around the kitchen with Scarlett in her arms, making shushing sounds.

'The baby does this all day and all night,' I told Tom.

'Bugger,' he said.

'Oh, Andrew!' Mom said, when she caught sight of me, frantic, as if she'd been waiting for me all afternoon. 'Fetch me that bottle, would you? On the counter. Hi, Tom.'

'Hello.'

I passed her the baby bottle, half-filled with water.

I wanted to suggest she try a pacifier, but maybe Scarlett was too young, or there was some other reason that I didn't know about. I didn't want to upset Mom any more by implying she didn't know what she was doing.

'Is someone here?' I asked, thinking of the van parked outside.

'Just the guy with the safe. He's installing a safe in the garage for Mark.'

'Sorry,' I said to Tom. 'It's kind of crazy around here.'

'No worries. I'm gonna . . .' He hooked a thumb toward the front door.

'Cool. See you at school.'

That night I was lying in bed, reading by the dull glow of my flashlight, when a gentle tap came at my window.

I wasn't sure what the tapping was at first, maybe a branch scraping up against the pane, but it kept happening.

Then a voice called my name. 'Drew! Drew, open up.'

I went to the window, pulled back the drapes and peered out to see Tom, dressed in shorts, a tank top and flip-flops, standing in the bushes in the cut-through between the front and back yards, his face illuminated by the moon. He had a knapsack slung over one shoulder.

I turned the lock on the sash window and lifted the lower pane. 'What are you doing?'

'I've got something for you.'

'Now?'

'Come out.'

The rhythm of my heart quickened—out of fear or excitement, I couldn't tell. Maybe both. I'd never snuck out a bedroom window at night. It felt like a scene from *The Goonies* or something.

I was only wearing tighty-whities, so I pulled on a t-shirt then eased the window open a little further and stuck a leg out. I was too high off the ground to jump, though, so I just dangled there while Tom stood among the hydrangeas giggling.

'A little help?' I said.

He dropped his knapsack to the ground and extended his arms. 'Just fall,' he said. 'I'll catch you.'

'No way!'

'Oh, come on. Don't be such a wimp. Just jump.'

I turned around and stuck both legs through the window, hanging onto my nightstand. I wiggled my hips until most of me was through, then let myself fall.

I landed more softly than I expected and managed to stay completely upright.

'See?' Tom said. 'Easy.'

'What are you doing here?' I brushed mulch from the bottoms of my bare feet.

'I told you: I brought you something.' He dug a hand deep into his knapsack and produced something small, black and rectangular; in the dim light, I couldn't quite make out what it was.

He thrust it into my hand. 'One for you and one for me.'

'What is it?'

'Walkie-talkie, dummy. Now we can talk whenever we want. Our parents don't have to know.'

'Where did you get these?'

'I made them.'

'You *made* them?'

'From a kit. I sent away for it. Do you know what to do?'

'I'll work it out.'

'Cool.' Tom shouldered his bag. 'See ya tomorrow.'

Even at twelve years old, I understood why he'd given it to me. I pictured the scene he'd witnessed at my house earlier that night and what he must have understood about my home life. I had a sudden urge to hug him.

'Tom?' I said in a loud whisper. He was almost at my front fence now.

He turned. 'What?'

'How am I going to get back in?'

Back in bed five minutes later, having negotiated myself through the window with a boost from Tom, I held the walkie-talkie like it was a nugget of gold, running my fingers over the raised bits. To get a better look, I shone the flashlight over it under the covers. It was actually dark grey, with a squat antenna poking out the top. The upper half was a series of raised horizontal lines under which the microphone and speaker must have been, and on the bottom half, the flat part of the panel had an orange square call button and, printed in white, a list of the international morse codes that represented each letter—'a' a dot and a dash, 'b' a dash followed by three dots and so on. I couldn't imagine using that.

It would take forever just to say the word hello.

I pressed the orange button and it made a loud beeping noise. Alarmed, I shoved it under my pillow, worried that Mom and Mark might hear.

Tom's voice came through. 'Drew?'

'Tom?'

'Hey, Drew!'

'It works!' I said, trying hard to contain my excitement and keep my voice low. 'Where are you? Are you almost home?'

'You have to say over.'

'What?'

'When you're finished speaking, you have to say "over" so I know you're finished.'

'Why? I'll just stop talking, then you'll know I'm done.'

'Because it's not like a phone. You can't talk and listen at the same time. You have to press the button to speak. But if you're pressing the button, you won't be able to hear me if I'm talking. Get it?'

'Yeah, I got it. Over.'

18

The next weekend, Tom took me to the bakery on Hesse where he ordered something called a sausage roll.

'I'll have the same,' I said, imagining that this was what Aussies called hot dogs.

Instead, the woman behind the counter handed me a brown paper bag with discs of grease on the outside. Inside was some kind of long pastry.

Tom squirted ketchup from a large pump container into his bag, but I declined, wanting to know what this thing tasted like on its own.

What I discovered was a wondrous, meaty, flaky pastry sensation. I was so used to the idea of pastries being sweet that the concept of herbed sausage meat rolled into a log and wrapped in pastry seemed, well, unnatural.

'Thanks for the walkie-talkie,' I said as we made our way

down Hesse toward the water. The sun seemed to bounce off every surface—every sign, every shop window, the hood of every car—making it impossible to be outside without squinting.

'No worries.'

'I wonder who came up with the name "walkie-talkie",' I said. 'It's pretty cool, right? Like, you walk and you talk. It's perfect, actually.'

'I guess.'

'What if we named other things the same way? Like, how you use it or what the thing does is what we call it.' I bit into my sausage roll. 'Like this takeout. You have to wait for it, right? Then you eat it. So it's a waitie-ateie.'

'Yeah. Good one.'

We passed through shrubbery and beyond the old railway station.

'Are there snakes around here?' I asked.

'Not everything is trying to kill you,' Tom said, as if he'd already told me ten times. 'But some things are.'

'Like snakes?'

He shrugged. 'There's black snakes. And tiger snakes. But leave them alone, and they'll leave you alone. They're probably more scared of you than you are of them.'

'I doubt that.'

Tom was systematically downgrading all the man-eating creatures I associated with Australia to 'fine' and 'easygoing'. I'd have to ask about spiders sometime.

Tom screwed up his empty paper bag and tossed it into a trash can. 'Snakes smell with their tongues. Did you know that?'

'Nope. I hate their eyes.'

'No eyelids, that's why. They never blink. Sleep with their eyes open. Freaky, huh?'

'Totally.'

We walked by the beach toward the bridge that led to Swan Island. Further along the foreshore, past the fish sheds, something large, lumpy and silvery brown was slumped over the sand.

Tom followed my gaze. 'It's a seal,' he said. 'Looks dead.'

The sausage roll churned in my stomach and I slowed my pace. I didn't want to see a dead seal. But Tom continued on, curious, and I was compelled to follow.

As we got closer the seal must have sensed us approaching because it turned its glistening head slightly. It tried to move its heaving body, too, but it couldn't.

Tom glanced at the ocean. 'Coulda got hit by a boat. Poor bugger. Back's probably broken.' He looked at me. 'We have to kill it.'

'What?' Panic rose in me.

'It's the only thing to do. If we leave it here it'll starve to death. Or maybe get attacked by dogs at night.'

His eyes scanned the area where the sand turned to long grass, probably looking for a heavy rock or something.

My lips began to quiver, my eyes to moisten. *How could we kill this poor, harmless creature?*

Tom walked off, returning with a short but sturdy-looking log.

'Do you want to do it?' he asked.

I shook my head.

The seal stared up at us, its glassy eyes frightened.

Tom took a deep breath, raised the log high in the air, and then brought it down on the seal's head.

When I got home from school the next day, Mom was standing outside Scarlett's bedroom door with a ginger-haired woman I didn't know. Behind the closed door, Scarlett was crying.

'This is my son Andrew,' Mom told the woman. 'Andrew, say hi.'

'Hi.'

'This is Corinne from the baby health centre.'

Mom stood there, bleary-eyed and tangle-haired, biting her lower lip, her fingers reaching for the doorhandle.

Corinne gently prised Mom's hand away. 'She'll stop. Just give it a minute.'

I walked into the kitchen, heading for the cookie jar. Only the ones with orange frosting in the centre remained. Had Mom eaten all the others?

'You should be an old hand by now,' Corinne said quietly.

'It wasn't like this with Andrew. He was good. And we were living in my in-laws' basement at the time, and David's mom was a great help. This one—I can't put her down or she'll start crying, so I end up walking around the house all day with her in my arms. I can't get anything done and this house is getting smaller and smaller.'

'Why don't you go for walks outside? You've got beautiful beaches on your doorstep.'

'I do, but she just screams and people look at me like I'm the worst mom in the world.'

'I'm sure they don't think that.'

'Oh, they do. I can see it in their faces.'

Scarlett continued to cry.

'She's just colicky,' Corinne said. 'She'll grow out of it.'

Scarlett's cries started to abate, as if she'd heard Corinne.

'When can I switch to bottle feeding?'

The nurse gave her a tight smile. 'The baby will get confused if you swap between breast and bottle.'

I squirmed at the word 'breast'.

'No, I mean, stop breastfeeding,' Mom clarified.

'Stop breastfeeding?' the nurse asked in disbelief.

'It's so painful.'

Corinne took a breath. 'You can take Panadol, but only Panadol.'

'Panadol?'

'For the pain. It's paracetamol. You buy it at the chemist.'

Mom nodded.

'Breast is best, dear,' Corinne said in the most condescending way possible. 'You must persist.' She eyed Scarlett's bedroom door. 'For her sake.'

All the talk about breasts was too much, so I sat myself in front of the TV and zoned out.

After Corinne was gone and the house was quiet, Mom placed her hands on her chest, wincing at the pain.

'Andrew, could you run to the drugstore and get me some . . . what did she call it? Panadol. Get me some Panadol.'

'It's Drew.'

'What's that now?'

'Drew. I want to be called Drew.'

'Oh.' She seemed confused for a moment. 'The carriage is at the front door. You can take the baby for a walk, if you want?'

'Is that a good idea?' I said doubtfully. 'She's asleep for once.'

'Sure,' she said. 'You'll be fine.'

I didn't want to do it. I couldn't do it.

'I'm going to ride my bike. It'll be faster.'

'Oh, okay.' She pressed a purple five-dollar bill into my hands.

I couldn't believe she'd suggested I take Scarlett out on my own. What was going on inside her head?

19

One Saturday, Tom came to my house because his mom was hosting a book club meeting and he wasn't allowed to make any noise.

We sat in my room, on opposite beds, talking about fishing. Scarlett was howling in the other room. Snivel, wail, snivel, ear-piercing wail. Situation normal.

Between us, on the nightstand that divided the beds, was the golden fish lure Tom had given me, resting on Dad's copy of *The Hunt for Red October*.

'You kept this thing?' Tom asked.

I didn't answer.

He picked up the lure, grabbed a black marker I'd left on the nightstand, and penned something on the underside of the fish. He capped the marker with a jab from the heel of his hand and returned both to the tabletop.

Scarlett's crying seemed to fill the house.

'Sorry,' I said. 'It's a bit hectic here right now.'

'It's fine.'

It wasn't fine. It was embarrassing. His house was so calm and his parents were so laidback. Gillian, I'd learned, had trained as an environmental scientist, and Gavin worked at the Ford car factory in Geelong in some kind of finance job.

'Wanna get a video?' Tom asked.

'Sure.'

In the living room, Mom was swinging the portable crib back and forth, Scarlett screaming inside. 'It's supposed to calm them down,' she said. 'Like they're still in the womb or something.'

'We're going into town,' I told her.

She turned and I saw wet patches over her boobs. I was conscious of Tom standing right by me and cringed.

'Mom.' I pointed to my own chest and then to hers.

She looked down. 'Oh,' was all she said, continuing to rock the baby.

We hiked up Mercer to Hesse, then entered Eddie's. We passed through the racks of clothes, shelves of art supplies and collection of toys to the back of the store, where the walls were lined with empty VHS cases—new releases for five dollars or five weeklies for ten. Movie posters adorned the walls above.

'Have you seen *Backdraft*?' Tom asked.

'Yep.'

'*Ninja Turtles II*?'

'Yeah.'

'Ooh! *Silence of the Lambs*.'

I shook my head.

He held up *Terminator 2*. 'What about this?'

'What's it rated?'

'Who cares?'

'I don't. Whatever you want.'

'We can watch it at my place, if you like.'

'Okay.'

On our way out of Eddie's, we encountered three girls coming in. I recognised them from school. All were in our class, but I only knew one of their names—Lauren.

'Hi, Marissa,' Tom said, casual as you like.

'Hey, Tom.'

Marissa wore a black bucket hat, like on that TV show *Blossom*, and a waistcoat over a white shirt. Her friend, the dark-haired one whose name I still didn't know, wore a pale-wash denim mini skirt with a matching denim jacket, and Lauren had a neon-printed crop top, big hoop earrings and a psychedelic scrunchie. Marissa was tall—you couldn't miss her. She seemed too sophisticated for sixth grade.

'Marissa's having a party,' Lauren blurted.

'Lauren!' Marissa gave her friend a playful swat on the arm. 'It's true, I am. It's my birthday. But I haven't decided who I'm inviting.'

'We'll come,' Tom said. 'Won't we, Drew?'

I nodded, dumbstruck by his confidence.

'In your dreams,' Lauren said.

'I can invite who I want,' Marissa declared. 'Mum already said.'

The dark-haired girl rolled her eyes. 'Whatever. I'm going to see if they've still got *Robin Hood*.'

'Urgh!' Lauren said theatrically. 'She wants to *marry* Kevin Costner.'

The girl disappeared into the store, leaving the four of us standing there on the sidewalk.

'What did you guys get?' Marissa asked.

I held up *Terminator 2* and *City Slickers*.

'Two new releases? There's your night gone.'

'We'll probably watch one tomorrow,' Tom said, although we hadn't discussed this. 'Drew's sleeping over. Aren't you, Drew?'

We hadn't discussed that either, but I nodded.

'Have you met anyone famous?' Lauren asked me. 'Like, film stars?'

I'd once seen the singer Prince through the window of a restaurant, but I didn't meet him.

'Jesse Ventura?' I said. He'd done an appearance at Southdale Mall and I'd seen him from a distance. I had no interest in meeting him.

'Who's that?'

'The wrestler!' Tom said.

'Oh. I met the cast of *Neighbours* last year,' Lauren said. 'They were in Geelong for something. It was so rad.'

I knew about *Neighbours*—it was a TV show set in Melbourne. It was on every night after the news.

'Cool,' I said, although I couldn't care less.

'Anyway,' Marissa said. 'We better go in before all the good videos are gone. See youse later.'

On the walk home, Tom told me he liked Marissa.

'Isn't she a bit . . . tall?' I asked.

'Who cares?'

'I don't know.'

'I reckon Lauren likes you.'

'She doesn't.' I wondered what made him think that, what social cue I'd missed. Maybe he'd said it to be nice, or because he had some other plan in mind—like the two of us going on a double date with Marissa and Lauren.

'Well, she will,' Tom declared. 'Once she gets to know you. Marissa's party's your in.'

I didn't know how to respond to that, trying to imagine what I would say to this girl and what the party would be like. Would it be a low-lit basement with kids making out in every corner? Maybe I could pretend I was sick so I didn't have to go.

'Want to go fishing tomorrow?' Tom asked.

'Okay.'

'But we have to go early.'

'How early?'

'Sun rises 'bout quarter to seven.'

Scarlett would be awake then. We would all be awake then.

'Okay.'

20

We were sitting on Queenscliff Pier by six-thirty. According to Tom, the sun was due to come up in eleven minutes—he'd checked the previous day's newspaper.

Tom chose a position a quarter of the way along the pier, where he'd set us up on two low stools with canvas seats and strange-looking fishing poles. A dozen other guys were there at that hour—sitting in camp chairs or on upturned buckets, jiggling their lines.

Despite the number of people, it was quiet. Nobody spoke, mostly because many of the guys appeared to be there alone. One guy used what looked like a homemade bamboo fishing pole.

The sun had not yet risen but I could see pale light creeping over the horizon to the east.

'There's a lot of people here,' I said.

'This is nothing. Two hours ago, it would've been packed. In December and January, people come at, like, nine o'clock in the morning to get their spot for the *next night*. It's crazy.'

We faced the south side of the pier, with views to the fort, the water tank and the black lighthouse.

From his bag, Tom produced an old margarine container with small, colourful lures. 'And they're not locals,' he added. 'They come all the way from Melbourne.'

'Must have to get up early.'

'Everyone's here for squid. You can use a normal rod but most people use these squid poles. Do you know how to tie a knot?'

'We do clinch knots. Is that what you do?'

'I'll do it.'

He tied one of the plastic fish to the end of the line and passed it to me; it was heavier than the ones I used when I fished with Dad in Minnesota.

'We want squid too,' he said. 'That's why we're at this end of the pier. It's the weed beds around here. They love 'em. They like shallow water too.'

He tied a lure to his own line and dropped it into the water. A gull squawked above us.

'Sometimes you'll see their ink, so you know where they are.'

'No bait?'

'You can, but these jigs are enough. You need to give it a shake to attract the squid. They think the lure's an injured prawn.' He demonstrated, flicking the jig in and out of the water. Along the pier, other anglers were doing the same.

'I love this time of day,' he said. 'So peaceful.'

Never in my life had I longed for peace and quiet as much as I had since Scarlett came along. I didn't know how Mom could stand listening to her crying all day. I guessed she had no choice.

In the near distance we could see the bluff, and the light from the black lighthouse winked at us every ten seconds or so.

All around, the sky was streaked in pinks and oranges, the wind whistling past my ears and blowing my hair across my face. On the beach, an old guy in trackpants led his German shepherd along the waterline, the dog sniffing at whatever the tide had dumped on the shore.

'When we get bored of this we can go to the end of the pier and try to catch a fish. It's good here for snapper. Salmon too, if we're lucky.'

Further up the pier, where the water was deeper, some guys used conventional fishing poles.

'You have to get a licence to fish in Minnesota,' I said.

'Why?'

I shrugged.

'How much?'

'Ten bucks or so.'

'Rip-off. What else did you do there—like, in the holidays?'

'Boring lake drives. Since Mark got back from Kuwait, he spends a lot of time in a hammock.'

The sky turned more orange. We kept jiggling our lines but nothing was happening. Nobody else along the pier seemed to be having much luck either.

'My dad and I used to fish for panfish off a dock in Minnesota,' I said. 'Hey, here's a cool fact. Catfish are covered with tastebuds instead of scales. The tastebuds help them find food because the water's so murky at the bottom of lakes.'

Tom's face lit up. 'Excellent!' He twisted his neck, facing eastward. 'Check it out, Drew.'

Behind us, the sun had breached the horizon, an orange ball of fire. The whole sky was aglow now and I'd never seen anything like it.

'How cool is that?' Tom said.

I wished I had a camera so I could take a picture and show Mom. She'd love it.

'Why did you call me Drew that first day we met?' I asked out of nowhere.

'Isn't that what people call you?'

'Most people call me Andrew, actually.'

'Like on your bedroom door?'

'Yeah.'

'I thought you said "Drew". Sorry if you don't like it.'

'No, I do.' Drew was who I was now. The Australian version of me. The kid who fished at the beach, talked on a walkie-talkie and was best friends with Tom Howell.

'Do you miss America?' Tom asked me.

I took in the sky—all its brilliant pinks and peaches and pumpkins and persimmons—and felt the warmth of Tom's shoulder rubbing up against mine as he jiggled his lure. And was that a tug on my line?

'Not *to-die*, mate.'

21

The morning after Tom's funeral, I ate a plate of bacon (non-crispy; the way Aussies make it) and eggs in the hotel restaurant—a long room, original floorboards in their natural colour. I sat inside, but double doors opened out onto a patio area with more tables and chairs. On one wall, a large wine rack towered almost to the ceiling. I scrolled through social media and news feeds on my phone. Eliot had emailed during the night to say she was a hundred pages into the manuscript and was enjoying it so far. I smiled, but then I realised she was probably just soothing my ego. Was I so needy that she felt she had to send these reassuring emails? Apparently so.

I hadn't slept well, jet lag still confusing my sleep–wake cycle. I must have drifted off sometime about 2 am but was startled awake by a gunshot. I'd been having a dream. I was back in

Mercer Street, Mark standing over me, his body swaying from the effects of alcohol, a gun in his hand.

After college, my dreams were always of childhood, as if I had grown up in the daytime but not the night. The events varied in these dreams, but I always woke with the same feeling of abandonment, as though the sunshine had left me behind. Some mornings it would take hours for that feeling to leave. And it was strange that the images which returned so vividly while I slept felt so distant in the waking hours. The morning sun would burn them away. I had no logical explanation for this. Why did my subconscious keep returning to my childhood when my conscious brain was doing its level best to forget it?

Back in my room, with the porch doors open, I FaceTimed Claire. It was nine-thirty in Queenscliff; four-thirty in the afternoon in Minneapolis.

'How was the funeral?' she asked.

'Good, actually. I'm glad I came. I only wish I'd come a month ago.'

'You didn't know this was going to happen.'

Behind Claire, through the window, a corner of Foshay Tower pierced the overcast sky. We'd celebrated our last anniversary there, eating eighty-dollar rib eye at Manny's.

'How's Tia?' she asked.

'Hard to tell. She's being strong for the kids.'

I thought again of what Henry had said at the funeral, the implication that Tom was struggling. We hadn't spoken again at the wake so I never got a chance to ask him about it.

'It can be a while before these things take hold,' Claire said.

'I guess.'

'Maybe now the funeral's over and life starts settling back into a routine without him . . . and with Christmas coming up.'

'Yeah.'

'How's the weather? Hot?'

'Yeah. Really.'

'Make sure you wear sunscreen. You don't want to fly all the way home with a sunburn.'

I hadn't thought of that. I had a cap but I should probably buy some lotion too.

'How's your conference?'

'Great. The speakers are wonderful and I've met some really inspiring people. There's a *lot* going on in social enterprises. It's quite exciting. But so much more to do . . . What's on the schedule for today?'

'Probably walk around a bit. I haven't really had a chance to see the town in daylight yet. I have the car, so I might go for a drive. Try not to kill anyone.'

She gave me a startled look.

'Driving on the other side of the road takes some getting used to.'

Her face relaxed. 'Of course. I forgot about that. Have you been past your old house yet?'

'Yeah.'

'How was it?'

'Fine. It was fine. Yeah, it was okay.' I nodded. 'It was okay.'

'Sounds like it,' she said dryly. 'Have you spoken with Tom's parents about . . . you know?'

'No.'

'There's time.'

'Sure. I know.'

'Might help.'

'Yeah.'

'Hey, take some pictures of your old haunts. I'd love to see.'

She glanced up from her phone—someone had come into the room. She held up a finger, gesturing for them to wait a moment. 'I gotta go, Drew. Call me later?'

'Sure.'

She kissed the tips of her fingers, then waved goodbye. The screen went blank.

I was twenty-two when Claire and I married. She thought we were too young, but I persuaded her.

Twenty-two felt unusually young in 2002, but in 2018 it seemed positively adolescent. I was in my senior year at Minnesota State when we met. I'd left Ely for college in Minneapolis at eighteen. The four-hour drive wasn't quite far enough away for me, but the in-state discount was too good to pass up. I spent most of my freshmen year alone in my dorm reading Hunter S. Thompson, Kerouac and Ken Kesey. In my sophomore year, my roommate, Jayson, practically lived at his girlfriend's place (she was a junior and lived in an apartment off campus). I loved going to sleep in the quiet and waking up alone.

I was lucky enough to score a single in my senior year. I hadn't dated much in high school or the first years of college. Granted, I wasn't much to look at—I had the toneless chest of a ten-year-old child and chicken legs that were only ever called upon to walk me from point A to point B, no running, jumping, kicking or sprinting required. Some girls thought I was nice; others thought I was too nerdy and weird. When they divided boys into friends and potential boyfriends, I was invariably relegated to category one.

And then I met Claire. A social work major, she was rooming with a girl in my linguistics class, Sarah Fecher, who introduced us at a dorm party. We talked all night—about what, I can't remember, because I'd discovered tequila slammers by that time, but I could tell she was ready to take on the world, even back then.

I built walls around myself, but she kept scaling them. I thought of her as I completed my British Literature course-work, as I ate quesadillas in the cafeteria, and as I stared at the bare light bulb on my dorm room ceiling.

The intensity of my feelings for her left me dazed and lightheaded. When I was with her, I became visible. I existed again in a way I hadn't since stepping out of the glow of Tom's friendship.

Claire and I went from seeing each other three times a week in the first semester to virtually living together by the second. We found common ground in the spicy foods we liked, the post-grunge music we listened to and the classic movies we watched. She somehow slipped beneath my defences in a way no one else could.

I worried that her Afro-Caribbean parents wouldn't approve of me, but those fears turned out to be baseless, and after graduation we rented a one-bedroom apartment together in Dinkytown. She had a graduate position with the City of Minneapolis and I worked part-time in a bookstore.

Her no-kids stipulation hung between us, but I was so desperate to spend the rest of my life with her that I would have agreed to anything. Insecurity had driven all the decisions in my life that I came to regret most.

After FaceTiming Claire, I popped a stick of Big Red in my mouth and trekked back to Tia's to collect the car. When I got there, I found Adam in the driveway washing what I guessed was Tom's car: a forest-green Subaru, maybe ten years old. A family SUV stood beside it, which I presumed was Tia's.

Adam's feet were brown and bare and he wore faded blue shorts that had either been laundered to death or spent too much time in the ocean. Or maybe they were brand-new and designed to look like that. Splashes of water dotted his t-shirt, pink and surf-branded, stretched out of shape at the collar and with a long tear along the seam under one arm.

Something about him taking care of his dad's car stilled me. What would happen to that car? Maybe he would inherit it. But then I remembered that the driving age in Victoria was older than in Minnesota—maybe eighteen? That was still five or so years away for him. And they could probably use the money it would bring if they sold it.

'Hey, Adam.'

He looked up. 'Hey.'

'You doin' okay?'

He nodded.

It was an automatic response. He couldn't possibly have been okay.

I reminded myself to tread lightly.

'Any plans for today?' I asked.

Adam dipped the sponge into a bucket of sudsy water and sloshed it onto the hood. 'Not really.'

'Bet you're glad yesterday is behind you.'

'Kind of.' Then, after a moment, he added, 'People just want to talk all the time.'

I rubbed my tired eyes. 'Is that your way of telling me to shut up?'

He went back to his work, soaping up the windshield, so I

took in the view across Swan Bay and its meadows of yellow-green seagrass. I couldn't see Swan Island from this angle, only the bulky mass that was the main part of the Bellarine Peninsula over the green water. The sun was low behind me.

'If you don't have any plans, how about showing me around town?'

'There's not much to show.'

He dropped the sponge into the bucket, splashing water over the driveway, then grabbed the hose, snaking it across the grass.

He twisted the sprayer to open it, squirting water over the side of the car he'd just finished washing, then tossed the hose back onto the lawn.

'Maybe I could show you some of the places where me and your dad used to hang out?' I suggested.

'No thanks.'

'Or buy you some food?'

At that, Adam looked up and regarded me quizzically. He wiped his hands on his shorts, leaving dark patches of water in streaks. 'I'll get my thongs.'

I followed Adam into the house. While he disappeared down the hallway I went to wait in the living area. Tia was there, ironing the same patch of shirt over and over while staring into the backyard. The sun streamed through the porch doors, slanting across the floorboards.

'Morning,' I said.

She looked up. 'Oh, Drew. Hi.'

Three neat piles of clothes sat on the table, balled socks huddled together at one end. I clocked a red Queenscliff Primary polo that must have been Missy's. The school shirt had changed little, although the black swan of the logo appeared to be in flight now.

'How are you?' I asked.

'As good as sober gets.' She smiled to let me know she was joking. 'I'm fine.' She stopped what she was doing and stood the iron upright on the wider end of the board. 'Fine,' she said a second time, for emphasis.

She looked better than she had the previous night. She hadn't applied make-up and her hair was pulled back in a simple pony-tail, but her skin looked clear and her eyes more alert.

'You want coffee?' she asked.

'No, thanks. I'm gonna head out for a walk with Adam, if that's okay with you.'

'Oh. Okay. Yeah, no worries.'

She sounded surprised, but I couldn't tell whether it was because I'd offered or because Adam had accepted.

Through the French doors I saw Missy sitting at the table on the back porch drawing in a binder book.

'Hey, thanks for letting me hang around last night.'

Tia smiled. 'I enjoyed the company. You sleep alright in the hotel?'

'Off and on. The wine helped, I'm sure.'

'Probably. I've got a nice bottle that we were saving for Christmas, but what the hell. Come back for dinner?'

I didn't want to say no, in case I offended her, but I didn't want to encroach any further on her hospitality either. Maybe she didn't want to be alone?

I wondered, then, where her other friends were. Were people stopping by with casseroles? Checking in to see how she was doing? Maybe they didn't know what to say, or figured now that the funeral was over she'd be okay.

'Are you sure?' I asked.

'\'Course.'

'Okay then, thank you. Hey, I might use the bathroom before we head out,' I said.

I wandered down the hall, passing Tom and Tia's bedroom, and Missy's room, then stopped at Tom's den, which I could identify as such by the framed fish-identification posters and photos of himself with particularly impressive catches. It was a small room, at the rear of the house, one wall lined with Ikea-style bookshelves. A small desk under the window overlooked a raised portion of the backyard.

A MacBook was closed in the centre of the desk. I wanted to open each drawer and look inside. Not to be nosy; just to try to get closer to him. To understand something more about the man he had become. I hadn't seen him for fourteen years. I really didn't know him anymore. I didn't know his political affiliations (if he had any), what food he liked to eat, what he thought about the Democrats winning back the House in the recent midterms, or the UK's upcoming divorce from the EU. Was he content? Was he living the life he'd hoped for? If you'd taken at face value the stories told about Tom at his funeral, you would think he was deliriously happy. But how a person presents on the surface rarely accords with what lies beneath.

Henry's words reverberated in my head. I had grown a thick skin over the memory of what happened in '92. Maybe Tom hadn't.

I let the thought sink away and took a closer look at the pictures of Tom on the wall. One, of him standing on the bow of his boat, was slightly crooked so I straightened it with the tip of my thumb.

I scanned the bookshelves, something I often did whenever I visited someone's house, finding my own book among the spy novels, the reference books and fishing compendiums.

The pages looked clean and smelled relatively new, although creases down the spine told me it had been read. I turned it over, as if I wasn't already intimately familiar with it and read the back cover blurb to see how it sounded after four years:

> Joby Tucker has finished college but still doesn't know what he wants to do with his life. So when his dad dies in a car wreck and his mom, Grace, suggests they drive the length of Route 66 in his honor, he agrees. But as they navigate the 2448 miles from Chicago to Santa Monica Pier, Joby discovers his mother has been masking a deep-seated depression for years, all stemming from an unnamed childhood trauma.
>
> And as they enter California at the end of their third week on the road, Joby discovers the shocking truth about his mother's past, about the father he thought he knew, and the lie they have been living with for decades.

The lie, it turned out, was not much of a shock to readers, most of whom, according to Goodreads, predicted the ending. Some thought the book was too slow; others said it lacked nuance. A particularly scathing one-star review called it 'bloated'. Another called it 'anemic'. Taken together, the two reviews made it sound like a distended, waxen corpse pulled from a lake.

These reviews had threatened to crush my soul for a time. I'd obsessed over them, wondering how the reviewers could have been so obtuse as to have missed the entire point of the novel. Wondering, too, how they could be so cruel. And, later still, wondering if they were right.

But even the good reviews were never enough. I should have known something was wrong when, after Eliot sent the manuscript to twenty-two editors, only one made an offer. It came from a mid-sized independent press based out of Cleveland called Old Wolfe Books, run by a veteran of the industry, Tony Wolfe. Tony had been chewed up and spat out by a handful of the big guns—Simon & Schuster, Penguin, HarperCollins—and several of the smaller players too, and was now determined to publish only books that 'spoke to him' and 'contributed something meaningful to the zeitgeist'. I'd never heard of Old Wolfe, but Eliot assured me it was a reputable publisher of mostly literary fiction. Among its stable of authors, three had won the American Book Award, two were finalists for the National Book Award, and a handful were American Library Association Notable Book winners.

Whenever I expressed any reservations about Old Wolfe to writer friends, I would get back: 'All you need is one to say yes.' But what if that one turned out to be a bad fit? If the other twenty-one publishers didn't believe they could turn it into a bestseller, why should I have trusted that Tony could? He tried, but he ran a small operation of two in-house editors (one of whom was his wife) and one overworked publicist who covered sales, marketing, distribution, foreign rights and anything else that didn't fit into the categories of editorial, accounts, legal or HR. They also employed a year-round intern who combed through the slush pile, and a couple of summer interns.

I believed that publishing a novel would bring an instant feeling of gratification, affirmation and fulfillment. That the world would suddenly open up to me, that I would never again experience self-doubt and that any other problems in my life would be effortlessly dealt with. I would be a Published Author and nothing would ever hurt me again.

For a time I hung on to that belief, even in the face of stagnant sales and sobering reviews. I can't remember the moment when that belief finally curled up and died. But it was sometime between the 'bloated' and 'anemic' reviews.

I reshelved the book and looked up at that picture of Tom and his big fish, and realised how obscene my thinking had become. Tom was dead and I was brooding over my publishing career.

Adam and I met in the hallway. He wore flip-flops and had added a cap. He hadn't bothered to strip off his wet clothes.

'You're not changing?' Tia asked him when we returned to the living room.

He shook his head.

'At least change your shirt. That one's wrecked.'

The hardness in his jaw made me wonder if he was angry at Tia for something.

Without a word, he tore his baggy t-shirt off and tossed it over the back of a chair. He grabbed one from the top of the pile Tia had just ironed and pulled it over his torso all at once, popping his arms out last. It was the same way Tom used to dress and something caught in my throat, as if the past and present had fused and Tom was standing in front of me.

Then Adam turned, breaking the spell, and headed straight for the door without a word to his mother.

When he was out of earshot, Tia said to me: 'About Adam, just . . .' She shook her head, giving me a small smile. 'Never mind.'

'I'll have him back to you soon,' I said.

22

Without discussing it, Adam and I headed toward Hesse Street, passing the church on the corner of Mercer and Hobson. It was ten o'clock and the church bells were ringing. Something sounded off about them, then I realised it was a recording rather than actual bells.

'Your mom said you're done with school for the year?'

'Yep.'

'In the States, high school starts in ninth grade.'

He raised an eyebrow. 'What about seven and eight?'

'We have middle school for that—sixth, seventh and eighth. Some places they call it junior high. Then four years of high school. Do you know what you want to do when you finish school?'

'I'm only in Year 7.'

He had a point. 'Your dad always talked about doing something ocean-related when we were kids, even in sixth grade. Guess he got his wish.'

'I thought we were getting food.'

I'd let myself forget the real reason he'd agreed to hang out with me. 'We will. I just had breakfast.'

He seemed to deflate a little and I thought, for a moment, that he might turn around and go home. But he kept walking.

We reached a bait shop at the corner of Symonds and Hesse. Across the road was a large patch of grass and, through the trees, I glimpsed a triangle of ocean. 'There used to be a gas station here,' I told him.

'Uh-huh,' he said with a good helping of sarcasm.

We continued straight ahead, over the railway line, toward the water.

'This is where your dad and I used to come to fish.'

'Here?'

I pointed east. 'Bit further along, actually. There was a pontoon here then. He said it was the best place during the day, if you could avoid the seals. Did you fish with him?'

'No.'

'Never?'

'Why are we talking about this?'

'Sorry.'

We kept walking east until we could see the fringes of Swan Island about half a mile across the water, a black helicopter hovering in the sky above it.

I gestured to Swan Island, jutting out my chin. 'My stepdad worked there.'

'Swan Island?'

I had his attention now.

'What did he do?'

'Never did find out. Something to do with weapons training, I think.'

'Is that what they do there?'

I gave him a smile. 'Isn't that the big thing about Swan Island? Nobody knows.'

He gave me a one-shouldered shrug.

'My stepdad was a weapons specialist, so he must have been doing something like that. He never talked about it, though.'

'Probably wasn't allowed.'

The storyteller in me appreciated the mystery of Swan Island even more now. That huge parcel of land, looming out there in the green water, activities unknown. So close, yet shrouded in mystery.

'Maybe these days there's more of a focus on counter-terrorism,' I suggested. 'Biological warfare, maybe.'

We walked on, the dry sand giving way under our feet.

'We had so much fun together,' I said. 'Me and your dad. We'd walk to the lighthouses, watch videos. He was always making things in his shed—remote-controlled cars, those little carts with the golf-buggy wheels.'

'Billycarts,' he muttered, as though someone was holding a gun to his head.

'Yeah. He loved the water too. I thought he knew everything there was to know about the ocean. He always had an interesting fact to share. Something wacky about some rare fish that nobody's ever heard of. I don't know how he knew so much. I don't think he read. Magazines, maybe. And there was no Google or podcasts to listen to.'

A group of boys carrying cricket bats passed us, tossing a tennis ball between them.

'What do *you* do for fun?' I asked him.

'PlayStation, YouTube. Normal stuff.'

'Do you ever catch the bus into Geelong? Hang out there?'

'Mum says I have to be fifteen.'

'What did your dad say?'

'Nothing.'

'On the weekend,' I began, 'we used to leave home in the morning and not get back till dark. Our parents had no idea where we were most of the time. And we were only twelve. I can't imagine kids doing that now.'

'Is that why I'm here? So you can talk about what you and Dad did in the olden days?'

Making friends with Adam was going to be trickier than I'd thought. But why was I trying so hard? I'd be gone in a few days and Adam would promptly forget me.

'What do you want to talk about?' I asked.

'Nothing. I want to eat.'

'Okay. Soon. Let's walk some more first.'

Adam led me up a hilly sand dune and along a narrow dirt trail, stepping over the tea-tree roots protruding from the ground.

Soon the silence took on an uncomfortable shape. I thought again about what a bad idea this was. Then, finally, once we'd reached the uppermost point of the hill, Adam spoke.

'Sand is the world's most-used natural resource after water,' he said. 'Did you know that?'

'No.'

'Well, it is.'

We walked on a little further.

'Have you heard about the sand mafia in India?' he asked me. I shook my head.

'The world's running out of sand. The kind we can use,

I mean. We make so much concrete now that it's using up all the sand.'

'What about desert sand?'

'Useless. For building stuff, anyway. The grains are too smooth—they won't lock together.'

'You know a lot about sand.'

'Not really. Did a project on it at school last term.'

So we were going to talk about sand. That was fine with me. Anything but strained silence.

'So it's the good sand that's running out?' I asked.

'Yeah. We're using it up faster than we can replace it. Much faster.'

'And whenever we have a rare resource that everyone wants,' I surmised, 'criminal elements want to exploit it—this mafia you're talking about.'

'Exactly. They import and export sand all over India. And they're kind of brutal about it, apparently. They've murdered, like, hundreds of people—journalists, environmental activists, police officers, government people. One reporter was hacked to death with machetes.'

'Jesus.'

'Right?' He turned to me. 'That could be a cool idea for a book.'

I nodded. 'The dogged journalist who risks his life to expose all this to the world. I can see it as a movie too. The pictures would be great—all that caramel sand against a blue sky.'

But I would never write that book. Big Sand was not a sector I could get passionate about.

'No two beaches have the same sand,' Adam said.

'I've never thought about it, but I guess that makes sense. Like the way CSIs can tell where a certain kind of dirt comes from.'

'Yep. And I know it seems like there must be endless grains of sand in the world, if you think about every beach in every country, but scientists reckon there are way more stars in the universe than grains of sand on earth.'

It was like being with Tom again.

'We've got some of the best sand right here in Australia. Have you heard of the Whitsundays?'

'Uh-uh.'

'There's this beach up in Queensland—it's called Whitehaven Beach—and it has the purest white sand on Earth. It's, like, ninety-nine per cent pure quartz sand. It's won awards. People say it feels like velvet, and never gets too hot to walk on because it's so fine.'

'Sounds beautiful.'

'It is. I've heard it is, anyway. And the water there is crystal clear.'

We continued along a walking trail that meandered through the dunes, passing gnarled and twisted trees, bent by the wind, their bark like crepe paper. An off-lead lab approached and Adam ruffled the fur behind its ears.

'I had a dog when I was a kid,' I told him. 'But I had to leave him behind when we came to Australia. I really missed him. By the time I got back, and we had to move . . .'

'We had a dog too. But he got out one day and disappeared. Someone found him near Swan Bay. Not hurt, just dead.'

'I've heard that old dogs sometimes run away because they want to die alone.'

He shook his head. 'That's a myth. They don't want to die alone. They get confused and can't find their way home. Who would want to die alone?'

★

Adam led me to an expanse of rock pools below the white light-house. He walked ahead of me, stepping across the craggy surface in his flip-flops. At one point he crouched down and I joined him.

'What's there to see?' I asked.

'There's usually lots of crabs—hermit crabs, shore crabs, red bait crabs.'

'What's that pink, spiky thing?'

'Sea urchin.'

In a crevice to my right I recognised periwinkles, although they were bluer than I was used to. I pointed to a group of shells stuck to the rocks in front of Adam. They were tinted in whites and browns and shaped like the bamboo hats Chinese field workers wore.

'Limpets,' he said. 'They're a kind of snail. People use them for bait, but they're hard to get. You have to sneak up on them.'

I went to reach into the water, but Adam grabbed my wrist.

'Limpets have super-strong feet. They can stick to your hand. But there's worse than that.'

'Like what?'

'Like sea anemone. They can sting if you touch them. But the worst thing? The most deadly creature in Queenscliff?' He paused for effect, then said, 'You know what it is?'

I shook my head; he was enjoying himself now.

'The blue-ringed octopus. No joke. Its bite's super poisonous; it can kill you. So watch where you stick your fingers.'

Tom had not been like this as a kid. Or maybe he was just as cautious, but he didn't want to scare me. Nothing was dangerous if you left it alone—that's what he always said. I'd carried that philosophy with me ever since: don't disturb the bear. Don't poke things that can turn around and destroy you.

★

147

For lunch we ate fish and chips at an outdoor table on the foreshore. They were just as I'd remembered, from the same shop, only triple the price. Battered fish, crunchy on the outside, gnarled potato cakes and fat yellow chips. We sat on either side of the table and spread the white butcher's paper over the wooden slats between us.

'Didn't realise how much I missed this food,' I told Adam as we licked salt from our fingers.

'It's the best.'

'Do you ever have egg sandwiches?'

'Gross. No.'

'Your dad never made that for you?'

'Nuh.'

'You missed out. It's a fried egg, ketchup—tomato sauce— and a lettuce leaf between two slices of white bread. You never had that?'

He shook his head.

'Huh. I thought it must have been an Australian thing. Maybe it was a Tom thing. We ate them all the time. It was the only thing we could cook. Do you cook?'

'Toast. Two-minute noodles.'

'I don't think that counts.'

We sat adjacent to the old Esplanade Hotel, which was now a brewhouse and whisky bar. It could have been 1992. I could have been sitting there with Tom, staring across the same ocean. Except I wasn't twelve, and everything was different. In '92, the view mirrored my life. The ocean was endless; it had no edges and it felt as if my life back then didn't either. I could do anything. But then my world closed in and got infinitely smaller and confined.

'I wish I'd stayed in touch with your dad more,' I said.

Adam shoved a handful of chips into his mouth.

'I didn't really know him as an adult. What did he like to do?'

'I don't know.'

'Oh, come on . . . what were his hobbies? What did he get up to on the weekend?'

'I said I don't know!' Adam stood. 'See ya later.' He began to walk away.

Quickly, I rolled up the grease-stained butcher's paper into a tight ball for the trash and chased after him.

'Hey, sorry, Adam. I didn't mean to . . .'

I threw the paper into a trash can and reached into my pocket, pulling out my packet of Big Red. I held out a single stick to him. 'Peace offering?'

'I don't like chewie.'

'You haven't tried this one, then.'

He stopped, looked at me like he was going to punch me, then held out his hand, sighing. 'What flavour?'

'Cinnamon.'

'*Cinnamon?*'

'Sure.'

'Weird.' He accepted the stick and tore off the wrapping. He folded it into his mouth and chewed. 'Tastes like a cinnamon doughnut,' he said.

'That's the idea.'

'Whoa!'

'What?'

'It just got hot.'

He smiled for the first time since I'd met him. A real smile— one that changed his whole face.

It was a small thing, this smile, but it shifted something inside me, levering open a door shut for too long. Maybe I could get through to this kid, after all.

23

On the way back to the house, Adam and I went by the local bakery. I needed a coffee; jet lag was still pressing in. I ordered a cappuccino to go and asked Adam what he wanted. He opted for an ice-cream cone and so followed the server to the end of the counter to the glass case where the flavours were lined up in rectangular tubs.

It was the same bakery from which I'd bought my first sausage roll with Tom in '92, although with a different name and completely remodelled interior.

I was standing back from the counter, waiting, listening to the hiss of the coffee machine, the clang of cutlery and the drone of chatter, when a woman approached me.

'Are you Drew Iverson?'

If I'd been in the US, I might have thought she was a reader who'd recognised me from the author photo on my dust jacket.

Here, it was more likely to be a local connection, but I couldn't place her.

'I'm Samara. Samara Osman?'

Samara was my age, black hair tied into a ponytail, dressed in a fitted black skirt that just reached her knees and a light blue shirt with the top few buttons undone.

'We went to primary school together,' she prompted.

Vaguely. So vaguely.

'I used to hang out with Marissa Davidoff and Lauren Holloway.'

'Samara! Of course! Hi. How are you?'

Not much of her face had survived childhood. Her hair was still jet-black and straight, her eyes cloaked in shadow, but the rest of her face had altered beyond recognition. I gave her a hug.

'It's good to meet you. Again.' She tipped her head and let out a goofy laugh. It was as if she were starstruck. 'I heard you were in town and when I saw you standing here, I just had to come say hello.'

'That's nice of you. Thank you.'

'I'm a big fan, too. Sorry, that sounds . . .'

Like an exaggeration? I didn't have big fans. A handful of readers, maybe, but not fans.

She looked around, wrung her hands, then let them fall loose, like she didn't know what to do with them.

I hadn't noticed him approach, but suddenly Adam was by my side.

'Samara, this is Adam—Tom's son.'

'Hi, Adam,' she said. She rearranged her face into something appropriately sympathetic. 'I'm so sorry about your dad, mate.'

He nodded, then licked the yellow ball of ice cream on top

of the cone. 'You're Charlotte's mum.' Adam turned to me. 'I'll be outside.'

I watched him leave, then turned back to Samara. 'So, you stayed in Queenscliff?' I asked. As soon as I did, I regretted it, because it sounded mildly like a judgement, which of course it wasn't meant to be. Maybe it even sounded rude, as if there might be a reason not to stay.

If Samara was offended by the question, she didn't show it.

'I did leave. But then I came back. Divorced,' she said, holding up a hand devoid of a wedding ring. 'My kids go to the same primary school as we did. Freaky, huh?'

'Yeah. Crazy. You getting a coffee?'

'Yes,' she said. 'Takeaway. I have to get back to work. Houses to sell.'

As she talked, and I watched her lips move and her eyes flicker, glimmers of her from twenty-six years ago returned to me.

'How long are you here?' she asked. 'Where are you staying?'

'The guest house on Hobson. Just till Sunday.'

'Well, I'd love to—'

She was interrupted by the server calling my name. I accepted the paper cup of coffee.

'Would you like to come over for dinner?' Samara asked. 'Maybe tomorrow? I'm not a great cook, but I'm sure I can rustle up something.'

I had nowhere else to be and it would be nice to have a legitimate excuse to refuse another offer from Tia, who clearly felt she needed to look after me; I hated to put her out but also hated to say no.

'That would be great.'

'Fantastic. I'd love to pick your brain about books and publishing. I *love* reading. Come at six. We eat early in my house.'

She gave me the address and I left to find Adam on the sidewalk, down to the cone part of his ice-cream cone, standing near a small group of bikers huddled around a table drinking coffee.

'You're famous?' he asked me after we'd turned the corner at Hobson.

I made a pfft sound. 'She's only read my book because we went to school together.'

I took my first sip of coffee. It was not an understatement to say it was exceptional—creamy, slightly bitter and mildly sweet from the frothed milk. And just the right temperature.

'Isn't it very good?' Adam asked.

My mind was still on the coffee. 'What?'

'Your book?'

I sighed.

'Sighing isn't denying,' he said with a completely straight face, then continued walking.

I smiled. I couldn't help it. Then I jogged a few steps to catch up with him. 'It's a matter of opinion.'

'What's your opinion?'

I took another gulp of coffee. Its texture was incredible—the way it held together. Was this standard for Australia or had I stumbled on the best coffee on the peninsula? That seemed unlikely.

'I *did* think it was good,' I said.

'What changed?'

I lifted the black plastic lid from the top of the paper cup and licked the froth underneath. 'Nothing, I guess.'

'So?'

'So . . . yeah, I think it's good.'

Adam gave me a look. 'Some things we can change; some things we can't,' he said, in a fair impression of my accent. 'Focus on the things you can, Drew.'

24

Back at the guest house, Leon stood behind the reception desk, tapping on his keyboard. He looked up when I entered, a smile at the ready.

'Good afternoon,' he said.

'Afternoon.'

'Enjoying your stay? Everything alright?'

'All fine. Thank you.'

He pushed his glasses further up his nose. 'What brings you to Queenscliff, anyway?'

'A funeral.'

He nodded, as though I had solved a riddle for him. 'Tom Howell. I thought as much.'

'You knew him?'

'Not well. I bought fish from him for the restaurant. Nice fella.' Leon raised his wispy eyebrows at me. 'Long way to come for a funeral, though. You must have been close.'

I nodded. 'What was he like?'

Leon looked at me, his eyes narrowing. I could almost hear his unspoken question. *Why would you come all the way to Australia for the funeral of a guy you barely knew?*

'He was easygoing,' Leon said. 'Always had a story to tell. Really knowledgeable about a lot of things.'

'Happy? Would you say he seemed happy?'

Leon shifted behind the counter, as if I'd asked him to rat on a friend. 'I guess . . .' he said cautiously. 'He seemed . . . How did you know him?'

'Childhood friend. It had been a while.'

'I see.' Suddenly, Leon held up both his hands. 'Wait there. I've got something for you.'

He walked through the foyer to the restaurant, emerging a minute later with a plate covered in aluminium foil and a stainless steel fork lying crossways over the top. 'Here.' He thrust the plate at my chest. 'With my compliments.'

'Thank you.' I took the plate from him; whatever was under the foil was still warm.

Upstairs in my room, I peeled the silver sheet off the plate. I wasn't hungry—I'd eaten fish and chips with Adam not long before—but an intoxicating aroma greeted me: garlic, chilli, ginger.

I set the plate on the nightstand and picked up my phone to see what was happening in the world. There had been a stampede at a rap concert in Italy, a shooting at a Christmas market in Strasbourg and anti-government protestors had turned violent in Paris. I shouldn't have bothered.

I lay on the bed. I wanted to sleep, but instead I read for a bit, then turned on the TV and flipped through the channels until I landed on an episode of *Lakefront Bargain Hunt*. An older couple were looking for a cheap vacationer in northern Minnesota, on Fall Lake, a little ways north-east of where I lived with my aunt while I was in high school. Ely was quite a sanctuary—Shagawa Lake at our backs and views of Bear Head Lake State Park from our front door. Our closest neighbour was a mile away.

Like most Minnesotans, Aunt Jem had a resourcefulness typical of those accustomed to harsh, unforgiving winters. She grew beets, cabbage, carrots and cucumbers, raised chickens and kept a menagerie of dogs, cats and pigs that roamed the house and garden at will. I would walk into the living room to watch TV and find a seven-hundred-pound pig at my heels. The house itself was incredibly messy, which added to my anxiety about living there. It didn't bother Aunt Jem to leave dirty dishes in the sink for days and newspapers scattered over every surface. Of course, my unhappiness had nothing to do with my surroundings. I didn't know that then, obviously. I thought it was the place—the school, the town, the local wolf population and the annoyingly quaint shops—that was the problem. I was blind to the beauty of the place, with its lakes and trees and parks; when you are depressed, your mind can imprison you, tingeing everything around you in grey.

It was on the banks of Shagawa Lake, under the soaring pines and quaking aspens, that I got drunk for the first time, lost my virginity to a chess clubber named Lanie (who dressed like a 1960s beatnik and listened to Hole and the Smashing Pumpkins) and smoked my first joint. (Unlike President Clinton, I did inhale, but it failed to affect me in any noticeable way so I never bothered with it again.)

So many things that shaped me happened by that lake. Getting drunk that first time was like a detonation of happiness. All the fear and miserable memories exploded into tiny fragments, and I felt freer than I had since elementary school. I laughed uncontrollably at everything and nothing, and I remember thinking that this was how I wanted life to be always. Joy, laughter, the itch to try new things, to bond with strangers, to skinny dip—uninhibited—in the cool lake. The absence of terror.

It was easy to hang out with outcasts because they *expected* you to be distant; it was virtually a prerequisite in their worlds. While other local teens spent their nights scarfing burgers at the Dairy Queen, watching MTV, having sex and committing wanton acts of random vandalism, we spent ours at the lake, getting drunk, debating the merits of the Kyoto Protocol and the O.J. Simpson civil trial, and listening to Bush, Candlebox and Collective Soul on boomboxes until the batteries ran out.

In all the photos I have of myself from those times, I'm either smiling, laughing or staring glassy-eyed at the camera. In every one of them I was drunk. Even when a night of drinking didn't end well—when I finished up hurling all over the forest floor or blacking out for hours—I still loved it. There was something gallant, I felt, in pushing my body to its limits. Drinking stopped me caring. I kept drinking because I wanted to care less.

I never thought it would wind up becoming a problem for me.

25

I'd learned my lesson the previous night so walked to Tia's for dinner. On the way, I stopped at the liquor store and bought a bottle of local rosé. I had no idea if it was any good, but I'd heard that decent wine was ridiculously cheap in Australia, so I trusted that a fifteen-dollar bottle (discounted from eighteen) was probably alright.

Via text, I'd floated the possibility of takeout to Tia, because I hated the idea of her having to cook for me on top of everything else, but she insisted. *I'm sick of leftovers and other people's food. I have to cook for the kids anyway. It's no trouble.*

I passed a florist and thought of stopping in, but that felt too much like I was trying to date her—plus the house was full of flowers already. Instead, I dropped into the bakery and bought four vanilla slices. I remembered them from when I'd lived in Australia: a brick of firm yellow custard between two thin layers of flaky pastry, topped with a hard white or pink icing that cracked apart when you bit into it. At the time I thought it was the best thing I'd ever tasted.

'You really don't have to entertain me,' I told Tia as I handed her the bottle of wine and the vanilla slices.

'I want to. To be honest—' She peered into the bag. 'Ooh, snot blocks.' She placed both the bag and bottle on the countertop.

'You were saying?' I prompted.

'What?'

'To be honest . . .'

'Oh. To be honest, it takes my mind off everything. Everyone is so sad. Not that you're not. But they don't really know how to be around me. And the change is . . . I don't know how to explain it. If you weren't here, my life would be exactly the same, only without Tom. But you make it different. And that's good.' She turned on the faucet and placed salad vegetables under the column of water—tomato, cucumber, green peppers. 'Besides, I'm putting you to work.'

I raised an eyebrow.

'Barbecue. Hamburgers.'

'Fine by me.'

'You like onions?'

'Sure.'

'Us too.' She opened the pantry and produced a couple of brown onions. 'What did you and Adam get up to today?'

'He didn't tell you?'

'He doesn't tell me anything.'

She peeled the onions and began slicing.

'We just walked around the town. I showed him some places Tom and I used to hang out.'

'I bet it hasn't changed much.'

'Not really.'

'How did he seem?'

'Fine.'

She raised her eyebrows at me—she wanted to know more.

'It took him a while to warm up, but we got there. I don't know if he just needed to get used to me or if he's usually like that.'

'He's usually like that. Lately, anyway. Probably since he started high school. He was such a great kid. So curious. Always asking questions, wanting to know the ins and outs of everything. I worked out pretty quickly that I couldn't just make up answers if I didn't know because he'd always catch me out. He's very smart, you know.'

'I can see that. And he's still a great kid. What were you like at his age?'

She gave me a brief, lopsided grin. 'The same, I guess. Gave my mother hell.'

She finished the first onion and started on the second. 'So, what did you two talk about?'

It felt as if she was fishing for something in particular. 'Regular stuff. Food, school, how he spends his time.'

She nodded, as if my vague answer confirmed something for her. Or put her mind at ease.

Her eyes were watering and she placed the backs of her hands over them and rubbed. 'He's been disappearing.'

'Disappearing?'

'Yeah. Takes off for hours; won't answer his phone. When he gets home and I ask him where he's been, he says, "Riding around."'

'Maybe he has been.'

'For five hours?'

'Has this just been since Tom died?'

'No, before too. He spends a lot of time on his own. I mean, a *lot*.'

'I did too as a kid. He doesn't have friends?'

'Some. But . . . I feel like he's slipping away from me.' She transferred the sliced onions to a large stainless-steel bowl. 'I don't even think he's cried yet since ...' She exhaled. 'Adam!'

'What?' he called from the other end of the house.

'Come show Drew how to light the barbie.'

This was nice—this casual shouting. If we were at home, Claire would have walked up the stairs and spoken to me at a normal volume rather than calling out from downstairs. Noise is good. It reminds us we're alive.

'Hang on!' he called back.

'I'm sure I can work it out,' I told Tia.

'It's tricky. The igniter doesn't work anymore so you have to use a lighter.'

'Okay.'

Adam appeared. 'Where's the clicky thing?'

'Where it always is.'

He gave her a droll look, but then his expression changed. He must have seen her red-rimmed eyes and assumed she'd been crying out of sadness.

'Third drawer,' she said.

As much as I hated thinking in these terms, it occurred to me that Adam was now the man of the house. A horrible responsibility—whether voiced or only felt—to put on a boy. Would he assume the role of protector? Of handyman? Would he be expected to cut the grass and change blown light bulbs? If he was anything like Tom at that age, he was no doubt more than capable, but it was a lot to dump on his young shoulders.

'Grab Dad's apron, too,' Tia told Adam. 'Bottom drawer.'

Adam placed the long-barrelled lighter on the countertop then slid open the bottom drawer. I watched as he lifted out the folded apron, clutched it to his chest a moment then, hesitantly, held it out to me.

We locked eyes.

'It's okay,' I said. 'I don't need one.'

'Of course you do,' Tia said. 'Take it.'

Adam looked at his feet as I took the apron from his hands.

He led me through the backyard to the barbecue—long and covered in a weathered black tarp that looked custom-made. He pulled apart the velcro strips at either end and whipped it off like a matador, tossing it onto the brick paving. 'Want me to light it?' he asked.

'I can manage.'

'You ever do the grilling?' I asked as the first jet erupted in a row of small blue flames.

'Nah. That was Dad's job.'

'I'd teach you, but I'm not sure I'd be up to his standards. Can you go ask your mom for some oil?'

'Sure.'

I lit the remaining jets.

I expected Adam to return alone, but a minute later the two of them emerged, Adam carrying a plastic bottle of vegetable oil and Tia with a glass of red in one hand and a small green bottle of Heineken in the other, the top already flipped off. She handed the beer to me.

'Go get the patties from the fridge,' she told Adam, then gave him a smile. 'Please.'

He rolled his eyes and headed back inside.

'And a cloth for this table!' she called out after him.

She placed her glass on a timber-topped patio table and sat on one of the cushioned chairs.

'Do you barbecue much at home?' she asked, taking a sip of wine.

'In the summer.'

'What do you cook?'

'Burgers. Hot dogs. I'm not much of a cook beyond that, although I do the bulk of it. Claire tends to work late so I've got pretty good at curries and hotdish. I've mastered my mom's booyah, too.'

Tia scrunched her nose. 'What's *booyah*?'

'It's like a thick stew. It's made with beef, chicken or pork, sometimes all three. Vegetables. Traditionally it was cooked outside in huge kettles, to feed the masses. It can be a whole production, taking a couple of days, but I don't go to all that trouble. With only two of us, it tends to become my lunch for the days after.'

Adam returned with a plate of ground beef rolled into large balls, and a tablecloth. 'Anything else, Your Majesty?'

'No, thank you, my favourite son.' She overplayed a smile and he ventured back into the house.

'I like him a lot,' I said.

'He'll do. Can't really send him back. You never wanted kids?'

Wanted?

'We decided against it.'

'I can't imagine my life without them. Especially now.'

I poured a puddle of oil over the hotplate. The lack of sizzle told me it wasn't hot enough.

'Utensils are in the cupboard underneath,' Tia said.

Missy emerged from the house wearing a princess dress and

one sparkly sneaker. The other shoe was in her hand. She held it out to Tia. 'Can you undo this for me? It's all knotty. Hi, Drew.'

I waved a wide spatula at her.

'*Please . . .*' Tia said.

'Please,' Missy repeated.

Tia went about untying the knotted shoelace.

'Should I cook all these?' I asked, judging the six balls of ground beef on the plate—it seemed too much for three people, especially when each one was the size of a tennis ball.

'Why not?' she said casually, handing her daughter the sneaker.

'Dinner in ten!' she called as Missy disappeared into the house.

I dropped the balls onto the hot plate. It occurred to me what it might look like—me standing at the barbecue, the kids hanging around, the wife looking on. This could have been my life had I stayed in Australia. Had I married someone who'd wanted kids. I took a long slug of beer.

I squished the balls onto the sizzling plate as Tia watched on, sipping her wine, as though this were all so easy and natural.

'There's footage of Tom's boat exploding on YouTube,' she said, apropos of nothing.

'Really?'

She pinched the bridge of her nose. 'Not *exploding* exactly. On fire.'

A gust of wind blew in off the bay, fluttering the napkins on the table.

'So you've . . .'

'Uh-huh.' She took a longer sip this time, almost finishing the glass. 'It's morbid, I know, but I can't help it. I keep watching, imagining him on board, and him . . .' She shook her head.

'Have the kids seen it?'

'I don't think so. They haven't said anything.'

I found it hard to believe they didn't know. Adam, at least.

'Maybe you should—' I stopped. 'Sorry.' I checked the burgers; turned them.

'I should do a lot of things, Drew, but I'm having a hard time figuring out what's the *right* thing at the moment.' A tear dripped down her cheek. 'I don't know why he was out there alone.'

'What do you mean?'

'He didn't have any clients that afternoon—thank God—so . . .' She shook her head. 'So why was he out there?' She seemed to be talking to herself.

I gripped the spatula tighter. 'How did he seem that morning?'

'Fine. Normal.' She lifted one shoulder. 'Good, actually.'

I'd heard that people who are planning to take their lives often seem content right before they do it because they know their pain will soon be over. But that might not have been the case here, I reminded myself.

'I'm sorry, Tia.' I wasn't sure if I was apologising for her loss or for not knowing what to say to comfort her. Probably both.

She acknowledged me with a nod. 'It's just harder now that . . . It's the waking. That's the worst part. Waking up and he's not there.'

The four of us sat around the wooden table on the deck and I wondered if I was sitting in Tom's seat. I must have been. I felt both honoured and like I was intruding. But being there, with Tom's family, wearing his apron, something paternal stirred inside me. And I saw a glimmer of hope for a future I hadn't dared imagine for myself.

Through the open doors I spied the Christmas tree standing in the corner of the living room. We hadn't erected a tree at home, only some smaller decorations around the house. Suddenly it didn't seem like enough. None of my life back home seemed like enough.

After we'd finished eating, Tia began to clear the table. I stood to help but she held up a hand to stop me. 'You cooked. Now you can relax. I'll stack the dishwasher.'

'Are you sure?'

'Of course.' She turned to Adam. 'Why don't you show Drew the stuff you've been making in the shed?'

Adam led me to the aluminium shed behind the carport.

The shed was large—you could have parked two cars in there—and along one wall stood a well-used workbench. Above it, tools hung from hooks on the wall: hammers, screwdrivers, handsaws. Several more were scattered across the workbench and floor.

I conjured up Tom there. Standing at that bench, chisel in hand, chipping splinters off a hunk of wood clamped in the vice, or sanding something to smooth perfection.

It was bigger and not as messy as Tom's childhood shed, but the contents were similar: fishing poles, various projects midway through completion, old toys the kids had grown out of—a pink Barbie car, a child's workbench made from plastic, the carcass of a bean bag without beans. I caught faint smells of the ocean; fish guts, no doubt. An old-fashioned fridge buzzed in the corner.

I leaned on the bench and crossed my arms over my chest. 'Did you hang out here with your dad much?'

'A bit. Not lately. He didn't really make stuff much anymore. Do you fish back home?'

'I used to. My uncle has a cabin in Brainerd Lakes. We used

to go there every summer. Fishing, waterskiing, cruising around on a pontoon boat.'

'What kind of fish did you catch?'

'Walleye, northern pike, trout. Sometimes we went in the winter too. Ice fishing.'

'Did you have to drill a hole in the ice?'

'Sure did.'

His eyes widened. 'Weren't you scared you'd fall in?'

'Nah. It's safe.'

It felt good to be impressing Adam with my own stories of the great outdoors, much like it had with Tom.

'So, where are these projects at?' I asked.

He showed me a few things he'd made: a bird house with a peaked roof and hole in the front; a four-foot-long planter that stood about eight inches high; and a small chest with a hinged lid.

'I like woodwork,' he said.

'I can see that. This is nice stuff.'

'Thanks. Hey, look at this.'

He handed me a length of PVC tubing, thick and capped at one end with a slimmer, longer piece connected to the other end. The longer end was maybe three feet long with a narrower conduit than the shorter end, maybe two inches, joined by an adaptor. The thicker part contained a red button.

'Now I know what happened to the igniter from the barbecue,' I said.

He smiled with half his mouth. 'This is from one my mate's dad was chucking out.'

'If you say so. What *is* this?'

'Here. I'll show you.'

He picked up a plastic bucket containing something I couldn't see and a three-foot-long piece of thick dowel. I followed him out of the shed, through the yard to a back gate built into the paling fence.

The gate opened out to a patch of grass that overlooked Swan Bay, the breeze delivering a strong seaweed smell off the water.

'Nice,' I said, taking in the view. A wedge of black swans in a 'V' formation soared over the bay, the white tips of their flight feathers in clear view, their long necks outstretched.

Adam set the bucket and dowel on the grass and I handed him the PVC contraption. He unscrewed the cap from the end and gave it to me to hold. Next, he reached into the bucket, produced a potato, and jammed it into the skinnier end, using the dowel to push it down. Flipping it over, he grabbed a can of hairspray from the bucket, and misted it into the thick end. Then he held out his hand for the cap, which he screwed back onto the bottom.

He glanced left and right, then lifted the whole thing, resting it on his shoulder like a rocket launcher.

'Stand back,' he said.

I took a step away, for a moment remembering that I was the adult in this situation but not having a clue what was happening or what I should do.

Adam pressed down on the barbecue clicker and, with a hollow *whump* sound, the potato shot out toward Swan Bay.

I don't know how far it went—maybe fifty yards—but it was a long way and the force of the projectile surprised me. 'Whoa!' I exclaimed.

'Cool, huh?'

'Ingenious.'

'Want a go?'

'Okay.'

He handed me the shooter and reached for another potato.

'How does it work?' I asked.

He pointed to the thicker end of the gun. 'Combustion chamber.' His fingers moved up to the longer, narrower section. 'Barrel.' He touched the barbecue clicker. 'Spark.'

'What does the hairspray do?'

'Starting fluid.'

That didn't explain it for me, but I didn't ask a follow-up. He opened the combustion chamber, gave it a spray from the can and replaced the cap. 'You can rest it on the ground if you want.'

I set it on the grass, tilting it forty-five degrees. 'Like this?'

'Bit lower. It'll go further.'

I did as instructed, bracing myself, then glanced at Adam, who nodded.

I pressed the trigger. The force was greater than I'd expected, but the feeling exhilarating. I had a lifetime aversion to guns, but this felt different. More like a sophisticated slingshot, although I was sure that if the potato hit something—or someone—it would do some serious damage.

'Good one,' he said. 'Again?'

I nodded. It felt naughty and childish, and I loved it.

Adam loaded the shooter again. This time, with more confidence, I rested it on my shoulder as Adam had.

I was more prepared for the blowback second time around, but it was even more exhilarating than the first. 'This is awesome!' I said.

'Whole thing cost me less than ten bucks,' he said. 'But hours of fun.'

'I bet.'

'Come on,' he said, beckoning me back through the gate. 'Before Mum catches us.'

Only then did it occur to me that what we were doing was borderline irresponsible and potentially very dangerous.

'You're not allowed . . .?'

He shrugged. 'It's fine.'

Back in the shed, he returned the potato shooter to its position leaning against the workbench. He showed me an antique-looking chest of drawers he was converting into a herb garden and talked about a couple of YouTubers he followed who, like him, spent their spare time turning junk into something useful.

Then I said, 'Is everything okay with you? I mean, apart from the obvious?'

He turned and fiddled with something on the bench as if it had just occurred to him that he needed to attend to it urgently.

'I mean,' I began, 'people have been saying—'

'People talk too much.'

'Your mom says you've been disappearing. Where do you go?'

'Now *you're* talking too much.'

I took a breath. 'Sorry, I'm no good at this. I'm not a parent.'

'No shit.'

'She's worried about you.'

'She doesn't have to be.'

'Yes, she does. She's your mom.'

He let the silence speak for him.

'Don't you think she's got enough to worry about?'

'That's not my fault.'

Jeez, this kid was hard going.

'Is this what works for you? This smart-guy routine?'

'Okay, Judge Judy. Court adjourned.'

He didn't speak for a moment, but then the hardness of his

face gave way to an almost indecipherable softening around his mouth. 'I go to the caves.'

I knew where he meant—hidey holes cut into the cliff face under the white lighthouse.

'Fair enough. But she'd probably appreciate a phone call once in a while.'

'No one uses phones for that.'

'A text, then. Whatever. You don't need to teensplain communication to me.'

He turned solemn, tucking his fingers under his armpits. 'Drew?'

The way his voice quaked, I could tell he was about to reveal something to me and I was suddenly terrified. He'd expect me to say something back—something adult and wise—but I didn't know how.

'I heard Grandpa telling Henry that Dad's accident wasn't an accident.'

'What do you mean?' I asked cautiously.

Adam picked up a stray length of twine and starting winding it around his finger, avoiding eye contact. 'That he did it on purpose.' The way his whole face slumped undid something in me.

My first reaction was to hose it down—to tell him that it was only speculation and not to worry—but that would have been disingenuous. The fact that he'd had to overhear it told me that the adults in his life were trying to hide something from him, but I knew from my own experience that kids understand a lot more than adults realise. I didn't want to be just another adult whom he couldn't rely on to tell him the truth.

'What do *you* think?' I asked.

He shrugged, but he didn't dismiss it out of hand, I noticed.

He must have sensed a grain of truth in it. Tom wasn't happy, and Adam knew that.

'I keep thinking about it,' Adam said with a catch in his voice. 'I keep imagining him doing it.'

I knew what that was like—to be unable to shift an image from your mind. I had pictured my own dad's last moments so many times when it happened, when I was only two years younger than Adam was now. Dad trying to negotiate with that guy. The gun going off. Dad falling to the sidewalk, clutching his stomach, blood seeping through his fingers.

Knowing the truth is better in these situations. The mind can travel to the most horrific places if left to wander.

But what was the truth? Maybe nobody knew. What was Gavin basing his supposition on?

'Have you asked anyone about it? Your mom?'

He nudged a coil of extension cord with the tip of his shoe, shaking his head.

'Why not?'

'She's sad enough. Maybe she doesn't know.'

That was unlikely. Even if it was just a rumour, she would know.

'Okay.'

'Do you think it's true, Drew?'

'I don't know, buddy.'

That was as honest as I could be.

26

All night, images of twelve-year-old Tom slipping from my grasp and sinking into the depths of a dark bay mingled with images of an adult Tom doing the same. The white light was there, flashing in my mind.

Adam's revelation had shaken my subconscious. I didn't know how to broach the subject with Tia the previous night so avoided it altogether after Adam and I emerged from the shed to eat our vanilla slices. Instead, Tia and I talked about TV shows we liked and cities we wanted to visit until another bottle of wine—the one she'd been saving for Christmas—was empty.

Now, as morning light glowed at the edges of the shades, I sat on my bed sipping instant coffee from a sachet I'd found by the electric kettle. I read one of Curtis Sittenfeld's stories. It was about a man who exchanged daily emails with his sister-in-law about classical music they liked. Neither spoke of it to the brother and it felt to them more intimate than was appropriate.

While I read, my subconscious idled. I had to talk to Tia. Adam was obviously upset by what he'd overheard; I couldn't just let it drop.

Morning, I texted her. *Thanks for dinner last night. Are you up for a walk on the beach?*

While I waited for a response, I took a shower.

By the time I stepped from the bathroom, a towel tucked around my waist, Tia had replied.

How about 11? I'm dropping Missy at a friend's.

I bought a couple of toasted ham-and-cheese croissants and a coffee from the bakery where I'd run into Samara and sat on a park bench overlooking the heads.

An orange boat bobbed on the horizon, waiting to guide a ship through the channel. I watched as the pilot boarded the ship. I envied the captain—to be able to cede control and let someone else do the heavy lifting for a while.

I met Tia at the lookout between the white lighthouse and the football club. Campers in trailers and tents circled the ground, but it looked to be purposefully organised that way—a strange location for a holiday park. Tia wore bug-eyed sunglasses, so it was difficult to read her mood, but she seemed upbeat enough, her smile on seeing me genuine.

We descended the wooden staircase to the sand, slipped off our shoes, and walked west along the tideline, the Point Lonsdale lighthouse in the distance.

'I remember walking this beach with Tom,' I told her. 'He said something about it constantly changing—the shoreline, I think he meant—and wondering what it would be like when we were old.'

Tia swung her arms gently, flip-flops dangling from the hand closest to me. 'I never pictured us walking on this beach when we were old.'

'No?'

She shook her head. 'We had an unspoken pact. Once the kids had moved out, we'd go back to New Zealand.' Her voice was dreamy, far away.

'You could go now,' I suggested. 'Make a fresh start.'

'I couldn't uproot the kids like that.'

Two boys, no older than ten, sprinted past us, racing to an invisible finish line.

'I don't think we ever would have gone,' Tia said. 'Even after they move out, kids still need you. And then if grandkids came along, I don't think I could bear to be that far away from them. Especially now . . .'

'It's not *that* far away.'

'Far enough.' She peered across the bay. A Melbourne-bound container ship was slowly making its way through the heads. 'This feels like home because it's my kids' home.' She looked amused. 'I'm not sure when that changed for me.'

'I've lived in one state my whole life, aside from the short stint over here.'

'Could you ever imagine moving?'

'Maybe out of the Twin Cities. Somewhere up north. But I can't see myself ever leaving Minnesota. Places like New York City, they don't interest me. Good to visit, but not to live.'

Tia smiled. 'I'm picturing you holed up in some log cabin deep in the woods with your typewriter, a coffee on the desk and a cigarette between your lips.'

I, too, smiled at that image. 'Maybe one day. If you swap out the typewriter for a laptop and the cigarette for a stick of gum.

I couldn't give up technology to live off the grid like some boho woodsman.'

I could see myself living simply—not a recluse, but sequestered away in a small town.

I stopped walking and turned to Tia. 'Adam overheard Henry saying that Tom's accident wasn't an accident.'

She nodded, the expression on her face not changing: it didn't come as a surprise.

'Is that what *you* think?' I asked, suddenly feeling empty inside as the potential for this to be true grew stronger.

Absently, she turned her wedding ring. 'I don't know.'

'Why would Gavin think that?'

'Tom was quiet. More so lately.' We started walking again. 'He liked being alone out there on the water. I mean, he was still great with people. We still went out socially. You know how he was—everyone loved him. But I could see that it was an effort for him sometimes.'

'What was?'

'Acting like the person they all expected him to be.'

'And what about with you? If you don't mind me asking.'

She shrugged. 'He was different, yes, looking back. But never angry or bleak. Normal. Well, what became normal.'

'Could he have been depressed?'

'He wasn't depressed,' she said emphatically. 'I would have known. Everyone's so quick these days to say someone's anxious or depressed, when it's just a rough patch or run-of-the-mill sadness. *Normal*. But, no, give them a diagnosis, prescribe some medication and send them on their way. He was going through a low time maybe, but he wasn't depressed. Not, like, clinically.'

How could she be so sure? People can be very adept at hiding depression, even from those closest to them.

I felt at once outraged that she knew about his change in mood and could talk about it so calmly, and also unbelievably sad—a new kind of sadness, now tinged with a sense of helplessness—because now it really seemed like it could be true: Tom had meant to die out there on the water.

'Don't you want to know what happened?' I asked. 'To be sure?'

'Yes.' Then she shook her head. 'No.'

'No?'

'It's too much now. I can't . . .'

I put my hand on her forearm. 'Tia . . .'

'If it's true,' she said, 'it means I didn't see it coming. I could have stopped it.'

'Maybe on that day. Maybe that one time.'

'I could have got him help.'

Although I couldn't see her eyes, I saw the tension in her jaw.

'Well,' I said, 'we don't know anything for certain right now.'

I knew something about Tom that I was sure she didn't—something that might shed light on his state of mind. I stood there on the beach, looking south toward the white lighthouse, clouds brewing over the sea and salty wind whipping through my hair, weighing my options. *How much to tell her?*

'I guess you know what Tom and I went through as kids?'

'He told me.'

'What did he say?'

She gave me a strange look: *Was there more than one side to the story?*

'I'm just interested in his take,' I said.

'He said your stepdad got crazy angry and your mum shot him to protect you—and that he saw the whole thing. Isn't that what happened?'

'Pretty much.'

She whipped off her glasses. 'What didn't he tell me, Drew?'

'Nothing. I, um . . .'

'Why are you hesitating?'

'It's painful. I don't like to . . .'

'I can understand that, but . . .'

'I was just thinking. That's why I hesitated.'

Changing my story. A telltale sign of lying.

'Thinking about what?'

'Wondering if maybe it affected him more than he realised.'

She replaced her glasses and we kept walking. 'He wasn't seeing a counsellor or anything. Are you?'

I gave her a questioning look.

'You were there too. It was your parents. How have *you* dealt with it?'

'I don't know. I just have.'

'You don't ever . . .?'

I shook my head. I never thought about it anymore. I worked hard to never think about it.

Tia took a deep breath. 'Sometimes I feel emotionally barren,' she said. 'Like I don't know how to love.' She twisted her lips, thinking. 'No, I know how to love; I don't know how to show it. Maybe I didn't show Tom enough love.'

'Don't do that, Tia.'

'My parents never showed us any emotion. I can't make the same mistake with my kids.'

'It's good to think about these things. Most parents don't.'

She squinted at me, as if trying to work something out.

'So, what are you going to do about Adam?' I said to change the subject, but immediately realised that it wasn't my place to ask. 'Sorry, it's none of my business.'

'No, it's a good question. I'll talk to him, I guess. I have to.'
She tilted her face toward the sun. 'I can't pretend I don't know
what he overheard. I just wish . . .' She put her hands on her hips
and blew out a long stream of air. 'I don't know what I'm going
to say, to be honest.'

'The truth's a good place to start.'

What a hypocrite. I'd been hiding truths from one person or
another my entire life.

'That's the thing. We don't know the truth.'

'And *that's* the truth. That's what you tell him. It doesn't
change who he—' I shook my head. 'Sorry. I'm not even a
parent. I can't imagine . . . I'm sure you'll work it out.'

I thought about my own experience. It's impossible to hide
things from kids, I knew. They see everything. Well, they feel
it, at least.

'If it helps,' I said, 'my mom told me exactly what happened
to my dad when he died. Did you ever hear about that?'

'Tom said something. A convenience store robbery?'

'An ATM. He was shot trying to help a woman who was
being held up. Mom didn't keep anything from me. And all
those details scared me. I had nightmares imagining it, but I was
always glad I knew. I wanted to know everything about him
because it made me feel closer to him. Not knowing, sometimes,
can be worse.'

'I'll keep that in mind.'

We continued a little further, stepping around sunbathers
stretched out on brightly coloured towels the size of bedsheets,
listening to the soft swish of the tide hitting the shore.

'Hey, is Adam around today?' I asked. 'Thought I'd see if he
wanted to hang out for a bit.'

Tia bit her lip.

'What?' I asked.

'Nothing.'

Maybe she was concerned I would talk to him about the circumstances around Tom's death.

'I appreciate you spending time with him,' she said, 'but I'm worried that . . . He's already lost his dad, and you're leaving on Sunday.'

'I know all that, but—'

'He's not around anyway,' she said quickly. 'They've got an end-of-school thing this afternoon.' She closed her eyes for a long second then turned to face the bay.

Why was she lying?

27

In the afternoon, after devouring a tray of mixed sandwiches from the bakery for lunch, I showed up at Tom parents' house on King Street unannounced.

Structurally, the house was the same, although painted a different colour these days. The silver birches in the front garden now towered over the roof, and once-tiny hedges were clipped to waist height.

The screen door opened and Gavin was there. He'd been at the funeral, of course, but seeing him in casual clothes and bare feet, his thick white hair rising untidily from his forehead, brought something back.

'Drew.' He said my name with a mix of surprise and delight. 'Come in.'

Passing through the front door, a rush of images from the past rose up; our school shoes kicked off on the stoop, video nights and egg sandwiches. Although the entry looked different—a new print above the hall table, wide floorboards instead of slate tiles—it smelled just as I remembered.

Gavin stood at the front door, allowing me a moment for it to sink in, then led me inside. 'Gillian's through here.'

The kitchen seemed smaller, and had been updated to all-white cabinetry, a black stone countertop and shiny silver appliances. It was a lot messier back then, too. Maybe they had more time to clean now that they were retired and it was only the two of them.

Gillian planted a kiss on my cheek then set about brewing tea in a sky-blue pot. I asked for water instead; I couldn't stomach hot tea.

The tea made, the three of us sat at the kitchen table.

'I still can't believe you're here,' Gillian said. 'Tom would have been so touched.'

At the funeral she'd worn make-up, a dress, but today she was the person I remembered, more or less. Her hair was whiter, her face more lined, but she still seemed like someone comfortable in their own skin. I wondered if she still rode a motorcycle.

'I'm sure he knows,' Gillian continued. 'Somehow.'

I didn't know what to say to that. My connection to Tom—in the physical world, at least—had been dissolving for some time, but some invisible wire connected us. Still, I couldn't claim to know him anymore, although I felt I understood the essence of him. A person couldn't change *that* much, could they? He was, at heart, the same when he came to the States with Tia. But what he became after that—a father, a business owner, an active member of the community—and whatever his state of mind was when he died, I was seeing through a thick plate of glass, unable to touch it.

'How much do you remember about the time you spent here?' Gavin asked. 'What year was it?'

'Ninety-two. Sixth grade.'

'That's right.' Gavin ran a hand through his hair. The physical similarities between Tom and his dad materialised: the shape of the head, the hairline, the eyes that took in everything.

'I remember an amazing amount, actually. I have a good memory anyway, but I guess being in a completely different place heightens the senses. And it was a period of transition for me as well—my dad had just died, Mom had married Mark, I became a brother. At the time, it seemed like a natural progression from one big change to the next. But when I think about it now, it was all very significant. And now that I'm here . . .' I couldn't finish the sentence because I didn't know how. Something floated, rising inside me, but I couldn't make out what it was or forecast where it would land.

Outside, in the yard, I could see a corner of the shed. It would always be Tom's shed to me. Were remnants of his handiwork still in there somewhere?

'What's it like being back?' Gillian asked.

I exhaled. 'Strange. It's weird to think that Queenscliff went on without me after I left—people kept moving in and out, stores closed, new ones opened. In my mind, it was suspended in time. Not that it's changed much.'

'We won't let it,' Gillian said. 'We fight to keep it as it is. We don't always win, of course—like with the marina—but it's pretty well preserved.'

Gavin picked up the thread. 'It's a catch twenty-two. Most locals don't want to see overdevelopment but, outside of summer, it's still a quiet place: not much money floating around to keep the local economy going. In the hotter months, of course, it's bursting with tourists, but businesses have to survive all year round.'

I couldn't imagine Queenscliff as a bustling place. In '92, summer vacation over, I could walk to the store and back and literally see only three people.

'The marina's brought money to the town, no doubt,' Gillian said. 'All those fancy boats—the floating gin palaces and the plastic fantastics. But there are costs, too. Social costs, aesthetic costs. In some ways, Queenscliff's lost that fishing village atmosphere. It used to be a people's harbour. Now . . .' Her gaze slid to Gavin. 'Well, it's very difficult for some of us locals to berth boats there.'

Was she referring to Tom? Was his business in financial trouble, struggling to compete with larger charter operations? Rising mooring costs?

'Where did you go when you left here?' Gillian asked. 'Back to Michigan?'

'Minnesota,' I corrected her. 'To another small town—in the north. It was too small for me at the time, but now that I'm older, I can see the charm of living in a tight-knit community.'

'We've had the same permanent population here for, what, thirty or forty years,' Gillian said. 'In terms of numbers, I mean. But the peninsula is growing. More estates going up around Ocean Grove and the like. It's getting expensive. The secret's out—all those sea-changers realising how good we've got it down here. It's even expensive to come for a holiday. It's all Airbnbs now.'

Gillian pushed a plate of cookies across the table and I chose one with chocolate chips.

'He never . . . Tom never spoke about anyone the way he spoke about you,' she said. 'Of course he had other friends—he wasn't a loner; I don't mean that—but no one as close as you two were. Maybe it was the age that you met, maybe it was what you went through together. I don't think he connected with anyone so deeply again until he met Tia.' She shrugged. 'Probably why he put a ring on her finger as fast as he could. Maybe he was worried he'd never find it again.'

Tom and I had both married very young—that hadn't occurred to me before.

'I've been spending time with Adam,' I said. 'He's a good kid. Reminds me a lot of Tom around that age.'

'They used to be so close,' Gillian said. 'But I guess most kids drift away from their parents in the teenage years. We pretty much lost Henry when he left home and moved to Melbourne, and he's only now starting to come back to us, now that he's more settled in his own life. He turned forty last year—that was a shock.'

'For you or him?'

She smiled. 'Both! But he's content now. It took a long time, but he found his way. He and Tom were never close growing up, but I sensed them connecting more in recent times.' She looked at her husband. 'Don't you think?'

Gavin nodded his agreement.

'It brings me such comfort that we've got those grandkids, though,' she said. 'They walk here sometimes after school. It's lovely.'

'Do you think Tia will stay in Queenscliff?'

Gillian flinched and I immediately regretted asking.

'Did she say something to you?' Gavin wanted to know.

'No, nothing. I just thought that, being from New Zealand . . .'

'She's not very close to her family,' Gillian said with certainty. 'They didn't even show up for the funeral! Although apparently her sister's coming to help out in the New Year, when the kids go back to school.'

Since sitting down, my stomach had been churning. The churning had now developed into sharp cramps in my abdomen. 'Okay if I use the bathroom?'

'Sure,' Gillian said. 'You remember where it is?'

'Yeah, I think so.'

I headed down the hallway, passing a photo of Tom and Tia's wedding and framed shots of Adam and Missy at various ages— Adam holding a wad of green playdough up to the camera and Missy sitting on the sand, peering up, a red plastic bucket at her side. There was one of Henry dressed in a suit at what looked like an opening—probably the premiere of one of his theatre productions.

At the end of the hallway, the door to Tom's old room was ajar. I pressed my hand against it, opening it wider. It had been converted to a kids' room with twin beds—for Adam and Missy, no doubt—and looked nothing like it used to. Even the carpet and window shade were different. I wanted to see Tom's clothes scattered across the floor, the loose components of remote-controlled cars strewn over the desk and one of our walkie-talkies resting on the windowsill. Nothing of him remained, and it felt for a moment as if our past had been erased.

A faint blast sounded, from Swan Island probably, bringing me back to the present day, and I pulled the door closed again.

I used the bathroom, but it brought me scant relief. When I returned to the table, the mood between Tom's parents had changed, and they both looked uneasy. What had they discussed while I was gone?

'Is everything okay?' I asked, pulling out my chair.

They exchanged an awkward glance.

'We know what really happened on Mercer Street,' Gavin said. 'Tom told us.'

Something inside me contracted.

'Oh.' I sat back down. Part of me was shocked that he'd told them—that they had known this entire time—but another part, a bigger part, was relieved that he hadn't borne that burden alone.

'Did he ever talk to anyone about it?' I asked. 'A professional?'

Gavin's expression changed then, turning harder.

'I'm not making a judgement here,' I clarified. 'Or questioning any of your decisions. I wouldn't have known what to do.'

I doubted if I'd ever learn how much Tom was affected by what happened on Mercer Street. Maybe it accumulated over time? Maybe he wasn't even aware of the source of whatever issues he was having?

'He was fine,' Gillian said with a quiver in her voice. 'He always seemed fine.' Was she thinking about what Gavin had told Henry?

'Tia said he might have been going through a rough patch lately,' I ventured. 'Did you get that sense too?'

'He was questioning some things,' Gavin answered in a sure-footed way. 'Was that really the career he wanted? Could he have been doing more? You know in high school he wanted to be a marine biologist?'

I nodded.

'I think he felt trapped,' Gavin went on, steepling his fingers.

'Oh, Gavin,' Gillian reproached him.

'I'm not blaming anyone here, Gill. But he had a family to feed. He couldn't just up and leave his business, could he? He had responsibilities.'

That felt like old-fashioned thinking to me. There are ways—studying part-time to get a qualification, winding up the business slowly until the new career takes off. Plus, Tia worked. She could have supported the family financially for a while. She would have done that for him.

I said goodbye to Gavin and then Gillian saw me to the door. I hugged her, then turned to leave, but she called my name.

'Are you . . . okay?' she asked. She meant fundamentally, I understood.

'Sure. I'm fine.'

'It was brave what you did. Protecting your mother like that.' She shook her head. 'What it must have cost you . . .'

I nodded, then turned and walked the brick path to the sidewalk. I had the distinct feeling that Tom hadn't told them the truth at all.

28

Mark hobbled into the kitchen one Saturday morning still dressed in his summer pyjamas. I'd rarely seen Mark in pyjamas. He was generally an early riser—showered, shaved and dressed before I was even awake. I was at the table eating Weet-Bix (I'd never heard of them before coming to Australia, but that's what Tom, and most of the other boys at school, ate for breakfast). Mom had Scarlett pressed to her chest, manoeuvring her this way and that, drawing sharp breaths when Scarlett did something Mom didn't like.

'You're shuffling around like an old horse this morning,' Mom told Mark.

She didn't look much better, her eyes hanging out of her head and her hair a tangled mess.

'Just overdid it at work yesterday,' he said. 'Have we got any Tylenol?'

'Panadol. It's the same thing.' She motioned to a packet on the counter.

He picked up the box, examined it, then put it back. 'Maybe Advil would be better anyway, for my kind of pain.'

'You're probably right. Andrew? Could you run to the drug-store, hon?'

Drew. 'Sure.'

With her spare hand, she pulled banknotes from her purse, examining each one before passing me a five-dollar bill.

I walked to Pardeys on Hesse. The bike would get me there and back too fast.

In the store, I scanned the shelves but couldn't find Advil. What did catch my eye, though, were lines of antique medicine bottles with the original labels on shelving above the dispensary.

'Can I help you?' a woman with frizzy hair and a pinched face asked. She wore a white coat.

'Have you got any Advil?'

''Fraid not. But I can give you something similar. Is it for you?'

'No, it's for—it's for someone else.'

'Your mum or dad?'

'Yeah.'

She handed me a box of Nurofen.

I walked home the same way I'd come—up Hesse, past the ice-cream store and Eddie's. As I turned the corner at Stokes I saw Lauren from school coming the other way.

'Hi,' she said.

'Hi.'

She wore floral tights and a crocheted crop top, a square of sunlight hitting one bare shoulder.

'Are you, like, *stalking* me?' she asked.

'No,' I said, sounding too defensive, even to my own ears. I held up the white bag. 'Just getting some drugs.'

She looked at me strangely for a second, as though unsure if I was trying to make a joke, then said, 'Oh. *Medicine.*'

'Yeah.'

'I was just kidding about the stalking stuff.'

'I know.'

Waiting on the road just near us was the horse and cart the local bakery used for home deliveries. I could smell the horse—a mix of manure and hay—and had to rub my nose.

Lauren shook back her blonde hair, which gleamed in the morning light. 'Are you going to Marissa's party?'

'I guess. Tom wants to go, so I guess I'll . . . yeah.'

'It's gonna be radical. She has *such* a nice house. Where do you live?'

'On Mercer.'

'Cool. So . . . did you have a girlfriend in America?'

'Ah . . .' Suddenly a circle of pink gum squished into the sidewalk long ago looked extremely interesting to me, so I pressed the sole of my flip-flop into it and twisted my foot. 'No, not really.'

Not really? There were no degrees of 'no' in this scenario.

'Me neither,' she said. 'A boyfriend, I mean. In Australia.' She laughed in a fake way, dipping her eyes. It was the first time I'd detected anything other than self-confidence on her face.

'Anyway, I have to get this home,' I said, holding up the bag.

'Righto. Guess I'll see you at school.'

'Guess so.'

★

On Monday, I arrived home from school to find Tom's mom sitting at our kitchen table. Scarlett was in the portable crib on the sofa, quiet for a change.

'Hi, Gillian,' I said, as if everything were normal.

'Hiya, Drew.' She grabbed a cracker from the plate of Ritz on the table. Mom's hostess skills had taken a dive since Scarlett had arrived.

Mom opened her mouth to say something, but closed it again without speaking. She must have been conscious, as I was, that this was all new—me calling my friends' parents by their first names and them calling me Drew.

'Just brought a few things I thought you might need for Scarlett,' Gillian told me. 'We don't need them anymore.'

It was weird having Gillian in my house—this meshing of my two lives. It felt as if I'd lost something; as if Mom had weaved her way into a secret part of my new world that I'd wanted to keep separate from this stifling house.

'She brought a mountain of spaghetti sauce too,' Mom said. 'What did you call it?'

'Spag bol. Bolognaise sauce.'

'Right. Bolognaise. Wasn't that nice of her?'

I wondered how this meeting had come about. Maybe Gillian was interested in getting to know my family. Maybe Tom told her to come.

It only occurred to me then that Mom had not made any friends in Australia. Her job was to stay home and look after Scarlett. Being at home all day without anyone to hang out with could be very boring; every kid knew that. (That's why we needed books!) It wasn't like she could talk to Scarlett.

Mark didn't have friends here either, I realised. Not that he'd had any in Minneapolis. He'd moved there from Fort

Hood to marry my mom, so he didn't really know anyone.

'Look at this, Andrew,' Mom said, holding up what looked like a complicated arrangement of padded straps. 'I can tie the baby to me in this contraption and still use my arms. Imagine all the things I can do now!'

The way she said it—her voice kind of delirious—I couldn't tell if it was a good thing or not.

I made myself a chocolate milk with Milo and took it into the living room with a banana and two cookies from the jar, which was almost empty again. I went to turn the TV on but hesitated. What if I woke Scarlett? I peered into the crib. She was sound asleep and looked so peaceful. I didn't want to disturb her. I took my food to the rug in front of the TV and turned the volume way down before switching it on.

Degrassi Junior High was on Channel 2, but I wasn't really paying attention to what Spike and Joey Jeremiah were doing. Instead, my ears tuned into the discussion between Gillian and Mom in the kitchen. Gillian's back was to me, but I could see Mom's face.

'I was the same with Henry,' Gillian was saying. 'I was *constantly* tired, doubted every decision, thought that every other mother was doing a perfect job and couldn't understand why I wasn't. I became sort of cuckoo. Had terrible thoughts.'

'Like what?' Mom asked tentatively.

'Like how good it would be to go to sleep and never wake up. Or to walk out the door on my own and just keep walking straight into the ocean.'

The look on Mom's face said it all—horror, alarm, recognition.

'Some days I would *beg* Gavin to stay home from work. The days were so long.'

'Andrew was such a good baby,' Mom said. 'But I was so

afraid of doing something wrong. I had this feeling like I had no business being left in charge of this little human being. I'd had no experience with babies. Neither had David. I mean, what lunatic gives someone with no idea what they're doing such an important job?'

'They tell you it's all supposed to come naturally,' Gillian said. 'As if we're born knowing how to look after a newborn. As if maternal instinct will get us through. What they don't tell you about is the craziness that can come along with it. No one talks about *that*.'

Mom bit off a tiny corner of cracker. 'It was my greatest fear—that I couldn't protect this helpless little creature from all the bad in the world. Or that I'd just be a bad parent to him.'

Gillian nodded, and Mom continued. 'I had so much I wanted to do when I finished college—go to Italy and Spain, maybe join a travelling theatre troupe. I loved acting in high school. But then I married David and we had Andrew straightaway. So that was the end of that.'

'You're travelling now.'

Mom gave her a weary smile. 'I'm stuck in the house most of the time. At least if I was in Minnesota, I'd have my mom to help. My sister Jemima. But here . . . Mark's gone all day, and when he gets home, he's . . .' She paused, pursing her lips as if to stop the words coming out. 'Everything's breaking down in this place.'

Gillian leaned forward. 'What do you mean?'

'The latch on the front gate's broken, one of the sliding doors sticks. In the bathroom—' She broke off abruptly. 'Sorry—you didn't come here to listen to me complain.'

Gillian's shoulders seemed to relax. 'You're allowed to complain. We all have to vent our frustrations sometimes.' She took a sip from her mug. 'Can't the army send someone to fix that stuff? It's their house.'

'Mark says he'll do it, but he never seems to get around to it. He's . . . distracted. He went through a lot last year in Iraq and all, and he's still . . . he's still processing it, I think.'

I wondered if Mom, too, was still processing it. I remembered her obsessively watching the war on TV, images of blasts lighting up a blurry green screen; it had reminded me of a computer game.

Gillian touched Mom on the forearm. 'It's not forever.'

That night, in bed, I listened as a small animal scurried across the roof, its claws tapping on the slate. It had the weight of a squirrel but I didn't know if Australia had squirrels. Its footfalls were too heavy to be a rat. I called Tom on the walkie-talkie.

'What's up?' he said. 'Over.'

I pressed the talk button. 'Does Australia have squirrels? Over.'

'Some, but they're not native. Why? Over.'

'There's something running on my roof. Over.'

'That'd be a possum. Over.'

'Oh.' That meant nothing to me, but I'd go to the library (the bookie-lookie) and find a picture of one. I pressed the button again. 'What are you doing? Over.'

'I'm in the shed. Why are you whispering? I can hardly hear you. Over.' Then: 'Are you in bed? Over.'

'Ah . . . no. Scarlett's asleep, that's all. Hey, I thought of some other words.'

'Oh yeah?'

'Yeah. How about heatie-eatie—what do you think that is?'

'The oven?'

'I was thinking the microwave, but yeah. What about a furrie-purrie?'

'A cat?'

'Yeah.'

'I've got one,' Tom said. 'Trackie-dakkies.'

'What's that?'

'Tracksuit pants!'

That didn't make sense to me, and I had a feeling it was something he'd heard before. 'Good one,' I said anyway.

'Hey, Drew?'

'What?'

'We forgot to say "over".'

I woke to Mom banging around in the kitchen, Scarlett crying in the background.

I threw off the sheet, slipped yesterday's t-shirt over my head and walked down the hallway. She was pressing buttons on the coffee maker Aunt Jem had shipped us from home, but it only splattered black droplets into her cup. Scarlett was lying on the rug in a diaper and dirty undershirt, and yesterday's newspaper was open on the table.

'Darn it!' She jabbed at the buttons again.

'Mom, let me try.'

She raised her hands in surrender and stepped away from the counter, pulling up the shoulder of her t-shirt, which had slipped down her arm. A lot of her clothes seemed too big now. Or she seemed too small.

I'd never used the machine but tried to approach it logically, checking if water filled the covered well and that it was switched on at the wall (the electrical sockets back home didn't have switches). I flicked the red switch to OFF and then ON again, but it only spluttered coffee, the same way it had for Mom.

'See?' she said. 'It's hopeless!' She turned to face the living room. 'Oh, for Pete's sake, shut *up*,' she shouted at Scarlett.

Fear stabbed me in the chest. Mom never got angry like that. She barely ever got frustrated. And it was not as if she could reason with Scarlett. Babies were like kittens in that way, I thought. You had to take care of them, but you couldn't control them. It was all take and no give, and there was nothing you could do about it.

I returned my attention to the coffee maker, listening to Mark on the phone to his mom in the hallway.

'I don't know, Mama,' he was saying down the line. 'That's what they said: he couldn't give blood because he'd been in the Gulf . . . I don't know. Something's wrong with his blood, that's all they said. Something they're not telling him . . . Yeah, *us* . . . The vaccines, maybe. I don't know . . . Listen, I gotta go. This is costing me a bucket . . . I will . . . Sure thing . . . Bye.'

Mark came in to the kitchen, his face a strange shade of grey except for the bags under his eyes, which were smudged red. Even in the short time I'd known him, I could see how much effort he put in to maintaining his body, and the contemptuous way he regarded men who didn't. He equated sickness with weakness.

The changes happened slowly. When he first came back from the Gulf, I sensed something different about him. He was not as tall, or didn't stand up as straight, maybe. He got tired quicker, spent more time sitting on the couch or lazing in the hammock. He'd become smaller, as if some part of him was missing—or had been taken from him.

Now, standing in the doorframe between the kitchen and front hallway, his defensive barriers—his height, his strength, his immune system—were failing him, and it must have been the worst thing he could imagine.

'My mom wanted to know if you got the birthday card she sent you?' he asked me.

I shook my head. My birthday was a month ago, just before we came to Australia.

'Bit late, I know,' Mark said. 'But she said she sent some money, so when it comes, maybe we can go shopping?'

'Okay.'

'I was thinking of maybe getting you one of those electric cars you talk so much about.'

I nodded. 'Yeah, that'd be great.'

'We can go for a drive to Geelong one weekend and you can pick one out.'

'Sure.'

He gave me a nod, then turned to Mom. 'Where are the . . .' He clicked his fingers. 'You know, the things to open the car?'

'The keys?' Mom said.

'Yeah. Where'd you put them?'

'Why would I put them anywhere?' she said in a raised voice. 'I can't even drive here!'

When he didn't respond, Mom said, more calmly this time, 'Have you checked your nightstand?'

'Of course I have.'

'Well, I don't know then, hon. Maybe in yesterday's pants?'

He left the kitchen, headed for their bedroom. A moment later, I heard the jingle of keys. He couldn't have checked his pants that quickly—they must have been on the nightstand all along.

The front door slammed and Mom slumped back into the kitchen chair. 'I just want coffee. Is that too much to ask?'

'I'll get it working, Mom.'

I took a breath, then turned back to the coffee maker.

'Sorry, hon. It feels like my brain has disappeared sometimes.'

Mom's mind was growing dark, and a quiet voice in my head asked how much longer we could go on like this.

The school day came and went as usual, except I won three games of downball in a row, which was my record. When I got home, Scarlett was crying in her room. Mom was sitting at the kitchen table, head down, with the tips of her fingers touching her temples. A pedestal fan blew loose strands of her ash-blonde hair into the air. I was holding a paper I wanted to show her—a story I wrote, set in Queenscliff during the gold rush. Mrs Lennon had stuck two gold stars on it, with the words: *We have a gifted writer in our midst. Keep up the good work!*

The story was okay, but it could have been better. An idea that was so big in my head always became smaller when I tried to write it down. I wished that wouldn't happen.

'Mom?'

She didn't stir.

'Mom!'

She lifted her head, looking at me strangely for a moment as if she couldn't place me.

'Do you have a headache?'

'Not a headache, hon.' She placed her palms flat on the table. 'A head fog.' She squeezed her eyes closed like she was trying to push her way through it. 'It's all pea soup in there. Screaming pea soup.'

Something was happening to her. Something not good. She was going soupie-loopie.

She stood, steadying herself with one hand on the tabletop. She was dressed in an old t-shirt she usually wore to clean the house. Scarlett's spit-up stained one shoulder. Damp circles covered her boobs.

'What's the time?' she asked me. 'I have to get your father's dinner on.'

I didn't correct her.

'It's only four, Mom.'

'Four?'

'Is Scarlett okay?'

'What?'

'I'll check on Scarlett.'

I carried my gold rush story down the hall, stopping at my door and peeling off both gold stars. I stuck one each over the 'A' and 'N' of 'ANDREW'S ROOM', then tossed the paper on my bed.

I continued on to Scarlett's room and found her lying in her crib, her face a scary shade of red from all the crying. There was something wrong with her. I'd heard words bandied between Mom, the baby health centre nurse and Mark—colic, reflux, something called glue ear. I heard them again and again but their meaning was lost on me.

I reached over the white slatted bars of the crib and picked Scarlett up, holding her upright against my chest like I'd seen Mom do. She smelled of poop and her face was hot.

'What's wrong, little baby? Are you hungry?'

I glanced at the changing table. Could I do it? I'd seen Mom change her diaper enough times. It couldn't be that hard. Just gross.

I laid her on the soft vinyl top of the table and, with one hand resting firmly on her chest, felt underneath for the box of wet wipes and then for a disposable diaper.

Scarlett was still crying.

'Hold up, little girl. Won't be long.'

I unclasped the studded buttons on her onesie and then pulled at the velcro strips on the side of the diaper.

Mustard-coloured shit smeared her girly parts and the tops of her thighs. I wiped the worst of it with the clean sections of the diaper and tied it into a plastic bag. Her skin radiated red. No wonder she was crying. I wiped her clean with a wet wipe then regretted that I'd already tied the diaper bag. I had to use a second wipe to get the job done properly then put the dirty wipes in a separate bag.

I'd seen Mom use lotion on Scarlett and so searched the table drawer until I found the blue tube of goo. I squeezed a marble-sized dollop onto my fingers and smeared it all around.

She wailed even more.

'I'm sorry, Scarlett. Not long now.'

I wiped the leftover cream on my school shorts, lifted both her legs by her feet and slid the clean diaper under her butt. With the diaper closed and the buttons on her clothing clasped back together, I lifted her off the table and cradled her in my arms. I nuzzled my face into hers, shushing her, rocking her, trying to make the crying stop. It wasn't working. I didn't want to ask Mom for help; she was making dinner now. And besides, I was Scarlett's brother; I could make her happy, I knew I could. I changed her position, standing her up against my chest so we were cheek to cheek. I walked around the room and started to sing softly—'Baby, Baby' by Amy Grant. I ran out of words so swapped to humming the tune. Within thirty seconds her crying had petered out but I continued walking, rocking, humming.

I kept walking right out into the kitchen.

'Mom, has she been fed?'

Mom stood at the counter slicing an onion into cubes. 'You'll have to make a bottle.' She used her knife to point to a large plastic steriliser on top of the microwave. 'Clean ones are in there. See the tin of formula?' A large gold tin sat on the countertop. 'One scoop, fill it to the line with boiled water from the refrigerator and into the microwave. Not long. She doesn't mind it room temperature. Okay?'

I didn't want to put Scarlett down; I'd only just got her to stop crying. I'd have to do it all one-handed.

I managed it, and within three minutes Scarlett was lying across my lap on the couch slurping away on the teat of the bottle.

This was my favourite Scarlett—the quiet one. The one who had everything she needed in the moment. Food. Comfort. Her brother.

I watched Mom from the living room, mumbling to herself. 'Now, I've fried the onions. Next step: tomatoes.'

Maybe Scarlett would go to sleep after this. But eventually, I knew, she would wake—and it would start all over again.

At five, when the house was quiet, the doorbell chimed.

'Andrew!' Mom called from the kitchen.

I rested *Brave New World* on the bedcover beside me and trudged down the hallway. Opening the door, I found Tom's dad Gavin standing there, a tool belt slung around his hips.

'Handyman calling,' he said with a grin.

Gillian must have told him about the jobs that needed doing around the house.

I introduced him to Mom, who was a sight in her stained cleaning t-shirt and flip-flops, and went back to my book.

For the next half-hour, while Scarlett slept, the whirr of an electric drill and breathy whistling came from whatever room Gavin worked in. It was a welcome change from Scarlett's wailing.

Someone tapped on my door and Gavin poked his head in.

'Anything need doing in here, mate?'

'Nah, I'm good,' I said.

'No worries. I'll be off then.'

I knew it was good manners to see someone to the door when they were leaving, and I couldn't rely on Mom to do it, so I stood and followed Gavin into the hallway. To my surprise, Mom was already at the front door, waiting. She thanked him, placing a hand on his shoulder. He put his hand over hers, glanced quickly up the hallway at me, then left.

That night, I sat on the rug in the living room working on my Olympics project for school, a bowl scraped clean of soup beside me. *Home Improvement* was on, but I wasn't really paying attention to it. Neither was Mom, who sat on the couch staring at the TV unblinking, her barely touched bowl of soup on the cushion next to her. I hadn't asked what happened to the marinara sauce she was preparing earlier.

'Mom, aren't you going to finish your dinner?'

She shook her head.

'But you love this soup.'

'Sick of it.'

She didn't seem to love any food anymore, surviving on cookies and coffee.

Mark arrived home then. Standing in the kitchen in his uniform, he said, 'God, Cathy. This place is a mess.'

Mom sighed languidly, as if doing so used her final shred of vitality. 'I just need someone to . . . someone to . . .'

Mom hadn't showered and she had a crusted yellow patch of baby barf on the shoulder of her top.

'Cathy, that person is you. You're the someone. You're home all day. What's for dinner?'

'Soup.'

'Again?'

One day, when she'd found some energy, she'd made a colossal pot of wild rice soup and froze it in Tupperware containers. Now we were living off it.

'I went to the store but I couldn't . . . The baby wouldn't stop crying. I had to come home.'

Mark stood there, waiting for a better explanation.

'I feel like . . . like . . . I can't do it, Mark. I've . . .' She looked down. 'I've been using baby formula.'

I hadn't realised she'd been keeping that a secret from Mark.

'But I thought . . . Mama says breast milk is better.'

'Well put her on a plane and send her over here!'

'Come on, Cathy. Be reasonable.'

'Reasonable? *Reasonable?*'

With that, she seized the spoon from her bowl and flung it at his head, droplets of soup landing on the rug. Mark ducked and the spoon ricocheted off the doorjamb.

'Jesus Christ, Cathy! What's *wrong* with you?'

29

Just as we did every morning, Tom and I met on the corner of Stokes and Stevens so we could walk into school together.

'What's up today?' he said as soon as he saw me.

I was sad, that was true, but how could he tell?

'Things are a bit rough at home.'

I'd woken to the sound of the vacuum cleaner roaring to life in the living room. Scarlett was crying, but that didn't wake me anymore—I must have become accustomed to it as I had to other sounds in the house: the bathroom taps clunking off when someone was done in the shower; the creak of the hallway floorboards. The thought of Mom cleaning again brightened my mood. But then, a few minutes later—the vacuum still humming, Scarlett still howling—I heard Mom shouting, 'Shut up, shut up, shut up!'

I flew out of my bed and into the living room; something told me I needed to hurry. Mom had Scarlett fastened to her chest in the strappy thing from Gillian and was clutching the long vacuum hose in one hand, her head tipped back in defeat.

'What's wrong?' I asked.

'I started the vacuum to shut her up, but it's not working.'

The blank look on my face must have said it all.

'They say the whooshing sound calms them down,' she explained. 'It's like being in the womb again.' She shook her head. 'More lies.'

I held out my arms. 'I'll take her for a bit while you vacuum.'

'I don't need to vacuum, Andrew!' she shouted at me. 'I need her to go to sleep!'

I didn't tell Tom any of this; I didn't have to because he already knew somehow. Or maybe it didn't matter.

As we neared the school gate he held his arm in front of my chest to stop me going any further. 'Let's wag,' he said.

'What?'

'Wag school. Take the day off.'

'Cut school?'

'Yep.'

We walked to the beach, but I kept looking over my shoulder, as if my mom, or his mom, or someone else's mom, or a teacher, or the principal, or any other person in town would see us and rat us out. I needn't have worried. There was literally nobody on the beach, so we took our school shoes off, tucked our socks inside, and set out in the direction of the white lighthouse.

'What's a seppo?' I asked him.

When I'd met Tom's dad for the first time a week or so before, he'd used this word and it had been churning through my mind ever since. He'd said it like, 'Oh, you're the seppo.'

'A septic tank,' Tom answered now. 'A *Yank*. It rhymes. Get it?'

I didn't. Why didn't he just say Yank? Or American, for that matter?

'I thought you liked rhyming words,' Tom said. He dragged one bare foot at a time through the sand, lifted it and watched the granules fall. 'Walkie-talkie.'

'Yeah, I do. I thought of another one when I was watching TV last night. The clickie-flickie. You know—for the remote? You click it and it flicks the channels.'

'Awesome. Hey, I can hold my breath underwater for fifty-six seconds,' Tom said as we followed the tideline. 'How long can you?'

'Don't know. Never counted.'

'Last year I could only do forty-one, but I practised in the bath and now I can do fifty-six.'

We sat on the sand just down from the football field, a few yards from the shore and peered across the bay at a ferry inching its way into port.

I had only eaten half of my bowl of Weet-Bix for breakfast so fished around in my backpack for my lunch box while Tom removed plastic wrap from a white-bread sandwich. 'What have you got?' I asked.

He peeled back the top layer of bread so I could see. 'Strass. Dead horse.' It looked to contain some kind of reddish-brown cold cut—baloney, maybe—with ketchup smeared over the underside of the bread.

'It's not really horse, is it?'

'Dead horse. *Sauce*. Rhyming, remember? I don't know what strass is. Probably pig guts or the arse of a cow, for all I know. What's in yours?'

'Peanut butter.'

'Smooth or crunchy?'

'Creamy. We call the other kind chunky.'

'It's like a different language. Isn't the world complicated enough?'

We looked out at the bay as a pilot boat zipped over the waves toward shore.

'We should camp out here one night,' Tom said between bites.

'Here?'

'Sure. You said you used to go camping all the time.'

'I know, but . . .'

'I'll bring an esky.'

'What's that?'

'You know, the box you keep your cold stuff in. Like drinks.'

'A cooler.' I thought for a moment. 'A coldie-holdie,' I proposed.

'Yeah. A coldie-holdie.' Tom surveyed the coast. 'Beaches are constantly changing shape because of the waves. I wonder what it will look like here when we're old men.'

I visualised me and Tom wandering along the beach with white hair and walking sticks, and smiled.

At home, Corinne from the baby health centre was in the kitchen, but this time Mom was showered, dressed and wearing lipstick. Scarlett was still crying, but Mom was telling the nurse that she had everything under control.

'She's really settled down. I have her in a routine now. Cup of tea?'

'No, thanks. And you're still breastfeeding?'

'Oh, yes. We've really bonded now. It's precious how that happens, isn't it?'

'It is, yes.'

'Lemon bar?' Mom brandished a plate of slices.

It was obvious to me that Mom was putting on an act, and the nurse either believed it or was pretending to because it made her job easier. She could check the box in her report and move on to the next mother at her wit's end.

Corinne took a lemon bar from the plate and smiled, exposing sand-coloured teeth. 'And what about the mastitis?' she asked.

'All cleared up. Those cabbage leaves you suggested really did the trick.'

'Terrific. Sounds like you've got everything shipshape here.'

Mom beamed. 'I really do.'

When she closed the front door behind the nurse ten minutes later, I could hear Mom's sigh of relief all the way from my bedroom.

At dinner, Mark, Mom and I sat at the table eating Gillian's microwaved bolognaise sauce with pasta shells while Scarlett howled in her bedroom. Mom had forgotten to cover the bolognaise with plastic wrap and the red sauce had splattered down the white walls of the microwave.

'Some of the guys are going for drinks tomorrow night,' Mark told Mom. 'Do you mind?'

Mom glanced down the hallway toward the bedrooms. 'Of course not. Go ahead. Go live your life,' she said without looking at him.

'It's okay. I won't go.'

'No. Please. Do it. Go. I *want* you to go.'

'Are you sure?'

'Just go, Mark.'

'If you're sure.'

She forked pasta into her mouth.

'You don't sound sure.'

'Shit, Mark.' She clanged her fork into the side of her plate and ripped a piece of store-bought garlic bread from the tray in the centre of the table. I'd never heard my mom swear before and it sounded so strange coming from her mouth, like a demon had taken control of her thoughts. Even her voice sounded different.

'I'm sorry, Cathy. I won't—'

'Oh, yes, you will,' she said. 'I won't have you blaming— Do it, Mark. Go out and have fun.'

We continued eating, forks scraping on plates, mouths chewing, baby crying.

Then, after a few minutes, Mark spoke again. 'Cathy, if you don't want—'

Mom rose abruptly to her feet, her chair crashing to the floor behind her. 'Go, Mark!' she screamed. 'Go!' She pointed to the front door. 'Get out of this house! Go! Leave me alone in this fucking prison!'

30

Tom borrowed a two-man tent from a kid at school and stashed it in his shed a few days before our sleep-out. It was mid-March; fall had arrived and the weather had turned cooler. We met at the fish-and-chip shop on Hesse at 7 pm and waited outside while they made our order. When we went back in to collect it, the fair-haired lady with the lazy eye asked, 'Chicken salt, boys?' and Tom said yes without checking with me.

We took our fried food, steaming inside the white butcher's paper, and walked back to Tom's place, the sky a dull and formless grey overhead.

'I thought you were staying at Drew's?' Gavin said when he saw me arrive with a backpack slung over my shoulder.

'We are,' Tom said. 'But we're eating here first.'

That didn't really make sense to me, but Gavin seemed to accept it. My mind shifted to the way Mom had rested her hand over his at our front door that day, but I didn't let the thought go any further.

In the shed, under the flicker of a fluorescent tube, we ate our chips, and I officially became a chicken salt convert. I had no idea what it was, and I didn't care. It was yellow and tasted kind of garlicky/oniony, with a hint of sweetness. I licked every last grain off my fingers.

We hung out for a bit, waiting for it to get dark. Tom showed me what he'd been working on for his mom's birthday. He'd painted an old picture frame white and screwed little hooks into the top part. 'It's so she can hang her jewellery,' he explained.

We packed the coldie-holdie with cans of pop (which I'd learned to call 'soft drink'), two 'tinnies' of beer from Gavin's fridge in the shed and two frozen icepacks to keep it cold. A packet of mixed candy from Foodland and a bag of salt and vinegar chips went into the backpack.

At nine, when it was dark, we each lifted one handle of the coldie-holdie and Tom carried the tent on his back, along with his sleeping bag. I had Henry's sleeping bag, and I'd packed extra-warm clothes in case it got chilly on the sand.

Tom had chosen our camping spot already. Or maybe he didn't even need to think about it; he just knew. It was on the shores of Swan Bay, not far from the pontoon where we'd first met.

He scanned the beach, walked a few more yards back from the tideline, then dropped the tent and backpack in a heap on the sand.

'Let's set up the tent now,' he said, 'so we don't have to worry about it later.'

Moonlight brightened the beach and I worried that someone might see us and tell us to leave, or even call the police.

But Tom was already pulling the tent from its long canvas bag and dumping metal poles and a small sack of pegs onto the cool sand.

'You know what to do?' he asked.

'Sure,' I said, trying to sound confident, hoping that Australian tents were the same as those back home.

'What should *I* do?' Tom asked.

I lifted the rolled-up ground tarp, held one end and cast it out like Mom did with sheets when she made beds. 'Take that end,' I told Tom. 'Flatten it out.'

I found the body of the tent, examined which way was up, and flung that over the tarp.

'Hold up,' I said, once it was flat. 'Let's face the door toward the bay so we can look out at it.' I threw him a tent pole. 'Straighten this.'

I did the same until we had two long, bendy poles.

I weaved my pole through the sleeve along the top and Tom copied so they crisscrossed, raising the tent body into its dome-like shape.

'Shit,' Tom said. 'I didn't bring a pillow. Did you?'

'No.' I said. 'We can just use our bags. Make our own . . .' I thought for a second. 'Beddie-headies.'

Tom nodded his approval.

I staked the four corners at a forty-five-degree angle and secured the tabs in the middle of each wall. Then I tossed the rain fly over the top like a blanket, attaching its points to the corners of the tent.

We stashed our gear inside but didn't go in right away. For now, we decided, we would sit under the stars and watch the sea roll in and out.

The surface of the bay was dotted with blobs of black—swans

sleeping with their feathers fluffed out for warmth and their heads and necks tucked underneath their wings.

'What are winters like here?' I asked Tom.

'I dunno. Normal. It can get cold.'

'But not, like, snow-cold, right?'

'Nuh.'

'It gets so cold sometimes in Minnesota that the governor calls off school.'

'Because it's too cold?'

'Because it isn't safe. This one time, a freak ice storm hit. You couldn't drive on the roads. We were on our way home from school and everyone had to pull over and wait for the snow trucks. It was so boring, so one girl got out of her car and, like, ice-skated on the road to entertain us.'

'Cool.'

'Yeah. Usually they're pretty good at getting snow off the roads. Snow falls real heavy and a huge army of these massive snowploughs comes and starts clearing the highways.'

'Excellent.'

'And we go ice fishing in the winter.'

'For real?'

'Yep. You drill a hole in the ice of a frozen lake and drop a line.' I was on a roll; I could sense I had Tom's full attention. Sometimes you don't realise how good or different things are until you're far away from them. 'We have cross-country skiing, too. It's like normal skiing except instead of going downhill it's flat, so you have to push yourself along.'

'We have that,' said Tom. 'Have you heard of grass skiing?'

I shook my head.

'Read about it in a magazine. Sounds cool, and you don't have to wait until winter. Do you go surfing?'

'We don't have beaches in Minnesota. Well, we do, but not the kind with waves. I've heard of people surfing on Lake Superior, though.'

'Surfing on a lake?' Tom sounded dubious.

'Sure.'

'America's weird.'

'Australia's weird.'

'Everywhere's weird, I guess.'

I scooped up a pile of sand and let it sift through my fingers. In actual fact, it was more like white shell grit than sand.

It felt defiant being out alone at night, on the beach, without our parents knowing where we were.

'Let's drink the beer,' I said.

Tom reached into the coldie-holdie and brought out the cans. I shished the tab on top and took a sip. It was absolutely disgusting—sour, bitter, tasted like old cheese. It reminded me of a sweaty sock.

Tom opened his and took a sip. 'Whadda ya think?'

'It's alright,' I said, taking another tentative slurp.

'Get the lollies, would ya?'

I rested my beer on the shelly sand and reached into one of the bags in the tent for the candy mix. I tore open the packet and threw a soft banana in my mouth, followed by a creamy milk bottle.

'Hand 'em over.' Tom said. I figured he was as desperate to get rid of the beer taste as me.

He tossed a few into his mouth without even checking what they were.

'The guy who invented the Milky Way and Snickers bar came from Minnesota,' I said.

'Really?'

'Yeah.' I could never match Tom in the trivia stakes, but I could try. 'We invented lots of cool stuff—Scotch tape, the pop-up toaster, waterskis, rollerblades.'

'Cool. I don't reckon anything was invented in Queenscliff. Do you like any girls at school?'

I popped a red frog in my mouth. 'Do you?'

'Sort of. Marissa.'

I pictured Marissa the way she looked that day we met outside the video store—angular, confident, big hair. Tom was the opposite: short, scruffy, not caring about his appearance. Maybe it was true that opposites attract?

Tom stared across the bay; the wind had picked up and the sand was cool under my butt.

'There are ships at the bottom of the sea out there,' he said.

'Shipwrecks?'

'Yeah. Four of them. Not here, actually. Near the heads.'

'How come so many?'

I wanted to hear stories of pirates.

'I told you. The rip.'

'Have you ever been out to see them?'

'Nah. There *is* buried treasure here in Queenscliff, but.'

'For real?'

'Yep. Benito's treasure. This guy Benito, he stole it from somewhere in South America in, like, eighteen hundred and something, and sailed all the way here and buried it in a cave on the shores of Swan Bay. True fact. People are always looking for it because it's worth millions. Just a few years ago, this company dug a massive hole, like a mine shaft, near the high school, looking for the treasure. And get this: to make sure the walls wouldn't collapse, they froze them with liquid nitrogen!'

'Whoa. What happened?'

'Nothin'. They found nothin'. They drilled some more holes earlier this year, but the council keeps trying to stop them.'

'Do you think there's really treasure?'

'Yep. A lot of other people do, too. One day they'll find it.'

We lapsed into silence, me imaging scooping up piles of gold coins and treasure, then letting it rain down from my hands.

'Hey, don't you want to know what it's like on Swan Island?' Tom asked. 'Like, what they do there?'

I didn't. I'd never cared about Mark's work. Or anything to do with the army, for that matter. 'Sure.'

'Let's go.'

'Where?'

'To Swan Island. Check it out for ourselves.'

'How? I mean, we'll never get through the checkpoint.'

'There's other ways.'

There were only two other ways, as far as I knew—by air or by sea. And I couldn't see us getting our hands on a helicopter.

Tom stood. 'Let's find us a vessel,' he said in a swashbuckling pirate's voice. He started off along the sand.

'What about our stuff?' I said, looking back at our tent.

'Don't worry. We're not in New York.'

I followed Tom along the shoreline, the chilly breeze blowing in off the water kicking up my hair at the front. I knew only one thing for sure—this was a bad idea.

We continued along the beach until we came to a pier. Floating in the water, moored to the dock, was a line of unattended rowboats in varying states of disrepair.

'One of these'll do.' Tom walked along the dock, checking them out.

'Do you know who they belong to?'

He ignored the question. 'Here,' he said. 'This one. Climb in and I'll push us out.'

He'd chosen the one kayak among the bunch, resting partly on the sand. My anxiety went into overdrive. Whose kayak was this? We hadn't asked to borrow it. What about paddles? *What about life vests?*

'Tom, wait.'

'What's wrong?'

Where did I start?

I stood on the beach, weighing my options: climb aboard this tiny, rickety craft or stand here like a wuss on the sand while he had all the fun.

'Come on,' Tom said. 'Let's have an adventure. What have we got to lose?'

Our lives?

I assessed the danger: I was an okay swimmer; Tom was probably an excellent swimmer. And an excellent seafarer.

'What about oars?' I said.

'Good point.' Tom surveyed the beach, then walked off. A moment later he returned carrying two sets of paddles over his shoulder. This kid was unbelievable.

'Don't suppose you found life vests?'

'Sorry, mate. Get in,' he said, lifting his chin in an upward nod.

I didn't move.

'Don't worry,' he said. 'It's shallow. Two metres, max.'

I stepped one tentative foot into the kayak and it rocked wildly under me. The craft was long and narrow and felt flimsy under my feet. The water suddenly seemed choppy, and so much louder in the dark.

I stood, trying to keep my balance while he passed me both sets of paddles.

Tom pushed the kayak off the sand and climbed in, stepping with slow, deliberate movements—getting his sea legs.

I put the paddles down, trying to keep the craft steady as he made small steps. He faltered and reached for me. I grabbed his hands and, together, we managed to find an equilibrium before sitting, me at the front and him at the back.

'Ready?' he said.

I nodded, resting my paddles across the width of the kayak.

'Have you ever done this?' he asked.

I shook my head. 'My dad usually paddled.'

'It's easy,' he said. 'If we work together.'

We pushed off and Tom plunged his paddle into the water to the right.

I followed his lead, sinking my paddle to the left.

'We need to go at the same time,' he said.

With the paddle in his hands, Tom rotated his leading shoulder forward, dropping the blade into the sea. Keeping his lower arm almost straight, he pulled against the shaft, propelling the kayak forward. I tried to do the same but came off looking embarrassingly uncoordinated.

'Don't jerk the paddle out at the end,' he said. 'You're lifting water. That's gonna make it harder and you'll get tired quicker. Make it smooth.' He demonstrated, slicing his blade out of the water.

We started off into the darkness, the smell of the ocean filling my nostrils.

After ten or twelve feet of mismatched paddling, the kayak bucking in the waves, Tom said, 'We're going off course. Let me paddle for a sec.'

I let him take over, peering off into the deep, black water that surrounded us. Dad had been so particular about boat safety.

'Thirty or forty people drown every year in Minnesotan lakes,' he'd told me. 'Another twenty die in boating accidents.'

I glanced back at Tom. His eyes were narrowed, the tip of his tongue poking through his lips, arms pumping hard. I was safe with him. Life vests or not, we would be fine.

In the distance, I could see lights on the island. It didn't look that far away, but I'd heard of people trying to swim across Lake Superior and failing. A few years back, a woman succeeded—the first person ever to do it. It took her something like fourteen hours. But distance across the water can be very deceiving.

As I stared ahead, I started wondering about security on the island. Did soldiers with guns patrol the beaches? I imagined one spotting us, an ear-piercing alarm sounding and a floodlight swivelling in our direction. Maybe they were trained to shoot on sight.

In the quiet, I heard what sounded like a soft honking.

'What's that noise?' I asked.

'Swans. In *Swan* Bay.'

I'd never known they made that sound.

'Apparently they sing a really beautiful song right before they die,' Tom said.

'Weird.' I glanced across the water, trying to see them. 'Maybe they're not singing. Maybe they're crying.'

With Tom paddling on his own (and me not hampering him anymore), we reached the dark perimeter of Swan Island within twenty minutes. I could see beaches, but I had no idea where Tom intended to land. And what would we do once we were ashore? Walk around? How much would we see? A bunch of barracks and mess halls? Maybe a shooting range? What would that tell us?

The fun was in getting there, I guessed. Seeing if we could do it.

All of a sudden, a loud noise sounded from the island and I ducked, as if trying to avoid a bullet. My quick, jolty movement shook the kayak and we tipped sideways, plunging us both into the cold water. I wasn't sure what was more shocking—the chill of the water or the fact that I was in it, way out at sea, in the dark. No life vest. But then my feet touched the sludgy bottom, seagrass tickling my ankles; Tom was right: it wasn't that deep after all.

I swam to the surface and wiped salty water from my face. I peered across at the island but couldn't see any reason for the noise; everything was dark and quiet. Maybe I'd imagined it? I couldn't see Tom but assumed he must be on the other side of the upturned hull.

'Tom?' I called. 'Tom!'

He didn't answer, but then, in the dull moonlight, his hand shot out of the water, waving madly.

I swam over to him, grabbing his hand, but he resisted. He resisted because he couldn't come any further. His legs must have been caught on something.

To my surprise, I didn't panic. My heart rate was steady and I knew, clearly, what I had to do.

I dived under the waves—closing my eyes, because I wouldn't have been able to see anything anyway. I reached out, finding Tom's waist. I kicked my legs to propel myself deeper, padding my hands down the leg that was long and rigid—the one I knew was stuck. Something thin and slimy had curled around his foot—a rope of some kind. I patted it from all angles, picturing it in my mind, feeling for where it had looped his ankle.

Using both hands, I loosened it enough so his foot could slip through.

Tom burst to the surface, heaving for air. He clasped the edge of the upturned craft with both hands, hanging on while he caught his breath. I trod water, waiting, realising only now that, although I had felt calm when I was under the water, my heart was racing.

'What was that?' Tom asked through heavy breaths.

'A rope, I guess.'

'Shit. That was a close one.'

We stayed there in the water, pulling ourselves together, Tom recovering his breath.

'Maybe we should swim back,' Tom suggested. 'It's not that far.'

The do-gooder in me didn't want to abandon the kayak we'd stolen.

'Let's turn it over and get back in,' I said. 'I'll row if you're too tired.'

He gave me an uncertain look, then swum around to my side to help me flip it back over. Once it was the right way up, he motioned with his head for me to climb in while he stabilised the craft with his hands.

For all my bravado, my paddling hadn't improved, and Tom had to take over after a few minutes of going in circles.

Back on the beach, the kayak and paddles restored to their rightful places, we lay on the gritty sand in our wet clothes and gazed at the star-studded sky.

'Thanks,' Tom said.

'No sweat.' I couldn't help but be proud of myself.

'Coulda stayed under for at least another thirty seconds,' he said.

After a moment I turned to face him. 'That was awesome,' I said, smiling.

He grinned. 'I know.'

31

I was shivering in my wet clothes, so we called it a night. We dismantled the tent and I headed home along roads bathed in moonlight, passing two uniformed soldiers stumbling down the street in front of me arm in arm.

When I arrived home the door was locked, so I had no choice but to knock. I couldn't stay out in the cold all night.

I didn't know what time it was, but it couldn't have been much after ten. The house was quiet—Scarlett must have been asleep—but a light shone from the other end of the hallway.

Mom answered the door. 'Ope! What happened to you?'

She looked dishevelled, a skin-coloured pad poking out from the V-neck of her t-shirt.

'I got wet.'

'I can see that. Did something happen with Tom? Why are you home?'

'Nothing. Don't worry about it.'

'Well, hon . . .'

Mark appeared in the doorway. Scary, *Jaws*-like music started playing in my head.

'What the hell is this? Do you know what time it is?'

Mom held up a hand but Mark brushed past her.

Why had I not thought ahead to this moment? Why hadn't I prepared my story?

'We were walking on the beach and I tripped over . . . into the water.'

'You were on the beach at this hour?' Mark said. 'Did Tom's parents know where you were?'

In the other room, Scarlett started crying and Mom shrank. 'Go get in the shower,' she said. 'We'll talk about this in the morning.' She disappeared down the hallway but Mark didn't follow.

'What if something had happened to you?' Mark said. 'You can't go walking around town by yourself at night like that.'

I wasn't by myself.

'Especially along the beach.'

'Okay. I'm going to get in the—'

'We're guests in this country, Andrew. Don't you forget that.'

'It's Drew!' I screamed at him. 'My name is Drew!' I marched down the hall and into the bathroom, slamming the door behind me.

After my shower I crawled into bed and listened to Mom and Mark talking in the other room.

'I know I'm breaking the rules by holding her all the time,'

Mom was saying, 'but I don't care. As soon as I put her down she cries.'

'Mama says you shouldn't—'

'I don't want to hear what your mom thinks, Mark!'

'Go to bed,' he said. 'I'll nurse her for a while.'

'There's no point; I can't sleep anyway. My body's forgotten how.'

'Oh, Cathy . . .'

'It's fine for you,' she said. 'You sleep. All weekend, lately.'

'Well, I have a full-time job and—'

'I have a full-time job too! More than full-time. Twenty-four hours a day with no break.'

'But when she's sleeping . . .'

'Shut up, Mark,' she snapped. She hadn't finished. 'What I'm doing here . . . It's—it's unrecognised'—she struggled for the next word—'unrewarded domestic labour!'

'Unrewarded?'

'Yes! I wish I was dead. At least then I'd get some rest.'

I'd never heard Mom talk like that before. The raindrops of misery had become a deluge.

I reached for Tom's lure and turned it over in my hands, avoiding the hooks, wishing my old dog Davey was here. I felt uneasy in the stomach and figured that's what people meant when they talked about homesickness.

I grabbed my walkie-talkie, burrowed under the covers and pressed the call button.

'Drew?'

'Hey, Tom.'

'What's up? Over.'

'Nothing,' I said. 'Did your parents . . .'

'Nah. Came in the back. They had no idea. Over.'

Lucky.

'That was fun, wasn't it?' he said. 'Over.'

'The best. Over.'

'Next time we'll prepare better. Life jackets for starters.'

'Floatie-coaties.'

'Yeah.' He laughed. 'Floatie-coaties. See ya later. Over.'

The Hardy Boys' *The House on the Cliff* was on my night-stand, so I picked it up. I'd almost finished. I opened to the bookmarked page but then closed it again and returned it to its place, switching off the light. I could go to sleep thinking about my own adventures now.

32

I stood in front of the bathroom mirror trying to tamp down the cowlick at the top of my forehead. I'd been to plenty of parties in fifth grade, but somehow this felt different. Maybe it had something to do with Mom not dropping me off and staying to chitchat with the other moms, like she would have in Minneapolis. This was *my* thing. I was going with Tom, and Mom didn't know where the party was, or who was going to be there. She didn't even grill me about parental supervision.

I considered my reflection in the mirror. I'd used too much gel—pink globby goo from a plastic jar—and now my hair was sticky and wet-looking. I stuck my head under the faucet, rinsed the gel out, towel-dried it and combed it the best I could. I should have gotten a haircut. But the party was in half an hour; there was nothing I could do about it now.

I went to the living room to say bye to Mom. It was five-thirty and Mark wasn't home yet.

I found her on the couch holding Scarlett, who was asleep. The TV was on, but she wasn't watching it. Instead she was staring at Scarlett as if trying to work out a complicated math problem.

'I'm going,' I told her.

She looked up at me, then back down at Scarlett.

'Rob Lowe is her daddy,' Mom told me. It didn't sound like she was joking.

'What?'

She gave me a conspiratorial look. 'Don't tell your father,' she whispered.

I exhaled. 'I'm going,' I repeated.

'Bye,' she said vacantly. I doubted she even remembered about the party.

As I walked out the door, I had an uneasy feeling. Mark would be home soon, I told myself. It would be fine. On the porch I hesitated again, but then descended the steps and went on my way.

Marissa lived in a grand old-style white house on Swanston Street that made me think of a fort. It was set back from the street and had a kind of square turret on top.

It seemed that every light in the house was on, creating a yellow glow around it. Overhead, the edge of the day was smudging up against the blue of evening.

Tom and I followed the stone path that led to the front door, which was open, and were greeted by a woman who I guessed was Marissa's mom.

'Hello, boys,' she said as we stepped over the threshold. She wore white pants that only just reached her ankles, a flowing, flowery top and big wooden earrings with birds painted on them. Her hair was even shorter than mine.

Tom and I had gone in together for the present. Gillian did the buying (a set of colourful bangles and a tray of eyeshadow in various shades, I was told) and I took ten bucks from mom's purse as a contribution. Gillian had wrapped the gift in pink paper and tied it with a pink ribbon ('I never get to shop for girls—it was fun,' she'd said). Tom made me carry it.

Now, standing in Marissa's hallway, I wasn't sure what to do with it.

'Everybody's out the back,' Marissa's mom said, pointing down the hallway. 'Go through. There's food and soft drinks. Help yourselves.' She reached out a hand to me. 'I can take that if you like.'

I off-loaded the present, the paper squished in one corner from where I'd been carrying it pinched between a finger and thumb all the way from Tom's house.

'This looks sweet,' she said and smiled at us. 'I'll pop it on the table with the others.'

We walked down the wainscoted hallway, through a very old house with very old furniture to match. Everything was dark and heavy-looking—tall armoires, overstuffed sofas, artworks in gold frames, frilly lampshades and theatre-style red drapes.

'Be cool,' Tom said as we neared the back door. I wasn't sure how he got the idea I wasn't feeling chilled and relaxed. Or, more to the point, what part of me wasn't hiding it well.

'I *am* cool,' I said.

'Tell that to your face.'

Stepping out onto the back patio, I felt decidedly overdressed in a blue button-down, folded to the elbows, and a pair of beige shorts with large pockets over the thighs. When I arrived at Tom's I found him in a pair of faded shorts and an ordinary t-shirt. Whereas I had spent twenty minutes deciding between two button-downs and whether to wear loafers or flip-flops, it looked as if Tom had grabbed whatever happened to have been in reach, probably off the floor, and put it on. I thought he would be the one out of place, but I was wrong. All the other boys standing in huddles in Marissa's sizable backyard were in regular t-shirts and shorts. The girls, on the other hand, had gone all out.

I spotted Marissa, towering over the other kids in a denim skirt and a crop top. Lauren of the bouncy blonde curls was beside her. She was wearing lip gloss, and I could see the outline of a sports bra under her halter top.

I'd found out that their dark-haired friend's name was Samara. She wore a bright printed tee tucked into pale-wash blue jeans with a black leather belt, heeled boots, and had her hair pulled back into a colourful scrunchie.

Music spilled into the night air, something by TLC or En Vogue; I always mixed those two up. Someone had strung balloons from the trees, and crepe paper streamers stretched from one patio post to the next.

On one side of the yard, rosy-cheeked boys talked to other rosy-cheeked boys. On the other side, shiny-haired girls talked to other shiny-haired girls.

'Let's go say hi to Marissa,' Tom said.

When we reached the three girls—Marissa, Lauren and Samara—they were laughing at something one of them had said. Lauren said, 'Gross,' but kept laughing. They stood near a table set with drinks, chips in large bowls and a plate of buttered bread with colourful sprinkles all over.

'Hi, Marissa,' Tom said. 'Happy birthday.' He gave her a hug. *Man, that kid had some balls!*

'Thanks, Tom. Hi, Drew.'

I lifted my hand in a wave. 'Happy birthday,' I said.

Marissa returned her gaze to Tom. 'My mum wanted to get a jumping castle,' she said. 'Can you believe that? Like I'm eight years old. She made fairy bread, which is embarrassing enough, right?'

'I like fairy bread,' Tom said.

I so envied Tom. He just said whatever he felt, even if it wasn't popular or cool. That's precisely what made him cool. Not many twelve-year-olds had that kind of confidence.

'We're getting pizza later,' Marissa added.

'Excellent,' Tom said. 'Cool house.'

'I might show you my room after,' she said with a playful smile.

Lauren's jaw dropped and she had to hang onto Samara to contain her combined disbelief and excitement.

Being at Marissa's party, surrounded by girls in short denim skirts and wearing lip gloss, I got the distinct feeling that I—that all of us in Marissa's backyard—weren't children anymore. Or that we soon wouldn't be. We were in our final year of primary school (kings of the school!) and next year we would be in high school. At the bottom of the heap again, sure, but on the fast track to adulthood. We were leaving the world of G-rated movies on the road to maturity—holding hands, kissing, drinking beer in tents on the beach, long bus rides on our own.

A kid with a flat-top haircut, flanked by another kid with a bowl haircut like mine, approached us.

'You're that Yank?' he said to me. His tone was inquisitive, tinged with a slab of macho aggression.

'What's it to you, Harro?' Tom said.

I stepped between Tom and the boys to let Tom know I could deal with it myself. The speaker's name was Brodie Harrison. I recognised him from school, but he obviously didn't know me that well.

'So, your dad works on Swan Island,' Brodie said. Like many people in Queenscliff, it seemed to me, his dad was in the army.

'Stepdad.'

My usual approach was to treat the Brodies of the world like you would a rabid dog—avoid eye contact in the hope that they wouldn't attack. But something buoyed me that night.

'What's he do?' Brodie asked. 'What do they do there?'

I told myself I should make something up. Something outrageous and sensational. The kids would gather around, listening to what I had to say. That's what Tom would've done. Be *interesting*. Be *entertaining*.

'They're building a bomb,' I said. 'A huge one.'

Tom glanced at me, eyes wide for a moment, until he caught on to what I was doing.

'What's it for?' Brodie's friend said, stepping closer. His name was Ned.

'It's so big, they had to build a special room for it, with six-inch steel walls in case something goes wrong.'

I sensed a couple of other kids moving in, standing behind Brodie in tight formation.

'It's underground, in fact. This room. And there's this retinal scanner at the door. That's how tight security is.'

'What's a—' Ned began, before Brodie cut him off.

'Eyes, you idiot. It scans your eyes.' He looked at me, a challenge in his expression. 'Go on.'

'You've heard of those WMDs Saddam Hussein was building

in Iraq? This bomb is ten times bigger than that, and can do a hundred times more damage.'

'What's it for?' Lauren asked. 'What are they going to do with it?'

'It's a secret, but I heard that they might use it to blow up the entire world. All at once. Only us in Queenscliff will be left.'

Brodie took a long look at me, then waved dismissively. 'That's bullshit,' he said. His eyes cut to Ned. 'He doesn't know anything.'

I'd pushed it too far.

The audience dispersed.

'Who wants a drink?' Marissa asked.

'Now everybody's gonna think I'm a liar,' I said to Tom on the walk back to my place at nine. It had been a soul-crushing two hours since the incident with Brodie. We'd left soon after Marissa had blown out the candles on her red velvet cake while we sang 'Happy Birthday'.

'Don't worry about that stupid ranga,' Tom said. 'He's as dumb as dog shit.'

It was small consolation; by lunchtime on Monday, the whole school would know.

If Tom had told that story, it would have come out as a big joke and everybody would have laughed. I should have been quicker. I should have said something like, 'Almost had you there,' instead of gulping and turning away. Confidence. That's what I needed. *Bravado*.

'What are you going to do when you finish school?' I asked Tom as we neared the highway.

'Maybe uni.'

'Then what?'

He gave a small shrug. 'Something to do with the ocean. Could be a marine biologist. I'd love to get a job at Sea World in Queensland. It's one of my favourite places. Or maybe something with computers. What about you?'

'I don't know. There's nothing I really like doing.'

'You like writing stories.'

'That's not a job.'

'Of course it is—author.'

'Not a job for normal people, then.'

'All those authors were normal people before they became authors, you know. Who says you can't be one?'

We crossed the main road and carried on by the general store on King Street.

'Maybe you could make a new dictionary,' Tom suggested. 'You like making up new words.'

That was true. 'But it would have to be, like, a fake dictionary. Words that we should have but don't.'

'What would be fake about it? If people use them, they're real words.'

I thought of words that people in my life used that I'd never heard on TV or in movies—Mom used words like 'uff da' and 'ope', and Tom said bickie, barbie and esky. Everything was shortened in Australia: postman became 'postie', mosquito became 'mozzie' and breakfast became 'brekkie'. And then there were those walkie-talkie words I'd made up.

By the time we got home to my place it was well and truly dark out. I found Mom asleep on the couch, Scarlett peaceful in her lap. I needn't have worried. They both looked exhausted and I wondered for a moment if I should take Scarlett to her crib and let Mom go to bed. But I knew from experience that if I disturbed Scarlett she'd probably wake up, start screaming, and never go back to sleep.

'Want a drink?' I asked Tom.

'Okay.'

The special cans of soft drink were in the refrigerator in the garage, so I headed out there, Tom trailing behind.

Mark was in the garage, sitting on a second-hand sofa he'd bought from a thrift store on Hesse. The safe door was open and he had something in his hands.

'Boys!' he said when he saw us. His mood was bright, and I knew what that meant. Beside the sofa, a large glass of whisky, no ice, sat on an upturned milk crate.

He wore a white undershirt and black trackpants. No shoes.

'How was the big party?' He was tapping his foot as though keeping time to a song that wasn't playing.

'Fine,' I said. 'Was Mom okay when you got home?'

'Sure, sure.'

As I got closer, I saw that in one hand Mark held an old dish towel that had once been white but was now stained in a mess of dark colours. In the other hand was his gun.

It was a small gun, much smaller than the long rifles he'd wielded in Iraq, the sandy desert in the background; I'd seen pictures. A modest black case sat open on the sofa beside him. It was the same one I'd seen on our first day in Queenscliff—the one he kept in the safe.

'Sleeping like a couple of old babies, they are,' Mark said. He took the rag and began polishing the gun gently, almost lovingly, as if it were made of thin glass. 'This here's a Ruger P90, boys. Investment-cast aluminium-alloy frame. Eight-round capacity.' His speech was slurred. 'Ruger's first forty-five ACP pistol.'

He looked up. 'You like guns, Tom?' His voice was too loud for the smallness of the garage.

'Sure. Yeah. Who doesn't?'

'Andrew. He doesn't.' Mark stopped polishing and studied the weapon for a moment, then he dropped the rag and picked up his glass of whisky from the crate. He sniffed, then rubbed his nose—he had another head cold.

'Is it loaded?' Tom wanted to know.

''Course it is,' Mark said. 'If I need to use it in a hurry, I won't want to be wasting time loading the damn thing, would I?' He took a sip of whisky, put the glass down, and went back to polishing. 'Safety's on, though.' He held it up for us to inspect, as if we wouldn't believe him otherwise.

'Let's go back inside,' I whispered to Tom.

'Can I hold it?' Tom asked. Maybe he hadn't heard me.

A blade of fear pierced me. Here was another example of Tom being more adventurous than me. His curiosity always won out, and I was scared that one day it was going to get him into serious trouble. But, then, he'd probably talk his way right out of it again.

'Maybe some other time,' Mark said, holding the gun aloft to examine it more closely under the flickering fluorescent light. 'It's every man's right to defend himself,' he declared. 'Don't you think, Tom?'

'Sure,' Tom answered. I could see already that Mark liked Tom a whole lot better than me.

I hated guns, like Mark said, and I definitely didn't agree that everybody should own one, if that's what he was getting at.

Mark lifted his glass again, took a swig, and then raised it in my direction. 'He doesn't like guns because of what happened to his daddy,' Mark said.

That was true enough, but I didn't like the way Mark pointed it out, how he shared it so casually. If that junkie hadn't owned a gun, I'd still have a dad.

'Ask me, that's the exact reason everybody needs a gun. His dad coulda offended himself.'

I presumed Mark meant *defended*, but I wasn't about to draw attention to his mistake.

'You should be proud, Andrew. Your dad was a goddamn hero. Not everyone woulda stepped in like he did. *He's* the one that deserves a medal.'

I didn't see it that way. What good was a dead hero? I'd rather have had a living dad. Thinking about my dad, tears threatened, but I blinked them back.

I hadn't told Tom the story of how my dad died—that he was passing an ATM when he noticed a guy robbing a woman who was trying to withdraw money. He stepped in to help and the guy shot him. I lost my dad. All the woman lost was forty bucks.

I tugged at the waist of Tom's t-shirt, but Mark wasn't done.

'They pin these medals on anyone. For much less, mind you.' He took another drink, looking at the seat next to him. I noticed then a second case on the cushion, this one holding a medal with a purple ribbon. 'They're real nice and everything. Shiny and all boxed up real pretty. All I got mine for was being there. Sure, I got wounded, but so what? You shouldn't get a medal for being wounded. If anything, you should get a slap about the head for being stupid enough to stand in the way of flying shrapnel.' He sniffed. 'I'm proud of it; don't get me wrong. But I wish I'd done something to deserve it. Something other than my job.'

Mark got injured in a friendly-fire incident on day three of the four-day Desert Storm campaign, when rounds of depleted uranium fired from a US tank struck his vehicle. He was awarded a purple heart.

'Ah,' he said, putting the drink down on the milk crate, liquid sloshing. 'What's the point?'

I didn't know what he was referring to. War? Rehashing the war? Giving out medals to wounded soldiers?

Satisfied that the gun was clean, Mark returned it to its case. He heaved himself off the couch, holding onto the workbench for support, and slid the two cases into the safe. The gleaming new safe looked so out of place in the dirty, dusty garage. Even Mark looked dirty and dusty, standing there in his stained shirt, scratching his chest. He closed the safe door, turned the key and placed it back in its hiding place inside a box of Redheads matches on the shelf above.

33

School holidays, as they called them in Australia, rolled around in April. The weather was still okay, but it was too cold to swim in the ocean. Early morning fishing wasn't as pleasant, either.

By the time I'd risen on the first Monday of the vacation, Mark had already left for work and Mom was in the kitchen, sitting at the table and staring at the refrigerator as if she expected someone to emerge from it. She wore a nightgown, ballooning around the collar, revealing one of her bare shoulders.

On the cooktop, steam rose furiously from a pot.

'What are you cooking?' I asked her.

'What's that now?'

'What's on the stove?'

I could see she'd set a large pot of water to boil. (The electric stove had thick black coils that heated to a bright orange—the *coilie-boilie*.) It couldn't have been to sterilise Scarlett's bottles because she did that in the microwave. And it must have been some time ago because only an inch or so of water covered the bottom.

'What?' Her eyes were vacant.

'Were you gonna cook spaghetti?'

She shrugged.

'It's only breakfast time, Mom. Where's Scarlett?'

'Asleep.'

I told Mom that I was spending the day with Tom, but she didn't seem to take it in. In a corner of the kitchen, the past three days of newspapers were still in rolls, bound together with thick red rubber bands.

'Are you gonna be okay?' I asked her.

'What's that, D?'

She thought I was my dad.

'Are you going to be okay?' I repeated.

'Sure. Go to work.'

I hesitated at the door, clutching the handle for a full ten seconds before walking out into the white sunlight.

34

Samara lived on a narrow street behind the Anglican church in a renovated Victorian with elaborate spindlework and jigsaw-cut bargeboards. Like everywhere in Queenscliff, it was close enough to walk.

A Christmas wreath, homemade from silver, green and red leaves scissored out of cardboard, hung on the door. There was a doorbell, a tiny brass one with a flimsy clapper, but my hands were full—a bottle of red wine in one and a box of wrapped chocolates in the other. I tucked the wine into my armpit to free up one hand and jingled the bell.

Samara answered. She was wearing an intricately patterned dress that hung loosely to her ankles and fancy tan flip-flops with beads threaded along the straps.

'Hi, Drew.' She twisted her head around. 'Girls! Drew's here!' She turned back to me and smiled. 'Come in.'

I handed her the wine and chocolates and followed her down a short hallway to the combined kitchen and dining area. The table was already laid for dinner, a foot-high white Christmas tree serving as a centrepiece.

Two girls with long black hair tied in braids came in, their faces downcast shyly, and presented themselves to me. Samara pointed first to the taller one, who must have been about eleven, and then to the shorter one, who was probably nine. 'This is Charlotte, and this is Hannah.'

'Hello, girls,' I said. 'Great to meet you both.'

'Hello,' they chorused. They looked at their mother expectantly.

'Okay, off you go,' she said. 'I'll call you for dinner.'

The girls disappeared again and Samara gestured toward a stool at the island.

A copy of *Saving Grace* sat on the timber countertop. Samara wasn't lying about owning it, and the heavily cracked spine told me she'd actually read it, maybe more than once. Or maybe she'd picked it up from a thrift store.

Saving Grace wasn't my first published work. The first time I'd seen my name in print was in my high-school newspaper, *The Harbinger*. I wasn't on the permanent staff but sometimes submitted articles. My debut was a creative piece about a haunted cookie stand (where you bought cookies not by the packet but by the bucketload) at the state fair. Seeing my name right there on the xeroxed page: I'd never known a feeling like it. It was a thrill ride at an amusement park—the kind of exhilaration you wished would never end. It was as if I finally existed. There I was, Drew Iverson, in black and white.

Samara caught me noticing the book on the counter.

'Thought I'd get you to sign it for me while you're here. Is that okay?'

'Of course. Yes.'

'It's a great book, Drew.'

She said it with a calm sincerity that told me she meant it.

'Thank you.'

It was best to be gracious; no need to show the persistent seed of ambivalence that had sprouted in my stomach and grown into a noxious weed. I wasn't sure when that happened. I remembered doing the final proofread of the typeset book before it went off to print, my heart billowing as I turned the final page. That had only changed, I realised now, because of what happened after: other people's reactions. Lukewarm reviews, low sales. It was still the same book. How had I allowed myself to be influenced by everyone else's opinions?

'Would you like a drink?' she asked, holding up the bottle I'd brought.

'Sure. Thank you.'

She reached into an overhead cupboard and pulled down a single wineglass. 'I ran into Miranda McCauley—*Mrs* McCauley—at the supermarket this afternoon. Do you remember her?'

I shook my head. 'You're not having wine?'

'I don't drink.'

'Oh, well, I won't either then.'

'You don't have to . . .'

'No, that's fine.' I should probably have a night off anyway.

'Take it home with you. To the hotel.'

There was no point refusing her; some people didn't like to have alcohol in their homes.

'I made this drink.' She reached into the fridge and took out a jug filled to the brim with a pinkish liquid, strawberries bobbing at the top. 'It's called strawberry limeaid. Try some?'

'Sure.'

'Miranda's still at the school. She's principal now. I told her I was seeing you tonight and she said to say g'day. She's read your book too. You're one of the school's most famous ex-students, after all. I don't know of any other published authors to come out of Queenscliff Primary.'

That wasn't the only thing I was famous for, I thought.

'That's really nice,' I said.

'She asked how long you were staying. I think she was hoping you'd come and talk to the kids.' She poured the drinks over ice. 'I've actually been following your career quite closely,' she said. 'The short stories you've published; the interviews.' She broke off two sprigs of mint and hung them over the edge of the glasses. 'When's the next book coming out?'

'Soon. Next year, I hope.' I took a sip of the juice and got a blast of lime, strawberry and an infusion of mint.

'What's it about? If you don't mind me asking.'

I repeated the awkward spiel I'd given the woman with the short-story collection at Tom's wake. Again, it was rambling and probably incoherent. I would really need to get my elevator pitch down for when Eliot started submitting it to editors.

'Sorry,' I said, after stumbling through too long an explanation. 'I haven't talked about it much. Haven't solidified how to describe it yet.'

'Don't be silly. It sounds wonderful. I'm sure it will be.'

'What do you like to read?'

'Anything. Everything. I actually trained as a librarian, if you can believe that. But being a corporate whore pays better.' She chastised herself with a shake of the head. 'I got involved with our local literary festival for a while too, but some of the personalities on the committee . . .'

'Margot with the three names?'

'You know her?'

'We met.'

'She was a bit intense for me. So now I just go as an avid reader.'

I took another sip of my drink, taking in the room. It was extremely tidy. If you looked closely, you could see where the fabric on the sofas was wearing on the armrests and scars of light scratches on the armoire. Maybe it was second-hand or had got banged around during house moves. Either way, everything was neat and clean. Heavy rugs and tapestry cushions gave the room a cosy feel.

'You work in real estate now?' I said.

'Yeah, we're in the shopfront right next to Eddie's. Used to be a shoe shop?'

I shook my head; I couldn't remember. 'What are the house prices like down here?'

'Astronomical. Although not as bad as Ocean Grove or Barwon Heads. The sad thing is, most of us who grew up here have been priced out of the market. Even shacks go for a million dollars. It's all ageing locals and cashed-up retirees from Melbourne.'

'So, not many young families like yours?'

'Unfortunately not. A couple of years ago the primary school was down to six students.'

'Jesus. I bet they had property developers sniffing around. That land overlooking the bay must be worth a bucket.'

'Uh-huh. But rural schools get a bit more protection from the government—low numbers aren't such a problem. Ready to eat?'

'Can't wait.'

'Girls! Dinner!' she called. Then, to me: 'I don't like cooking at the best of times, but it's much easier in summer. It's more like preparing than cooking—cold meats, salads. So much easier. Although two years ago I bought a slow cooker and that's changed my life. I just throw everything in before work, and when I come home all I have to do is cook rice and voilà: dinner. I'm thinking of investing in an air-fryer next.' She looked at me, trying to gauge my reaction. 'Sorry—I'm rabbiting on about nothing.'

The comfort of domestic life had a romanticism to it that I was sure didn't exist in real life, especially for a single parent having to do everything on her own—not only the cooking (three meals a day!), but laundry and cleaning, chauffeuring.

The girls walked in as Samara removed plastic wrap from two large bowls of food and carried them to the dining table.

'I bought the chicken already roasted,' she admitted. 'Couldn't quite get myself organised today.'

I held up my hands: *fine with me.*

'I've tried roasting them myself but it's not worth it.' She placed a platter on the table and tore off the aluminium foil covering. 'Girls, get what you want to drink. Or you can have some of this punch.'

The older one peered into the jug, shrugged, and sat at the table.

The food was delicious—some kind of cauliflower-based salad with chickpeas, something small and red (pomegranate?) drizzled with a thick white dressing. The other was just as vibrant, with colourful vegetables—tomatoes, cucumbers, radishes—and fried bread torn into bite-sized pieces tossed through.

'Do you girls play sports?' I asked, since that was what most Australian kids seemed to do.

Neither answered, looking to their mother for guidance. She responded for them. 'Hannah wants to play football, but I'm trying to talk her into soccer instead—too many injuries in football. And Charlotte plays netball, don't you, Charlotte? They're both in Nippers.'

'Nippers?'

'Surf lifesaving for kids. It's mostly about beach safety and surf awareness, but they compete in carnivals, too. It's big in coastal towns. But they only do it in the warmer months. Football's a winter sport.'

'The Queenscliff Coutas,' I said. 'I remember.'

'Still got a strong loyal following, although they haven't won a premiership since 2013.'

Again, I found myself at a table for four: the two parents and their children eating a meal, chatting about everyday things— the life that so many men my age had.

After dinner, Samara and I sat on a small, decked area in the miniature backyard, sipping her punch. She'd done an impressive job with the small space—a fine-leafed vine crept up the rendered walls and a mixture of seasonal flowers in painted pots dotted the perimeter in clusters. She'd opened an old metal trunk, bolted it to the wall at chest height and filled it with trailing colour. I snapped a picture of it with my phone for Adam, thinking of his herb-filled dresser. The girls had fled to their rooms, and Samara told me about moving back to Queenscliff.

'I didn't like anything about Melbourne or my life there. I didn't like the noise or the speed or our house or our neighbour-hood or the other school mums or that I couldn't go to the local shops and run into people I knew. It was all so anonymous. Hard to believe you can be lonely in a place where you're surrounded by people.' She sipped her drink. 'Anyway, when I found out my husband was cheating, I grabbed the girls and got out of there as fast as I could. It was such a relief. An excuse, really. No one could've blamed me. I mean, how could they? My husband cheated; of course I should leave him. But I loved him. Definitely enough to move past his cheating. But I didn't want to live in Melbourne and he never would have moved. We'd agreed that we'd stay in the city until the girls were finished school and then we could move wherever I wanted. But that was eight, nine years away. I couldn't wait that long.' She took in a deep breath and let it out again. 'I don't regret it for a second. I miss being married, but there were more important things.'

More important things than keeping your family together? Being with the person you loved? I couldn't think of anything so important that I would leave Claire to achieve it.

We talked about books, about writing, and then she brought up Mercer Street.

'I had nightmares about it as a kid,' she told me. 'I can't imagine what it did to you. Your poor mum. And, for you, I felt so . . . I don't know. I didn't know you that well, but then that happened, and you took off so suddenly and none of us ever saw you again. It scarred us.'

After leaving Queenscliff, I hadn't thought once about the impact of such an event on this close-knit town. I thought about Tom, of course, and other parts of my life here, but not about the lasting stain my family left behind.

'Then there was Tom,' she said.

Tom was the only one left in Queenscliff who had been in the house on that day. People must have looked at him differently, hounded him with questions, wanting a front-row seat to the horror. What an albatross that must have been to carry, not to mention his own pain. I rubbed my stinging eyes.

'You okay?' she asked.

'Sure. Just jet lag. Did you go to high school with Tom?' I wanted to know more about what became of him.

'Yeah. Queenscliff High. Well, Bellarine Secondary College, as it became known. That's where we all went. But we were the last ones. The Queenscliff campus closed after us.'

'What was Tom like then?'

'Um . . .' She took a sip of the limeaid, looking across the backyard. 'I guess he was a bit different. There was what happened at Mercer Street, of course, plus his best friend had moved away. He had lots of people around him; he always made friends easily. He *seemed* fine. But you never know, I guess.'

'And what about later on? Have you had much to do with him over the years?'

'I've only been back four years or so, but I saw him around the place. I knew he had the charter business, met his wife a few times at school fundraisers or whatever. Hannah and Missy are in the same year. Speak of the devil.'

I followed Samara's line of sight to the back door where the girls stood shoulder to shoulder, a blend of anxiety and excitement on their faces.

'I know that look,' Samara said to them. 'Ask away.'

The taller one nudged the shorter one.

'Can we have dessert?' the smaller one asked.

'Sure. There's ice cream. Can you do it yourselves?'

They nodded in unison then turned to leave.

'Wait!' Samara said. 'Aren't you forgetting something?'

They looked at each other, then something clicked into place for the older one. 'Would you like some, Mummy?' she asked.

'No, thank you, sweetheart.' Samara glanced at me, raising an eyebrow.

'Not for me. Thank you.'

The girls scampered into the kitchen and I watched as they pulled bowls from a large drawer and a tub of ice cream from a freezer below the refrigerator.

I wanted to ask more about Tom—to get an outsider's perspective—but I was wary of revealing baseless suspicions, so I dropped it.

Suddenly, I felt something bubble and loosen in my stomach and I knew I didn't have much time. *Oh god, not now.*

'Bathroom?' I asked Samara, already on my feet.

'Down the hall, between the girls' rooms.'

I tried not to be too obvious about quickening my step as I hurried along the hallway in search of the toilet. I found it easily and, thankfully, the lid was already up. I spun on my feet, yanked my shorts and boxers down in one swift jerk and planted my ass on the seat just as a violent splash jetted from my body and into the bowl. *Jesus!* I was thankful the girls were far enough away in the kitchen not to hear my gushing discharge in full chorus. I stayed only for a minute or two, opened a small casement window for fresh air, and washed my hands with lots of liquid soap pumped from a stone-coloured dispenser.

As I headed back up the hallway, my stomach still out of order, I realised then that I'd come to Samara's for more than just the free meal and some company. I wanted another connection to my twelve-year-old life in Queenscliff—someone else who knew Tom as I did back then; someone other than Tom's parents. Maybe to confirm that my memories were real. That it wasn't all a dream or a story I'd heard. I wanted someone to validate my existence here.

'What ever became of Marissa?' I asked as I resumed my seat. 'And Lauren?'

'Lauren, I don't know. She went to high school with us but moved away after that. Her family too.'

'What about Facebook?' I asked.

'Haven't been able to find her. Guess she doesn't want to be found. Marissa married a guy who manages a furniture store in Geelong. That's where they live now. I ran into her a year or so ago and—this is going to sound really unkind, but . . .' She paused, as if deciding what to say. 'It's funny how you imagine that the popular kids in school will always be popular and that they'll just coast through life the same way they seemed to coast through school.'

This reminded me of a story I'd read in Sittenfeld's book that afternoon called 'A Regular Couple', about a woman who, while visiting a ski resort, runs into a mean girl who tormented her back in high school. Although immensely popular at school, the girl had turned out to be very ordinary—married to a regular guy and mildly jealous of the narrator's success as a writer.

'And now?' I asked.

'She's normal. Completely normal. Wife, mother, standard family pressures. She even *looks* normal. No more glamourous than the next working mum. When your kids are having problems at school, you want to tell them that school has nothing to do with the real world. But you can't; they wouldn't believe it. I wouldn't have believed it at the time either, I guess.'

I thought about that. 'High school *is* like the real world,' I said, 'if you really think about it. You have your hierarchy based on wealth or looks or intelligence. You have the bullies and the victims. You have to learn to survive.'

'That's true, I suppose. Although what we value changes—individuality becomes more important. In the real world, standing out is more respected than fitting in.'

At the counter, the girls were taking it in turns to scatter sprinkles from a shaker over their bowls, missing some of the time, giggling, trying again. I couldn't suppress a smile, but it hurt a little.

Samara held up what was left of the pitcher of punch, but I shook my head no. She poured the last of it into her own glass, strawberries and rings of lime toppling in. 'I read somewhere that you went to university with C.J. DeBono,' she said.

'You've been stalking me online?' I asked with a grin.

'Fact-finding,' she answered, mirroring my smile. 'You're the only famous person I can claim that I knew as a kid. I was interested.'

I wanted to point out that I wasn't famous. Although perhaps I was in this town? Infamous, maybe.

'I went to grad school with him.'

'I love him. Haven't got his new one yet, but I can't wait. Do you two still talk? Do you read each other's work and give notes?'

I nearly laughed out loud but restricted myself to a smile. 'Not exactly. We're not in touch.'

'Oh, that's a shame. There's a sadness about him, don't you think?'

'In his writing?'

She shook her head. 'In *him*. I mean, when you listen to him in interviews he comes across as very confident and speaks very eloquently about his work. But when you look at photos of him . . . I don't know. He has sad eyes. Robin Williams had sad eyes, too, and look what happened to him.'

I hadn't noticed. About Christian or Robin Williams. But then Tom was in my head again, and what Adam had told me about him. Did Tom have sad eyes? I didn't think so.

'He's not married either,' Samara continued. 'His last two long-term partners were writers as well, and they both left him.'

I knew this about Christian. I'd put it down to his ego being too big for another person to fit inside any house he occupied.

'I think it just got too cold for those women,' Samara said, 'having to write in his shadow. That's tragic, don't you think? That someone would leave you not because you're a bad person, or even a bad boyfriend, but because their own ego is too fragile.'

'We don't know if that's why they left him.'

'*I* think that's why.'

'He needs to find a partner who isn't a writer.'

'Probably, but that doesn't mean he hasn't been hurt in the process. It's almost like he was punished for his success. I feel sorry for him.'

This didn't accord with my petty, envious image of C.J. DeBono. In my head, I believed that he—that all commercially successful writers—lived a perpetually joyful life full of wonder and excitement, his mental health fully intact. What, after all, could he possibly have to worry about? If he ever got down or depressed, all he needed to do was to read one of ten thousand gushing reviews of his work . . . or check the balance of his bank account.

I was about to say something glib, like how I was sure all that money and fame might have cushioned the blow, but I couldn't imagine Claire walking out because she couldn't live with the career goals that were most important to me.

A person's life is rarely as it appears on the surface, I thought. Mine wasn't. And maybe Tom's wasn't either.

★

When I arrived back at the guest house, the lobby was deserted, but I found Leon sitting alone in the public lounge, cradling a glass. A bottle of Glenfiddich sat on the coffee table beside him.

It was too hot for an open fire, but the option was there. How comfy it must have been to curl up in there with a book in the winter months.

'Drew,' he said, flashing me a smile.

If this was the US, he wouldn't dare presume to use my first name. But this wasn't the US, and I kind of liked it.

'Had a good evening?' he asked.

'I have, thank you. Caught up with an old friend for dinner.'

Leon smiled.

'Did I say something funny?'

'Sorry, I just thought of Hannibal Lecter . . . *I'm having an old friend for dinner.* What have you got there?'

I had returned from Samara's with the bottle of wine. 'Pinot noir.'

'Were you heading up to your room to drink it alone?' He raised his palms. 'No judgement.'

It suddenly felt like a good idea.

'Come,' he said. 'Sit. Have a drink with me. That way neither of us will look so pathetic.'

I entered the lounge area.

'You don't need a corkscrew, do you?'

I checked the bottle—screw-top. 'No, but maybe a glass?'

He placed his drink on the coffee table and heaved himself off the couch. 'Oh, you Americans. So conservative.'

I wasn't sure if he was joking, but then he gave me a conspiratorial smile.

'Back in a jiff.'

Leon was still dressed in pants and his work shirt, but he'd removed his badge. Was he technically still working? Maybe he lived in the hotel. The front desk was unattended at night but I'd noticed a cell phone number pinned to the wall so that guests could call in an emergency; it was probably Leon's.

I settled into the couch opposite his and, while twisting the cap off the bottle, took in the shelves of books surrounding us. How could you ever be bored or lonely when you had books to keep you company?

Above the fireplace was an artwork that I recognised as being famous, but I couldn't name the artist. It was a cubist work—a distressed-looking woman wearing a red hat, the image discernible but out of proportion.

When Leon returned, wineglass in hand, I said, 'Thank you for the food, by the way. It was delicious.'

He handed me the glass. 'I didn't know if you were vegetarian, so . . .'

I poured a generous glug of pinot while he took his seat again. 'It was sensational.'

'Why, thank you,' he said. 'I used to be a chef. Had my own restaurant in Melbourne. That's the kind of dish I used to make all the time.'

He raised his glass.

'Cheers,' I said.

I took a sip of wine, and with it arrived the comfort of knowing what was ahead—what always followed that first sip—and my habitual yearning to pursue it to the end.

'I've never tasted Asian food like that,' I told him.

'Most of the Chinese food you get in restaurants here is from the south of China—Cantonese food. What I cook is the stuff I grew up eating, from Sichuan Province.'

'I never knew eggplant could taste like that. Is that what you serve in the restaurant here?'

'We're more mainstream—contemporary meals and pub classics. I have input, but I know what it's like to have someone else dictating your menu. Celia knows her clientele. I mostly stay out of it.'

'Sounds wise.'

I could already feel the wine warming my stomach.

'You're a writer,' Leon said. It was a statement of fact.

I must have given him a puzzled look because he said, 'I googled you,' then took a slug from his glass. 'I took a few creative writing subjects at uni myself. Enjoyed it, but I wasn't very good. I did like the process of pulling apart novels, though— getting to the crux of them, revealing their underbelly.'

I didn't want to talk about writing anymore tonight, so I pointed to the painting over the fireplace. 'Is that yours or did it come with the place?'

'It's mine. It's a Picasso. Well, a print, of course.'

'She looks very unhappy.'

'She's crying. That's a handkerchief in her hand. He painted it at the height of the Spanish Civil War based on a photo he saw of a woman holding her dead baby.'

'Cheery.'

'He created a series of them: this weeping woman. The second version—the best one, if you ask me—is held by the National Gallery of Victoria. You should visit it in Melbourne before you head home.'

'Maybe I'll do that.'

'The likeness is from a woman called Dora Maar. She was a photographer and Picasso's lover for almost ten years. He always painted her in these kind of tortured poses. He said he was following a vision that was forced on him. As if he had no control over his art. He abused her, though. Physically.'

I'd never heard this about Picasso. 'Is that well known? About the abuse?'

'Yes.' He looked at me. 'Do you think we should judge a person's art based on who they are as people?'

'No,' I said without thinking. 'Is the art any better if it's painted by a nice person? Any worse because it's painted by an asshole like Picasso?'

My mind reached for C.J. DeBono. Could I ever read his work without letting my personal feelings for the man sully the experience?

'It's been a bad year for male authors being accused of sexual harassment or inappropriate behaviour,' I said. 'I can think of four high-profile ones just off the top of my head. Some of their agents and publishers have dropped them.'

'Does that mean you'll stop reading their novels? Should bookshops refuse to stock them?'

'No. That would be a kind of censorship. Or *cancelling* as they say now. People can stop buying them if they want. But sometimes you have to separate the art from the artist.'

'Is that what you do?' He gave me a searching look.

'I don't know.' I took a sip of wine. '*Shakespeare in Love* is one of my favourite movies. I'm not going to stop watching it because Harvey Weinstein was a producer.'

Leon glanced back at the painting. 'His abuse of women doesn't seem to have hurt the value of his works.'

Was he talking about Weinstein or Picasso?

Leon pursed his lips. 'Do you believe in the old adage that if you want to know about an artist, all you need to do is look at his art?'

My body of work was a scramble of half-hearted short stories, manuscripts that nearly killed me, tales that read as if written by someone I didn't know existed, or maybe had purged, and pieces that bled on the page. If you assembled all those manuscripts and short stories—abandoned and finished—and the pieces I wrote for the MFA program, what would you learn about me? What would they reveal?

'No.' Somehow we were talking about me and my writing again. Another subject change was in order. 'Why'd you make the move to Queenscliff?' If he'd had a restaurant in Melbourne, I presumed he'd probably lived there too.

Leon passed his hand through his thick black hair. 'My partner and I ran the restaurant together. He looked after front of house, and the kitchen was mine. When he died, I went into crisis mode. I mean, it wasn't always sunshine and roses. We fought—like any couple, I guess. But I learned to love him for who he was and forgive him for who I wished he would be.' Leon seemed to lose his train of thought. 'Anyway, then I bought this place. A sea-change. Isn't that what everyone's doing now? I thought this couldn't be so different from running a restaurant.' He blew out a stream of air. 'How wrong I was.'

Leon's words began to jumble together. I had some catching up to do, so took another generous sip of wine.

'I almost lost it last year,' he added. 'This place. Thought I could do it all on my own.' He looked at me. 'Spoiler alert: I couldn't.'

'What turned it around?'

'I recognised my shortcomings and asked for help. If you knew me, you'd know that didn't come easy. I'm a proud person. But if I hadn't swallowed that pride, I'd be broke and without a hotel right now. You'd be sitting here talking to some much more successful, capable and no doubt more handsome man who'd be running it in my place.'

'I'm sure that's not true. He wouldn't be as handsome as you.'

He smiled. 'Thank you, kind sir.' He refilled his glass, took a swig. 'Good lesson, that. Just . . .' He searched his mind for the right words. 'Letting go. Accepting things as they are. Jeremy was gone. I wasn't coping. Sometimes, when we're so beaten down, when there's nothing left in the tank, that's when we're on the cusp of becoming our strongest. We don't have any fight left in us and we see that all the small stuff—the petty arguments, life's little disappointments, bad service in a shop—is just not that important. We start to appreciate the small wins; the little, well, *niceties* around us. We find that the things we were protecting so vehemently didn't need protecting at all and were actually stopping us from living fully.' He held up his glass to me. 'Perspective, my friend, that's what a catastrophe gives you.' He smiled to himself. 'And all it took was letting go.'

'Easier said than done, Leon.'

'Indeed,' he said. 'Although you don't have to give up what you want. I don't mean that. But getting that thing you want won't magically solve all your problems.'

Heavy-limbed and back in my room, the wine cosy in my belly, I placed the near-empty bottle of pinot noir on the desktop and kicked off my loafers. I worked the top two buttons of my shirt loose then pulled the whole thing over my head, tossing it across the arm of the club chair. I flicked on the bedside lamp and sat atop the covers, looking at Tom's lure on my nightstand. I picked it up, turned it over a few times and put it back. Was something really wrong with Tom? Or was the fire a genuine accident?

I needed to stop thinking about it, so I picked up my Curtis Sittenfeld book, extracting the boarding pass I'd been using as my bookmark and placing it on the bedcover beside me. 'Volunteers Are Shining Stars' is about a young woman who helps out in a shelter for women and their children. A new volunteer rubs her the wrong way, and she ends up physically lashing out at her. Although the narrator never admits this, or even acknowledges it any way, it's about jealousy. She is jealous of this new volunteer's relationship with a young kid she herself has become enamoured with.

I closed the book and tapped the screen of my phone, the light from it projecting onto the grey walls surrounding me. I wanted to text the picture of Samara's suitcase garden to Adam but didn't have his number. Adam. What could I do to make sure this experience of losing his dad didn't make him even more angry at the world? Was there *anything* I could do? I was leaving in two days' time.

I FaceTimed Claire, who was getting ready to start her day.

'How's everything?' I asked.

She'd fixed her hair but not yet applied make-up.

'Great. What's happening down under?'

I looked down, pulling at the waist of my pants.

'Hilarious,' she said.

'*I* thought so.'

'Are you naked?' she asked.

'I'm wearing a grin,' I said, overplaying a smile.

'I see you've been sampling Australia's . . . *beverages.*'

'And meeting some great people,' I said. 'Had dinner tonight with an old classmate, then a drink with the owner of the hotel I'm staying in. It's good.'

'I'm glad.'

We looked at each other through the screen a moment, then Claire spoke again.

'How are you really doing? Any big feelings you want to talk about?'

Claire couldn't help herself, slipping back into counsellor mode whenever she detected something was off with me.

'Such as?'

'I don't know. I'm sure it's a lot to process—being back there, Tom's funeral.'

'I'm fine.'

'Really?'

'Really.'

Claire was the only one with whom I'd shared the truth about what happened on Mercer Street. We never discussed it, but it was always there—that unobstructed view she had into my psyche.

'Been spending a lot of time with Adam,' I said. 'Tom's son. He's great, once you break through the walls.'

Claire picked up her phone and carried it to the bathroom. 'Sounds familiar.'

I snorted a laugh. 'Anyway, I feel a real connection to him. I don't know if it's because he's Tom's son—maybe he reminds me of Tom as a kid—or because I lost my dad at a young age too. Either way, we've really hit it off.'

While I was talking, Claire had placed her phone on the bathroom counter, angling it upward, and begun applying foundation.

'Sounds like you're getting quite attached to this kid, Drew.'

'Yeah.' I took a breath. 'Claire?'

'What, baby?' She reached for something else in her make-up bag.

'Did we make a mistake deciding not to have kids?'

Spending time with Adam, something had changed in me.

'*I* didn't.'

'There's still time, you know. You're only thirty-nine and—'

'Drew,' she said, looking directly at the phone. 'You're going through a lot of emotions right now. Maybe you're looking for an anchor. But, baby, this isn't it.'

I didn't respond. Where had this come from all of a sudden?

'You'll feel differently when you get home,' she said.

I didn't think so.

35

I woke early, my body finally in step with the sleep–wake cycle. I showered, dressed in a pair of utility shorts, a Hamline t-shirt and sneakers, and brushed my teeth. I jumped online and changed my Melbourne hotel check-in date to Monday, giving me an extra day in Queenscliff. Something was holding me there, some unfinished business to do with Adam, Tom and what happened in the past.

I found Leon at the front desk with a glass of tomato juice, his eyes bloodshot, and asked if I could extend my stay another night.

'Of course,' he said. 'But I couldn't face another session like last night.'

'You build up a resistance to it,' I said.

He keyed something into his computer. 'I've got to stop treating my life here as if I'm always on holidays. Or as if I'm trying to bury something. I'm not quite sure which it is.'

For most of us, it was the latter, I thought but did not say.

Leon placed both hands flat on the desktop as if needing to prop himself up. 'My father always said you should only drink to feel happier, not as an antidote to sadness. We could all probably take something from that, I reckon.'

I climbed into the car without so much as a coffee in my belly and headed north, following the green road signs to Portarlington. It was virtually a straight line north from Queenscliff, and I travelled the twenty minutes through unchanging green fields, the road hissing beneath the tyres, infrequently passing a winery, a B&B and a horse stud on my way to the northernmost tip of the Bellarine Peninsula. It was good to be in the car and moving, my wrist draped over the steering wheel.

Claire was immoveable on the subject of producing junior Iversons. The details of the previous night's call with her were gone, but the gist of her unyielding response stayed with me. Maybe when I got back to Minneapolis, once we'd discussed it face to face, she would bend. My arguments would be convincing—she could keep working and I would stay home and raise the kid (kids?). It wouldn't affect our lifestyle; I would do all the donkey work.

I drove into Portarlington, past an elementary school, a pub and a vet clinic, until I reached the town centre, which I pinpointed as the spot where the historic Grand Hotel over-looked a ye-olde bandstand and the bay beyond it. When I saw the first sign advertising a bakery, I parked the car at the crest of a graded grassed area that descended to the water. I shut off the engine. It was 9 am by now and my stomach told me I must eat. But instead I sat there in the car, watching a man push a baby buggy along the street while he sipped a coffee. Without me realising it, the idea of having children of my own had been playing like a quiet but persistent tune in my head for years. For the past few days, a new future silently took shape in my mind.

I locked the car with the remote and crossed the street. Inside, the bakery was abuzz with diners—mostly old people and parents with young children, the only ones up at this hour in a vacation town on the weekend. They ate eggs and bacon on large arcs of toasted sourdough and bowls of what looked like granola and yoghurt. The smell of fresh coffee beans hung in the air.

Behind a large cabinet that also served as the counter, the staff busied themselves attending to a steady stream of patrons. I ordered a cappuccino and something called a bee sting—a bun filled with thick yellow custard and topped with flaked almonds.

As I waited for my coffee, my phone beeped with a text from my agent: *Is now a good time to talk?*

Eliot had finished reading *Woodland*. She wouldn't be calling to talk about anything else. Unless, of course, *Saving Grace* had been optioned for film. But that was unlikely, since nobody had read it.

I texted back: *Will call you in a few.*

With my coffee and a small white bag in hand, I crossed the road and descended the sloping green to the shore. The old pier I remembered was still there but decommissioned. Running alongside it was an upgraded version—a concreted, double-laned platform that, if you asked me, lacked the charm of the original. But it was well used, providing access to the Melbourne ferry and a cavalcade of private boats moored at one of two docks that jutted out from the main structure.

Official signs announced that the old section would soon be dismantled, condemned as unsafe because parts of it were separating from its foundations, and I felt a baffling sense of loss. Why was I so nostalgic for a pier that, really, meant nothing to me?

Sitting on a bench, gazing across the bay toward Melbourne and sipping my coffee, I figured it might be a long conversation with Eliot, so I decided to enjoy these few minutes before receiving what would be either good or bad news. I really had no idea what she might say. She might love it, call it a work of genius, the best thing I'd ever written. Or maybe she wouldn't get it. Or was it possible she'd already sold it? No, she would have told me about offers—and it had only been a week.

I placed my cup on the bench beside me and tore open the paper bag nestled in my lap. Dabs of custard clung to the bag's inner lining. I swiped my finger along the inside and sucked the custard off, then I scooped up the whole thing and took a bite. Another taste sensation delivered by the Bellarine Peninsula. The bun was light and sweet, like a brioche, and the top glazed with a honey syrup. 'Where have you been all my life?' I asked aloud.

I ate only half the bun; drank only a third of the coffee. Who was I kidding? I couldn't stand the anticipation, and my stomach confirmed it.

I tossed the cup into a nearby trash can but hung on to the remaining bun. Opening Eliot's text, I pressed the phone icon to dial her number and began walking along the pier. It was breezy, but the sun already radiated warmth. People wandered past carrying small foam boxes and parcels wrapped in paper, no doubt containing fresh seafood.

It was Saturday morning in Australia, but late on Friday afternoon in New York City: the end of the working week, but Eliot would no doubt still be at her desk for an hour or so. If it were me, in Minnesota, I'd have been watching the clock for the past hour, waiting for it to hit five so I could crack open a beer, ready for my pizza to arrive.

'How you doin', traveller?'

I was anxious to jump right in—to hear her thoughts on my manuscript—but I could pretend I wasn't desperate and needy for a few minutes.

'Pretty good. Nice to get away from the frost. You should see it here—it's like a postcard, if you can remember those. And the best coffee you've ever tasted. I didn't know coffee could be this good. And I don't mean high-end, expensive stuff. Just from regular cafes.'

On the pier, I passed men fishing alone, tackle boxes and thermoses at their feet. Pelicans soared above.

'Sounds heavenly. We're in for a relatively warm December, they tell us—up around forty. And wetter than usual. Not much snow heading our way.'

We were talking about the weather. Could it be any more obvious that we were avoiding something?

'I took Ashleigh and Nicolai to see the lighting of the tree at the Rockefeller Center,' Eliot said.

'Oh yeah?'

Ashleigh and Nicolai were her grandchildren.

'It didn't disappoint. Diana Ross shone. Although poor old Tony Bennett is a bit past it now. It was cruel bringing him out, really. Anyway, I do love the city at the holidays, despite the cold—not to mention the crowds of shoppers.'

All Eliot's talk of snow and Christmas magic washed over me. I was standing in shorts, looking out over a blue sea. It didn't feel at all like Christmas, and I was beginning to sense a quiver in my hand, as if I'd suddenly developed a tremor.

'So, what did you think?' I asked, wanting to end the pain. I considered adding 'of my manuscript', but why else would she want to speak with me?

'It's a great story, Drew.'

I felt something inside me lift or, more accurately, decompress. As if my whole body was clenched but could now unknot.

'The imagery of the LA landscape is breathtaking,' she continued. 'And what you're saying about Hollywood is interesting. Skylar is a well-drawn character.'

Eliot followed this praise with a beat of hesitation and I wondered what was inside it. She went on. 'But it feels like you're trying too hard—that you're trying to be another writer.'

Well, yeah, a decent one this time around.

'I wanted it to have a minimalist tone,' I said. 'Like Cormac McCarthy.'

The wind picked up, whooshing through the phone's speaker. I quickened my pace toward a sheltered area further along the pier.

'Unfortunately, that shows. The writing is guarded. It lacks vulnerability. It feels almost, I hate to say this, but *desperate*.'

I took a seat on a bench under a small tin roof, walled with clear, hard plastic, trying to take in the fact that the manuscript I'd spent three years on wasn't cutting it.

'It's got good bones, Drew. But you're holding back. The way you've written it . . . it's not breaking through. I mean, I commend you for what you're trying to achieve, I really do. But I just don't think it's working. It feels disingenuous. It lacks emotional honesty.'

Disingenuous. Lacks emotional honesty. The words swam around my head.

'So, what does that mean? What are you saying, Eliot?'

'I don't think I can sell it in its current state.'

In front of me, birds were diving into the water hunting for breakfast. For a fleeting moment, I felt like joining them—plunging into the sea to wash away the sting of Eliot's words.

'You're not going to send it out?'

'That's what I'm saying.'

The bee sting curdled with the coffee in my stomach, making me want to hurl.

'Can't you just—'

'Drew, you'll thank me later. Sending it out like this would put both of us in an awkward position and may diminish the odds next time.'

I turned away from the phone and exhaled, taking in a family of three, the parents swinging their toddler between them as they walked. The mother was pregnant again.

'Drew?'

'Is it salvageable, do you think?'

'That's up to you.' She paused, and I didn't fill the silence. 'I don't know what's going on with you right now, but you have to move beyond what you *think* this novel should be and let your instincts drive the story. You have to work out what's stifling you emotionally—because something is—and then let go of it. You're not going to connect with Grady's internal transformation until you do.'

After ending the call, I continued to walk the pier, the breath gone from my lungs. I had an urge to toss the damn phone in the bay. I was normally so good at controlling my emotions, pushing them down, and I'd had so many rejections in the past that I had learned to expect them; anything else was a bonus. But not personalising these disappointments—what a ridiculous concept for a writer, or any artist, to contemplate. It was always personal, no matter what anyone tried to tell you. No matter what you tried to tell yourself.

I turned at the end of the pier, where the path hooked to the right and narrowed alongside a stone-walled jetty. A handful of boats—mostly older, smaller vessels in need of repair—were moored there. Some looked as if they hadn't been touched in years, wood splintering, rust creeping up the sides.

I must have walked for ten minutes in squalling wind, shielding my eyes from the sun with a flat hand, before I reached the tip of the breakwater. I had gone as far as I could, and now there was nowhere else to go but back. But I wasn't ready. I wanted to stay there, sitting on that breakwater forever, never having to think about writing or becoming successful or seeing my name on the *New York Times* bestseller list.

So I sat, the beginnings of a headache gripping my temples, dread swimming in my stomach.

I thought I'd prepared myself for this rejection, running through Eliot's possible criticisms in my mind: *it's a bit slow at the beginning, it sags in the middle, the end needs tightening.* In my head, I was ready for this, but nobody had bothered to tell my heart.

A child negotiating the rocks on all fours like a crab slipped past me. He might have been Missy's age. I wanted to hug him, to let some of his childhood innocence seep into me. To make things better. Children always made things better.

Woodland needed too much work. I should just trash the whole manuscript. I couldn't start again. It would be too painful, too hard to let go of the ninety thousand words I'd already written. What would I cut? What would I add? How would I know?

I'd thought this manuscript was exceptional. Not a work of genius, perhaps, but a standout. Something fresh and singular. Clearly, I lacked judgement. My barometer for what constituted good writing was woefully out of whack.

I had nobody I could talk to about this. Claire didn't

understand. She was a good listener but couldn't offer any helpful advice because she didn't get it. She'd say something soothing like, *Don't worry; it'll all work out.* She might even suggest I take a break, which was out of the question. It had already been four years since *Saving Grace* was published and I'd spent the past three on *Woodland*.

I really had no idea what to do. *That's up to you,* Eliot had said. I needed some distance from it; I needed to take a step back and get some perspective.

For one crazy moment I considered contacting Christian. But I needed a pep talk and I doubted he would be the one to give it to me. He'd probably never had anything he'd written rejected.

What this manuscript needed, I thought, was to be taken out back and have done to it what Tom did to that seal back in '92.

When I was a kid, I loved words. I delighted in learning about their etymology and how meanings or usage changed over time. I played those walkie-talkie word games with Tom.

But now the words didn't seem enough. Worse, they taunted me. They held so much power—the ability to make my dreams come true . . . and the ability to destroy me. I'd once felt I had a kind of synergic relationship with them. They had always been good to me; I could always rely on them to lift me up. Now, words were my captor. They no longer listened to me or did what I wanted them to do.

We were no longer friends, words and me, because they had betrayed me.

I climbed the hill to the car and drove straight back to the guest house in Queenscliff, planning to slip under the covers of my bed and stay there for the day. But when I arrived, a housekeeper was vacuuming my room, the bedsheets in a white pile on the naked mattress, so I slid on my sunglasses and a Twins baseball cap and headed to the beach instead.

As a novelist, it is always in my power to change the ending. The more hard-fought it is, the more satisfying to the reader. As authors, we must erect obstacles in the way of our hero achieving their goals. Often, the hero doesn't know what that goal is, but when they discover it, achieving it is the only thing that will truly fulfil them. They almost always reach that goal, but not without some great sacrifice. That's the nature of a true dilemma—choosing the lesser of two evils. The hero has to decide which one he is most able to bear.

But in real life it's not so easy to change the ending. In a novel, the stakes are not real. Nobody really dies or has their heart literally broken. In the real world, when people get hurt it stings. Sometimes, the wounds never heal.

What scared me most about Eliot's thoughts on *Woodland* was that I couldn't see what was wrong with it; those failings that Eliot could identify so clearly were invisible to me. I could try to explain it away—I was too close to it; it was all in my mind but I hadn't articulated it on the page—but the truth was I lacked insight.

Without registering it, I'd walked up Hesse, along King, down Swanston past Marissa's old house and beyond the former nuns' home to the beach. As I hit the sand, I called Claire.

'Hey, you,' she said. 'What's up?'

'Nothing. Just wanted to hear your voice.'

'Oh. Everything okay?'

'Sure.'

'Where are you? Sounds windy.'

'At the beach.'

'Lucky you.' A pause stretched out between us. 'Drew?'

'Yeah?'

'Are you still thinking about our conversation? The one about having a kid, I mean.'

'No, but yes.'

'Can we get into this when you get back?'

'Sure. But you could keep working, you know. I'll stay home. I'll raise the kids.'

'*Kids?* We've already moved on to multiple children?'

'One would be lonely, don't you think?'

'Drew, no.'

'This won't affect us; our lives can go on as normal.'

'All expectant parents say that. It's never true.'

'Our house is big enough. We won't have to move.'

'Drew . . .' She sighed down the phone. 'I know you're craving a sense of security right now, but this is not it.'

I didn't respond.

'Aren't things good? Aren't *we* good?'

I closed my eyes. 'Well, *I* am, but you could probably work on yourself a bit,' I said with a smirk in my voice.

She took a moment, I hoped to smile, then said, 'I won't change my mind. I'm sorry. This is what we agreed.'

It felt like a one-two punch in the guts but there was no point in pushing it.

'Hey, did you hear back from Eliot about your book yet?' she asked.

How did she know? What could she sense in me?

'No,' I lied. I lied because I was too ashamed to admit to the person who had supported me all this time—financially, emotionally, hopefully—that I had failed. I wanted to tell her that I was sorry for allowing her to have faith in me, sorry for promising that I would become someone she could be proud of, that I could live up to my end of the unspoken bargain we had as a couple, sorry that she had backed the wrong horse.

We wrapped up the call with small talk, but it felt strained. The book was on my mind. Kids were on my mind. If I was ever going to raise children, it could not be with Claire. I was approaching forty with little to show for my time on Earth.

On the beach, kids dressed in bathing suits, high-visibility yellow swim shirts and yellow caps with their name Sharpied across the side, ran back and forth in short bursts between flags. Another group were in the water, kneeling on surfboards, paddling. I recognised Hannah and Charlotte among them and then scanned the huddles of parents on the beach for Samara. I found her sitting alone on a blanket on the sand, her shoes kicked off, reading.

My first thought was to avoid her—I didn't want to speak to anybody—but then she looked up and caught my eye, as if she could sense me there, and gave me a wave.

I made my way over, dragging my feet through the sinking sand.

'Good morning,' she said once I was within range.

'Hello. Thanks again for last night.'

'No worries. How'd you sleep?'

'I slept well, actually. I guess I'm over my jet lag.' I didn't mention the bottle of pinot noir, which had no doubt aided my slumber.

She scooted over to make room on her blanket.

I couldn't sit; I was too jittery, arbitrary thoughts competing for space in my brain . . . the call with Eliot, the call with Claire. 'How about a walk?' I suggested.

'Okay.' She stood, left her book on the blanket and pocketed her keys and phone.

Samara took one last look at the kids on the beach, now assembled in lines, shoulders back, looking like they were in a cartoon version of a military exercise.

'What were you reading back there?' I asked once we'd started off toward Point Lonsdale.

'*An American Marriage.* You? What are you reading at the moment?'

'A short-story collection. Curtis Sittenfeld.'

She shook her head. 'Haven't heard of him.'

'She's a woman.'

'Called Curtis?'

'Yeah.'

'How American. Any good?'

'Yeah, great, but . . . I don't really read for pleasure anymore. I can't.'

'That's sad.'

That dream I had of being a famous novelist when I finished school was a lofty one, not to mention a little crazy, but I did work for it. I practised writing like you might practise a musical instrument—an hour a day, whatever words came to me. And I read like mad. But not like I did when I was a kid. Not for pleasure. I started reading like I was studying for an exam, taking note of how the author depicted a landscape, stopping to examine my feelings about a character or a scene to try to work out how the author had managed to mould me, to make me feel the emotions they wanted me to. I wished I could read for the joy of it again.

Samara must have detected something in my voice.

'Is everything alright with you?' she asked.

I was about to blow her off—to say something about being tired—but only a few minutes before I'd told her I'd slept well.

'It's a lot of things.'

Tom, Adam, leaving Queenscliff, never having kids of my own, the manuscript. I thought of what Leon said about swallowing pride.

'I spoke to my agent and she's not sending out my latest manuscript.'

'Oh, Drew. I'm so sorry.' She squeezed my upper arm with her hand. 'Did she give a reason?'

'She doesn't think it's ready.'

The thought of returning to Minnesota with nothing resolved, feeling worse than when I left, made my entire body sag. I couldn't face the thought of reading that manuscript ever again, let alone working on it more. I didn't have the heart for it. I suddenly hated every word because none of them were any good. *I* wasn't any good.

'I'm sorry,' Samara said again. 'That's really shitty. Could you get a second opinion?'

'Not really. She's my agent.'

'I mean about how to . . . change it.'

I kicked at a broken piece of cuttlefish. 'I don't really have writer friends.' One of the reasons for that, if I had to admit it, was because I felt superior around unpublished writers and inferior around established ones. My contemporaries were other failed authors. We could get together and trade stories of literary disappointment.

'Why not?' Samara asked.

I pressed my lips together, trying to unravel the reason. 'It's hard to be friends with other writers,' I said. 'I know it shouldn't be, and it would be nice to think of us as this happy community that supported each other at every turn, but there's so often a blurry line, trying to find a path between hurt feelings and support. It's hard to be happy for someone when you're miserable yourself, even if they are a close friend.'

She nodded, encouraging me to continue.

'With the established ones, I look at their success and, instead of feeling happy for them, I feel disappointed for myself.' I looked at her. 'I've never admitted that to anybody.'

'I can see how that would be hard. When I got pregnant the second time, I had this friend—a really close friend—who had been trying for years. In the meantime, I'd married, had Charlotte and now I was pregnant with Hannah. I was scared to tell her. How sad is that? I had all this joy, but I didn't want to upset her. We drifted apart. I don't think she ever had kids in the end.'

'We have very fragile hearts, us humans. And egos.' I needed to talk about this. And for what seemed like the first time, I wanted to. 'Often, when I'm sitting at my desk trying to write, all of sudden I get these visitors—self-doubt, anxiety, panic. They come into my den and pull up chairs, forming a circle around me, and start to jabber on about how shit I am, how I have no business being a writer and will never amount to anything.'

'Lock your door. Don't let them in.'

'Easier said than done. They have a secret key.'

'Drew.'

I knew what I wanted *Woodland* to be. It was all there, in some inaccessible part of me, but I couldn't translate it to the page. Wasn't that what Eliot had said? It had the potential to be an amazing book about ambition and love and passion and desire, but I was not the writer to make it so. I didn't have the talent. I should focus instead on a less ambitious project that relied more heavily on plot to move the story forward, not try to say something new about how we lived today—the pressures of success and the unspoken implication that if you weren't visible, if you weren't lauded, you weren't successful.

'That's how I felt about dating again,' Samara said. 'After you've been burned, it's *hard*. It's like standing naked in the middle of the street and saying, *Start firing.* But you have to give it a chance. It's hard to open up to people. It can feel exposing. But if you don't, you'll never truly connect with anyone. And if you don't connect, you don't live.'

Connection. Hadn't Eliot said something about that? Leon had alluded to the same thing.

'Vulnerability is the first thing people look for in you but the last thing you offer up,' Samara said. 'In others, it's seen as courageous. In yourself, it's weakness.'

We kept walking, not speaking for a moment.

'I'm a lot more open to dating now,' she said. 'The way I see it, there are going to be successes and there are going to be failures. And you learn from both. You have to have the failures to appreciate the successes. Are the failures really failures? Maybe they're just getting me closer to knowing what I want. Maybe they're constructive.' She glanced skyward. The morning cloud had cleared. 'I needed to let go of my preconceived idea of what my perfect partner is—his age, what he looks like, what kind of career he has—and just go with the flow.' She glanced at her phone. 'Sorry, but I'd better head back.'

'I might keep walking for a bit.' Kinks were fixing in my gut and I needed to walk them off.

'Sure. I'll see you later. Don't skip town without saying goodbye, okay?'

I continued along the beach, stepping over kelp the tide had dumped on the sand, until I hit the Point Lonsdale Primary School.

I'd never thought I'd be one of those poor saps who only had one novel in them. Like the music industry, the literary market-place was oversupplied with one-hit wonders. Not that *Saving Grace* had been a hit. The popular wisdom is that first novels are largely autobiographical, but second novels, well, they're the real test. Can this dude create something out of nothing? Second novels make or break a writer because they ratify an author's talent and their worth in the publishing world.

I sat on the beach, watching kids building castles from damp sand moulded into turret bucket shapes, turning my manuscript over in my mind. Then, after ten minutes, fed up with the frustration of trying to find a loophole I could slip through that would make it all magically work, I dialled Eliot's number.

'I don't know what to do,' I told her.

'Drew, you have to work out what it is you're avoiding,' she said. '*Woodland*, in its current form, feels small. And you are not a small writer.'

I couldn't compute what she was saying; I didn't know how to turn her meaning into a solution for this manuscript. I wanted her to tell me that I could move a few scenes around, sharpen the dialogue in chapters 4 and 9 and be done with it.

'Whether you realise it or not,' Eliot continued, 'you got into this game for the pain. All writers do. But there are two kinds of pain, Drew: pain that you use and pain that uses you. Storytellers have to coax out the heroes inside them—*and* the monsters.'

I turned and started walking back along the sand. In front of me was the white lighthouse, standing there, doing its job, not asking for anything in return. Maybe a novelist should be like that—give more than they expect in return. Jake Heriot popped into my head.

In the summer between my junior and senior years of high

school, I took a job at the State Theater at the top of the hill on Sheridan, in Ely, where I met a guy named Jake Heriot. We were co-workers, spending hot afternoons behind the concession stand or sweeping up milk duds and Skittles from the floors of the movie theatres.

Jake wanted to be a screenwriter. He went to DePaul in Chicago but spent summers at home in Ely. He was serious about screenwriting and never questioned that he would get there. I'd never googled him to find out if he actually had or not.

One day, as I was loading the popcorn machine with orange butter from a large white tub, I asked Jake about his chances of making it.

'Someone's gotta write them,' he said. 'Why not me?'

'But you're from Ely.'

He laughed. 'So? You think all screenwriters grow up in Hollywood?'

'I don't know.'

He flicked his head, flinging long mousy brown bangs out of his face. 'All you have to do is write a good script and convince someone to buy it.'

'How do you do that?'

'Get an agent, for one.'

'What do they do?'

'They sell it for you. And take their ten per cent.'

Another day, on my break, he caught me sitting out back, reading *Norwegian Wood*.

'You really like reading, huh?'

'Sure. Don't you?'

'I like it enough, but I prefer movies.'

'You're in the right place for that.'

'You bet. Why else would I spend my summer earning

minimum wage when I could be out biking or kayaking? No, man, I'm *studying*. When I'm not here, I'm at the DVD store, or in my basement watching DVDs.'

'What kind of stuff do you . . . study?'

'Horror. But good horror, like *Scream*. Man, I loved that film. It was like a breath of fresh air blowing into the stale landscape of 1980s horror. It was self-aware; it laughed at itself, and the genre as a whole. Wes Craven is a genius.' He bit into his hot dog, hair flopping over his eyes. 'I'm gonna reinvent the genre. It's got a bad name because of scream-fests like *Halloween* and *Nightmare on Elm Street*. My horror's gonna be *smart*. I'm not writing my stuff like a classic horror film, which is all about getting the biggest fright. I'm writing stuff with real depth—absorbing characters, scenes you can't turn away from—but they happen to be scary too.'

He pulled out the seat opposite me and sat. I turned my book over so I wouldn't lose my page.

'We're at a serious low point in the history of the horror genre right now. We came out of a golden age and now we've got shit, mostly. Okay, so we had some of those, like, classy psychological thrillers—*Jacob's Ladder*, *Misery*—but they're the exception. We're in an evolutionary period. The eighties were all about slasher films; now we're more focused on the thriller genre. *The Silence of the Lambs* showed the kind of sophistication that can be brought to a horror flick.' He took another bite of his hot dog. 'You write?'

'A bit.'

'Fiction?'

'Maybe.'

'Well, remember this, Salinger. There's nothing wrong with genre. People look down their noses at it, sure. That's why you need a fresh take. Don't try to imitate others. Reinvent. Reawaken. Don't write some arthouse trash just because it might become a "critics' choice". Write the stuff you want to read. If you love it, if it moves you, it'll have that effect on someone else too. On lots of people. Never be embarrassed about what you like.'

I glanced at *Norwegian Wood*, splayed across the table.

'Look at the most popular movies this summer,' Jake went on. '*Men in Black*, *The Lost World*, *My Best Friend's Wedding*, *Batman and Robin*, *Con Air*. There won't be an Academy Award among them, but *damn* do people like 'em.'

Jake had given me this advice two decades ago, and I'd been trying to write something 'worthy' since college. But I'd forgotten Jake's definition of what makes something worthy: *If you love it, if it moves you, it'll have that effect on someone else too.*

It was all there, somewhere deep inside. But I needed to find the pressure valve, pull the release lever, and let it hiss through me.

36

When I got back to the hotel, I found Adam, on his bike, no helmet, riding in a figure eight in the street outside. He'd been waiting for me.

'Whatcha doin'?' I asked.

'Nothin'. Riding around.'

'Uh-huh.'

'What are *you* doing?'

'Nothing. Walking around . . . Buy you a milkshake?' I suggested.

'Sure.'

He rode his bike and I followed, heading toward the foreshore to a cafe wedged between the men's and women's sides of a toilet block. It was a kiosk named Harry's in '92—Tom and I had bought bags of chips and cans of soda from there—but it was now a cafe called Nelly's.

Adam chose a table by the window. A tall waitress with Pippi Longstocking braids brought glasses of water and placed menus between us. She couldn't have been more than twenty. 'Back in a tick.'

I gave the menu a cursory glance—waffles, toasties, burgers, wraps. 'Want some waffles?' I asked, but he shook his head. 'Iced chocolate?'

'Okay.' He folded the paper napkin on the table in two, then again.

The waitress returned, slipping a small notepad from the front pocket of her denim shortalls, and I ordered an iced chocolate for Adam and a cappuccino for me.

We handed the menus back to the waitress.

Again, Adam unfolded the napkin then folded it once more.

'Something on your mind, Adam?'

'No.'

'It's the weekend. Any plans tonight? With friends, maybe?'

'Nah. Probably just stay home.'

'Okay.'

He glanced out the window, at me briefly, then went back to his napkin-folding.

'How do you know if the feelings you're having are normal?' he asked.

I pressed my shoulder blades against the back of my chair, the pressure to respond with something insightful building. I crossed my arms. I uncrossed them. My brain trawled its banks for a life lesson that Adam could use now and take forward. But I had nothing.

'Every feeling is normal,' I said. 'I mean, if you're having it, then it's normal. For the person having it, at least.' I tried again. 'What I meant to say is, if you're having it, it's real.' Was that what I meant to say? 'Why do you ask?'

He shrugged. Then, after a full ten seconds, said, 'Maybe some feelings *feel* normal, but that's only because we've been having them for so long. And now we don't think they're strange anymore, but we should. Because they're not good feelings. But how can you tell the difference?'

He was talking about losing perspective—how we become accustomed to living in a certain way and so, eventually, fail to find fault with it.

I said, 'Do you ever get a cut or something, and you put a bandaid over it, and then when you take it off, the skin's all wrinkly underneath?'

'Yeah.'

'And it's only when you take the bandaid off, and you let the air get to it, that it starts to heal properly?'

'Yeah.'

'I guess feelings, especially sad ones, are like that. It's good to protect them for a while—when they're fresh and raw—but at some point they need to be exposed to light so they can get better.'

'Are you saying I should let them out?'

'I guess I am. If you tell someone, like your mom, then they can help you work out if they're normal or not.'

I wondered then if Tom had spoken to anyone about his feelings. Maybe he didn't need to. Maybe he *really* needed to.

The waitress returned with our orders and I sipped my coffee. Sublime.

'What's up with you today?' Adam asked. I mustn't have spoken in a while.

'Nothing.' I didn't need to burden him with my problems on top of his own. 'I guess I'm just thinking about leaving you all.'

He hmphed. 'Why would you want to hang around here? Everyone's miserable.'

'I don't know. I don't feel ready to leave.'

'Why?'

'Something's . . . unfinished.'

He gave me a look: *Don't bullshit me.*

'I got some bad news about a manuscript. That's all.'

'What news?'

I exhaled. Did he need to know this? Did I even want to talk about it? It seemed so unimportant compared to what he was dealing with.

'What news?' he repeated.

I took another sip of coffee, delaying. 'I sent my agent something new before I left the States and I just heard back from her this morning. Apparently, it needs the literary equivalent of rebuilding Europe after World War Two.'

'So it sucks big hairy dog balls?'

'Well . . .' I snorted a laugh. 'She doesn't like it.'

'Do *you* like it?'

'I thought I did.'

'This feels like déjà vu,' he said. 'Now you don't like it because your agent doesn't? Did it change after you sent it to her?'

He had a point. But so did Eliot. I wrote this book to have it published. Now it wouldn't be. Not in its current form, at least.

'It's not that simple.'

'Okay.' He slurped iced chocolate through the straw.

I felt the need to explain further—to say that if she didn't like it, it was as good as dead in the water, because I couldn't send it out on my own. I couldn't undercut her like that. Plus, I valued her opinion. I wanted her to like it. But I didn't say anything like that.

'You know that term *déjà vu*?' I said instead. 'The French have another term, *jamais vu*, which means the exact opposite: where something familiar feels foreign. Like something *should* be recognisable but it feels like it's being experienced for the first time.'

Adam leaned back in his chair, milkshake glass in hand. 'You know what's interesting about that?' he said. 'Nothing. You're changing the subject.'

'Yes.'

'Because you don't want to talk about your book.'

'Right.'

'Well, I think you're looking at it wrong,' he said. 'It's like all that stuff I muck around with in the shed—some of it works out, some doesn't. I probably learn more from the stuff that doesn't.'

I nodded. 'Do you read, Adam?'

'Nup.' He played with his straw, swivelling it around the bottom of his glass as if on an axis.

'I read nonstop as a kid. Characters in novels were my friends; the worlds of the stories were my playground.'

He made an 'L' shape with his forefinger and thumb and held it to his forehead. *Loser.*

I really loved this kid.

'I didn't have a ton of friends in high school,' I said. 'But I didn't want to.'

'That's what all the Nigel-No-Mates say.'

'I mean, I had *some* friends. I was drawn to the outsiders—the oddballs like me; kids who avoided fashion trends, read Vonnegut and sat around on the tailgates of their dad's pick-ups smoking. But these oddballs introduced me to authors and musicians and movies and attitudes and values and ways of thinking that made me feel, I don't know, *there*. Like maybe there was a place for me somewhere.'

'You think I need weirder friends?'

I shook my head, even though I knew he was messing with me. 'Books open you up to places you'll never go, people you'll never meet, thoughts you might never have had otherwise. They really can be—forgive me—life-changing, if you let them.'

'You're not as convincing as you think, Drew.'

Was it time to give up? Surely there was a point I was trying to make. I had another stab at it.

'All my friends were pumped about sticking it to the man. Calling out injustices as they saw them. I didn't have strong opinions about *anything*. And that made me feel kind of like a non-person. Like I didn't stand for anything. What do you stand for?'

I looked at him, awaiting his answer while he reached for the bottle of ketchup at the end of the table and started to rotate it on the spot.

'What?' he said, as though he'd missed something. 'Was that a real question?'

'Yeah. What's something you know, for sure, to be true?'

He didn't seem to be considering it, staring at me blankly instead. 'You're a very intense guy.'

'Come on. What do you believe? In your bones?'

Maybe I'd delved too deep, was being a boring old man again, but I wanted to fire him up, to help him find something he could be passionate about.

Adam sighed. 'I believe that fish and tomato sauce should never share a plate.'

I smiled. 'Fair enough.'

He returned the ketchup to its place at the end of the table.

'Drew, all this stuff with your writing, it sounds . . . I mean, why do you keep doing it to yourself?'

I drained the dregs of another spectacular Peninsula coffee. 'When I was a kid, sometimes all I had was books. They— don't snicker—kind of saved me at times. I want to give that to someone else. It's the least I can do.'

Even as I said it, it didn't feel like the complete truth.

'And to do that, you have to sell a lot of copies,' Adam said.

'Yeah, but it's not about fame. It's about achieving something big. Big enough to fill . . . to make up for . . . to . . .' I shifted in my seat. The phrase 'enough for three' swam around in my head. Where had I heard that? 'I never did believe in the idea that if you can help one person, it's worth it. I want to speak to lots of people. *Then* it will be worth it.'

Adam pushed his empty glass to the side of the table. 'What if the only person you help is yourself? Will that make it worth it?'

The sun was casting long shadows eastward as I walked along- side Adam's bike to the fringe of the foreshore park, where we stopped. Swan Island leaked through the gaps in the trees.

'My stepdad? The one who worked on Swan Island? I didn't find out until years later what he'd been through in the Gulf War. Well, *because* of the war.'

'PTSD,' Adam said. 'I know.'

'Maybe. But it was more than that for a lot of those guys. The US government didn't know what to expect from Desert Storm, so they pumped all the GIs full of vaccines to help them survive a biological attack—nerve gas, anthrax. These were unregulated vaccines. And too much, too soon. And they didn't know this at the time, but the facilities the troops bombed in Iraq released these toxins into the air that ended up really affecting their physical health—rashes, stomach problems, joint pain, memory loss—probably from the exposure to chemicals. None of this is proven or officially acknowledged, of course, but it's affected too many veterans to be a coincidence. Or to be all in their minds, like some officials tried to say.'

Adam considered this in silence.

'What I guess I'm saying is . . . about your mom . . . about giving people a break . . .'

He held up a hand. 'I get it. Good story, too. I really got into the world wars in primary school.'

'Lotta boys do.'

'It's weird how quickly we forget the past and keep making the same mistakes, don't you reckon?'

37

That night, I bought a takeout pizza for dinner. I noticed when I'd got the fish and chips with Adam that our old pizzeria—right by the fish-and-chip shop—was gone, and I wondered what had become of the gently spoken Italian guy, Pete, who ran it.

So I bought my pizza from a dinky place near the brewhouse and carried it to a bench in the foreshore reserve. It was quiet down there at 7 pm, but still sunny, and I watched as a young dad pushed two kids on the swings, alternating between them as the kids urged him to push them higher. The air was warm, but a cool wind chilled me as I sat shrouded in the shade of a large triangular pine tree.

It wasn't until my early twenties that I looked into Gulf War syndrome and began to understand what Mark and a lot of his comrades-in-arms went through not only in Iraq but, more tragically, after they got home. Many of them weren't believed—their symptoms dismissed by defence force doctors as psychological or as something unrelated to the Gulf.

Maybe I could have forgiven him for what he took from us a lot sooner had I understood better what was taken from him.

I couldn't finish the last slice of pizza and tossed the grease-stained box into a trash can. I left the shade and the children behind and headed for the street, having to stop once, bent over with my palms on my knees while a beastly stomach cramp had its way with me, then took myself into the brewhouse directly opposite. Maybe the company of strangers would take my mind off everything.

It was Saturday night and upbeat music I didn't recognise spilled through the open doors of the historic two-storey building. People filled the pub section at the front—glasses of beer glistening in the setting sun—and I passed through them on my way to the bar. Queenscliff's pubs meant nothing to me as a child; I hardly even noticed them and never went inside one. They were a part of the town reduced to exhibits in the museum of my memory. Now I had come full circle.

At the bar, I asked for their largest glass of tap beer.

'A pint?' the bartender checked. He was young, with a dark beard, and wore his long hair in a knot on the top of his head.

'Yeah, a pint.'

I took my beer and made my way through the crowd. It was a real mixed bunch—old, young, locals, holidaymakers.

I'd never been to a bar on my own. I was always with Claire or classmates in college, and ever since. All our friends these days were like us—professional couples in their thirties, no kids, whom we'd met through Claire's work or who were old friends of hers who had partnered up. There were other friends—college friends of mine, couples when we were in our twenties—but they'd moved away, or had kids, or split from the person in the coupling whom we'd liked better. I'd had one good friend, Hamish—a guy I'd met while working at the office supply store—but he was the CEO of his own digital advertising agency now, attracting eminent clients, making great money, having lots of success. I often found myself too busy to see him.

When one pint was finished, I ordered another, then another, talking with random people who were willing to welcome a Yankee into their circle for a round or two.

When you tell people you're an author it instantly sparks their interest—it sounds mystical and exciting, and I enjoyed the glow of their misguided admiration, however superficial. But then I watched them as they interacted with each other—knowing looks, inner-circle references I didn't understand, the shared histories of old friends—and disappeared into my beer glass. The glow of their admiration was fleeting, stark against the tight bonds of their friendships, deep and everlasting.

Some fragment of me I hadn't acknowledged for a long time ached to be a part of it, to share something intimate about myself in order to get closer; to understand them better; to have them understand me. To be part of their gang, even if only for one drunken night.

Then I found myself at the bar again, fumbling through my wallet, presenting a ten-dollar note. 'Enough for three,' I told the barman.

'For three drinks?' he asked.

'No,' I said.

He looked at me for a moment. 'Okay, mate. Maybe it's time to call it a night.' He moved along the bar to the next patron waiting to be served.

But still I didn't leave. I found someone at the other end of the bar to serve me and stayed until the muscles in my neck began to weaken and voices blurred to the point where I could no longer receive, or contribute, anything coherent.

I made my way to the main doors, pressing my fingertips to the doorframe for support. I stumbled out, losing my balance, and fell into the arms of a woman. White wine sloshed over my shirt and hers but nothing about it concerned me. She held me in her arms a moment and something about her reminded me of a younger Claire—the version from our college days, the version who couldn't keep her hands off me. I nuzzled my nose into the soft part between the woman's shoulder and neck and inhaled her scent, which transported me back twenty years. A firm grip on both my shoulders pulled me away. A man stood before me, no older than twenty-five, blond hair shaved to skin over his ears, with much longer strands slicked back on top like the lads in *Peaky Blinders*. His face was alight with fury.

'The fuck you think you're doing, mate?'

I turned back to the woman, as if she could offer an answer. She didn't seem concerned, but it occurred to me what I'd done, and how it must have looked. I reached out a hand—to say I was sorry—and took her by the wrist.

The guy again placed his hand on my shoulder, only one this time, and spun me around. Then his fist was coming at my face and there was no time to do anything. The rock of his knuckles slammed into my nose and mouth and I stumbled backward, crashing into one of the timber posts that supported the upper-floor balcony. But I was still on my feet.

Another man shouted. 'Oi! You two! Go home!'

I blinked, trying to orientate myself, thinking I should leave but not sure how to make that happen. My face ached and bright discs of blood blotted my white t-shirt.

The man who had shouted was at my side then, leading me forcefully up the street by the elbow, my feet shuffling to keep up with him.

Noises of protest erupted behind me—a woman saying, '*He* started it'—but by then I'd been pushed a distance away from the doors and was standing alone on the sidewalk.

I didn't look back, afraid of what it might trigger, and began a wobbly walk up Gellibrand, my brain sodden, my nose throbbing. My feet fell out of step and I found my body falling but righted myself just in time.

I was in no state to walk so stopped for a moment and took a breath. I wiped blood from my nostrils with my forearm and leaned against the cold steel of a parking sign for a spell until my head stopped swimming. I could still hear raised voices at the pub, mixed with the pulse of the music.

Shame got me moving again, propelling me up the street. I rounded the corner at Hobson, my hotel in sight. But then I stumbled off the path, losing my footing. I tripped on something—a tree root protruding through the earth maybe—and felt myself going down. I thrust my hands out, thinking they would protect me from the fall, but they flailed in front of me, as if I had no command over them, and my face was suddenly colliding with the unyielding trunk of a tree. I fell to the grass, rolling onto my back.

Even if I'd wanted to move, I couldn't have. So I lay there, looking up at the dark sky, barely visible stars giving it a translucent glow, the faint music from the pub echoing around me.

Suddenly I was sixteen again, in Ely. It was winter. I'd slipped on a strip of black ice on the way home from the lake and was lying by the side of the road, shivering in my denim jacket, staring at the dark sky, which was twinkling quietly with muted starlight. I was drunk then, too, had probably hit my head. I didn't want to move, so I stayed put, mesmerised by the stars, the cold stinging my ears and nose, wondering if I was about to die. The roads were deserted and nobody knew where I was. I was freezing at first, but then started to grow warm, and I registered that as a symptom of hypothermia. It wouldn't be so bad, I'd thought then, if I died right there on the side of the road. What did I have to live for? *Who* did I have to live for? And hypothermia, I'd heard, was not an altogether unpleasant way to go. I closed my eyes and felt myself drifting.

'Y'alright, mate?' a man's voice said.

My eyelids fluttered open. Standing over me was the guy from the pub who'd punched me, the moon pushing silver through the tree's canopy and onto his face.

'Enough for three,' I told him.

'What?'

'Enough for three.'

He leaned over and extended his hand, like he was challenging me to an arm wrestle. I couldn't work out what was going on, so curled my body into a ball, as if that would protect me.

'You're fucked,' he said. 'Here. Gimme your hand.'

In Ely, when I'd slipped on the black ice, nobody had come to my aid. It was the story of my teenage years and that was fine. That was how it had been since then, but that was mostly on me.

'Come on, mate.'

I ran my tongue over my upper lip, tasting blood, and exhaled. Then I gave him my hand and let the guy who'd just punched me pull me to my feet.

38

The ringing of my cell phone startled me awake. Light streamed under the shades, as if the day was trying to push its way into the room, but it felt like I'd only just drifted off. I couldn't remember climbing into bed.

I retrieved my phone from my pocket. Tia. 'Hello?' My teeth were furry, my eyes gritty and my brain woolly. Something was wrong with my upper lip.

'Adam's missing,' she said in a thin voice she was struggling to keep even.

I sat up, yawning, and my jaw clicked as if I'd dislodged the joint. 'What do you mean, missing?'

'Here's not here! What else would I mean by *missing*?'

I checked the time on the bedside clock: 7.49. 'Did he sleep in his bed?'

'How would I know? It's never made!' She sighed down the phone. 'He was here when I went to sleep.'

My phone bleeped and I pulled it away from my ear, squinting at the screen—only seven per cent of battery life left.

I placed it back against the side of my head to hear Tia say, 'His phone's still here. So's his bike.'

I wanted to ask if they'd had a fight or if they talked about the possibility that Tom's death was a suicide, but it wasn't the time and wouldn't have helped. Then I remembered what he'd said about hiding out in the caves. 'I think I might know where he is. I'll call you back.'

I changed into a blood-free shirt, snatched up one of the complimentary bottles of water from the bathroom for my parched mouth and headed out into the steely morning, leaving my phone charging by the bed.

Though I suspected Adam would be at the caves, dread seeped into my stomach.

I moved faster than my body wanted to, turning the corner at Hesse and following it all the way to the crest, through the roundabout and past the fort and football club. Fragments of the previous night flashed through my mind—getting punched at the pub, falling onto the grass, the guy hoisting me up. He must have helped me to the hotel, but I couldn't remember that part.

I descended the stairs to a narrow path edged with creeping greenery, a low wave wall on the beach side and a rusted square-wired fence on the other. Beside me, the water extended to another peninsula; a ferry slugged its way through the heads. On my left, thatches of shrubbery rose toward the white lighthouse.

The ocean hummed in my ears as I passed the first of two small, enclosed concrete observation bunkers that would have once been used to keep watch on the open sea channel but now resembled graffitied mini-dungeons. The path ended with a break in the wave wall and a few steps down to the sand. But I needed to go further. I scaled the three-foot-high concrete and bluestone wall, which could take both of my feet standing together but without much wiggle room.

I kicked off my flip-flops for better purchase and negotiated the wall on the balls of my feet, arms wide for balance, squinting against a spark of sunshine.

Fifty yards along, the wall curved around to the left, passing the second concrete lookout, the sand now ten feet below me on the bay side, rocks covering the beach where Adam and I had explored the rock pools three days earlier.

Rounding the bend, I made the two-foot drop to the land side and traced a thin path beaten into the sand alongside the wall to a small clearing a few yards from where the wave wall ended, crumbling to the sand below.

I angled left and treaded a small rise through more shrubbery to a cave, maybe eighteen feet wide by eight or ten feet deep, scooped out of the sand-coloured cliff face.

Adam was alone inside, sitting on a rock, drawing circles in the sand with his finger. Behind him, clear plastic cups littered the base, no doubt from kids coming here to drink and smoke and whatever else teenagers did in secret places in 2018.

He looked up when he sensed me there. 'What happened to you?' he said.

'I got here as fast as I could.'

He wore shorts and a hoodie, so he'd probably left home before daylight, when it was cooler.

'I meant your lip.'

Absently, I touched my mouth. It was tender under the press

of my finger, and I could feel the bulge where it swelled. 'Had a disagreement with a tree trunk.'

Adam went back to his circles. Someone had lit a small fire at some point and the remnants of charred branches blackened the sand in a rough circle near his feet.

'Come on,' I said. 'Can I at least get a pity laugh?'

He glanced up, but his expression didn't change.

I bent at the hip so as not to hit my head, entered the cave and sat next to him, setting my flip-flops and the bottle of water on the sand. 'Been here long?'

He shrugged.

'Your mom's looking for you.'

He didn't answer.

I reached into my pocket, hoping I'd left a pack of gum in there. I had. I offered him a strip and he took it.

'I changed my travel plans,' I told him. 'I'm not leaving until tomorrow.'

He raised his head. 'You're not going?' A tinge of hope infused his voice. Was that why he was hiding out in the cave? He didn't want to have to say goodbye?

'Not today, mate.'

Adam frowned. He took a breath. 'Do you think my dad killed himself?' He stared at me then, daring me to lie.

My head throbbed; I wasn't ready for this conversation and was in no state to have it, but Adam was, so I had to suck it up.

'I don't know, buddy. Maybe we'll never find out, which'll be hard to live with, I know. It's horrible growing up with unanswered questions.'

He nodded, looking away as a tear dripped down his chin.

I remembered then something Tia said—that Adam hadn't cried since Tom died. Now he was, and I didn't know what to do.

Hug him? Say something positive? Being a parent would be so stressful, I thought, never knowing what to do or say to make things better when you'd had no one to do that for you.

I switched course. 'Your dad and I tried to sneak over to Swan Island once,' I said.

Adam looked up, wiping his eyes with the sleeve of his hoodie.

'It was his idea, of course. I was scared out of my mind. We stole this little boat. What do you call those things?'

'A dinghy?'

'No, the other one.'

'Kayak.'

'Of course. Kayaks.' Minnesotan lakes were full of them—I'd drawn a mental blank. Maybe I had a concussion? 'Well, we *borrowed* it,' I continued. 'That's how he put it. It was the dead of night. The water was cold and we didn't even have life vests.'

'What happened?'

'We got most of the way there but then I got spooked and we fell in. Your dad's foot got caught on something and he almost drowned.'

Adam's face livened up. 'Dad never told me that story.'

'I've got a hundred more. He really showed me . . . He came into my life at a time when . . . I don't know . . .' My head hurt, and it was only getting worse. I tried again. 'When I came to Australia, I'd just lost my own dad the year before and Mom was having a baby with her new husband. I didn't know anyone. I didn't have any friends. And even when I did meet your dad, he had to coax me away from my books and show me how to live a bit. I was kind of a nerd.'

'Shocker.'

'Right? Anyway, he brought me out of my shell. Taught me about friendship, I guess. And I really didn't understand what we had until it was gone.' I exhaled. 'Then, somewhere along the way, I forgot what he taught me. I didn't have any real friends after him. I was scared to get close to anyone.'

Something registered behind Adam's eyes but he didn't speak.

'It's been great getting to know you a bit,' I said.

He sniffed. 'Yeah.'

That was all I was going to get out of him, but it was enough. I passed him the water bottle. 'You should probably hydrate after all that crying.'

He shoved me with his shoulder but took the water bottle anyway. He may even have smiled.

'This place is depressing,' I said, standing into a crouch until I could move beyond the cave's ceiling. I brushed sand from the seat of my shorts. 'Let's go do something fun on my last day.'

A moment later he emerged from the cave and we stepped over large sand-coloured boulders between a break in the crumbling wave wall to the beach.

'Race you to the pier?' I said.

Before he had a chance to answer, I broke into a run, my flip-flops in my hand, and he took off after me.

I slowed when I sensed him slipping behind, but then took off faster, my feet sinking into the sand as we neared the pier neck and neck.

I redoubled my effort and beat him by less than three feet.

We were both exhausted, though, collapsing onto the dry sand, struggling to catch our breath. I couldn't remember the last time I'd run like that.

'You're slow,' I said.

'You had a head start!'

Something about the whole scenario felt very familiar and I couldn't repress my smile.

Adam placed a hand over his heaving chest. 'Whatever you need to tell yourself.'

Fifty feet away, an abandoned kayak bobbed on the choppy water, tied to the dock.

'Want to go for a kayak?' I asked him.

'Haven't got one.'

'No worries. We can *borrow* one.'

He gave me a roguish smile and jumped to his feet. He ran toward it, me following close behind.

We climbed aboard. A single paddle lay longways in the hull.

I pushed us off from the mossy timber post of the dock and the motion upset the equilibrium of the boat. It tipped and we both fell out, having not even left the pier.

It was shallow, so we stood immediately. Then I noticed a smear of blood on Adam's forearm.

'Shit. What happened?' I said.

He held it up to investigate. 'Cut it on the post. A bolt sticking out maybe.'

The wound looked deep, and the blood kept coming. 'Wrap your t-shirt around it,' I said. 'We'd better get you home.'

39

Our clothes were still soaked through by the time we reached Adam's house. Standing on the porch, he called for his mom.

'What the hell happened to you two?' Tia said from inside. She opened the screen door.

Adam looked at me, a half-smile on his lips.

'We fell in the water,' I said.

'I can see that. In your clothes? Drew, your lip. And—oh my God, Adam. Your arm!'

Adam had put his wet hoodie back on with the sleeves pushed to his elbows, his t-shirt wrapped around the cut.

I could have lied to Tia; Adam would have backed me up. But what example would that set?

I ran a hand through my wet hair. 'We were kayaking out to—'

'Kayaking? Whose kayak?'

'Just listen, Mum!'

'I don't know whose kayak,' I admitted. 'We borrowed it to go for a row.'

She blinked rapidly, as if something had lodged in her eye. 'Without life jackets?'

I nodded.

She grabbed Adam's arm and tugged the sodden shirt off, examining the wound. 'This is going to need a stitch. You,' she said to Adam, 'get in the shower.' She looked at me again, fire in her eyes. 'You stay here.'

She followed Adam into the house, her hand between his shoulder blades, pushing him along.

A moment later she returned, a bath towel in hand. She threw it to me but I didn't react in time and it ended up flung over my head.

'What the hell were you thinking? Why didn't you call me as soon as you found him?'

I shook my head to let her know I wasn't thinking at all. 'I wanted to do something fun with him, and my phone—'

'And almost get yourselves killed?'

She was emotional, overreacting. But she had a point.

'You can't replace him, Drew.'

'I'm not trying to be his father.'

'I think you are. But not for Adam. For yourself. Adam is not Tom. You can't go back and . . .' She shook her head.

I knew what she was saying—I missed my boyhood friend, a friendship I'd never managed to match since. I wanted it back.

'I'm sorry, Tia.'

'You're the adult here. You're supposed to protect him, not use him to fill a void.'

'I know. I'm sorry,' I said again. It didn't seem enough, but it was all I had. I ran the towel over my sopping hair.

'Why did you come, Drew?'

I looked into her eyes, trying to interpret her meaning, because I wondered, deep down, if she already knew the answer.

Tia planted her hands on her hips. 'It's a bloody long way for the funeral of a person you'd seen once in twenty-five years and really didn't know anymore. What were you looking for?'

It was a good question, one that I'd not properly considered because my brain had satisfied itself with the obvious answers— to show respect, to say goodbye to Tom.

'Does it have something to do with what happened on Mercer Street?'

I shook my head. *I don't want to talk about that.*

She held my gaze for a moment longer but then gave up. 'Well, whatever it is, a part of you is stuck there. And you're not going to sort yourself out until you deal with it.'

She snatched the towel from my hands and went back inside, slamming the door behind her.

I beat a slow path back to the guest house, clouds gathering in the sky overhead.

So this was how I was going to leave Australia: things worse than when I came, nothing resolved, my manuscript in the toilet, no hope of having children of my own.

I was stuck. Where, I didn't know. Or maybe it was when— stuck in Queenscliff in '92, like Tia had said. Maybe bogged down by the failure of my first novel. Death surrounded me and I was sinking in it; Tom was dead, my book was dead, my relationship with Tom's family was dead. I was in no-man's-land, as if I'd tripped but not yet hit the ground.

I slowed as I the passed the liquor store, an illuminated sign flashing OPEN.

Inside, a man sat at the counter, alone. I stood there on the sidewalk, wet shorts clinging to my thighs, looking at the lines of bottles calling to me.

Writing was the lock that kept the gate to my past firmly closed, keeping all those memories at arm's length and out of my head. It protected me from having to let them in. But now the gate had blown open, the wind hissing around my ears, the past circling me, taking up all the space.

I kept walking, and as I crossed Hesse, it started raining. All of a sudden, it was coming down in waves. I took refuge under a covered bus stop outside the historical museum. Thunder sounded, then the lightning started, cracking open the clouds. Not forks of lightning, but sheets. Flashes of bright white light. *White light, white light.*

I sat in the bus shelter, watching water gush down the gutters, bringing leaves and debris. It was the same bus shelter I'd sat in with Tom on that momentous day twenty-six years ago. Something snagged in my mind, and then I saw it. A box of matches floated on the water, carried down the gutter toward the drain. In a flash, it was all there again. The matches. The spark of light.

The past and the present suddenly fused together, as if this sodden box of matches had been the only thing separating them.

It was Easter. Tom and I had taken the hour-long bus ride to the movie theatre in Geelong to see *Hook*. It was cold and wet, and there wasn't much else to do. After the movie we bought

Big Macs and fries and ate them on the bus on the way home, stepping off at the very bus stop where I now sat in the rain.

When we arrived at my place on Mercer, the sky darkening above us, the house was silent except for the TV, its blue light flaring and fading across the living room walls. 'Mom?'

No answer.

We dropped our backpacks at the front door and made our way down the hall to the unlit kitchen, where we found her sitting at the kitchen table, Scarlett wrapped in a blanket in her arms. Mom was staring into space and Scarlett was quiet. The light from the open microwave door was the only thing illuminating the room.

Something was wrong. I felt it distinctly, the way an animal senses a drop in air pressure before a storm. On the counter, Mom had peeled and cut potatoes into halves, the knife still sitting alongside the timber cutting board.

She didn't stir as I stepped closer. I looked into the microwave—red pasta sauce for dinner had splattered against the white lining of the internal walls and door.

'Mom?' I said again. When I touched her shoulder, she looked up, eyes as blank as a doll's. 'I had to heat the baby's milk,' she said.

'Okay.'

She held Scarlett to her chest so all I could see was the white of her blanket, covering her entire body.

'I can do it, Mom.' I could see Scarlett's bottle already filled, ready to heat, sitting on the countertop.

I realised then that Scarlett still hadn't made a noise. I went to touch her, to pull back the blanket, but Mom tightened her grip, pulling Scarlett even further up her chest.

'Is the baby okay?' Tom said from behind me. I'd forgotten he was there.

Mom continued to stare blankly ahead. I tried once more to touch Scarlett and, again, Mom pulled her close, but this time I insisted.

'Mom, let me see.'

Mom relented then, loosening her grip. I peeled back the blanket to find the underside covered in red. Scarlett's head was half gone, as if it had exploded, and blood poured from her eye sockets.

I screamed.

Tom was at my side now. I looked at Mom, then at him, his face panic-stricken. He glanced at the open microwave door, smeared in red, then at Scarlett and then at me, and I knew that he'd figured it out too.

'Mom! What happened? What did you do?'

Tears sprung to my eyes and I snatched Scarlett from my mother's arms, placing her gently on the table. The blanket fell open, revealing the extent of the damage to her little body. She was dead. So, so dead.

'I was supposed to heat the milk,' Mom said in a faraway voice.

The reality of what happened—of what Mom had done—sat so heavy in my stomach that it threatened to drag me to the ground.

Just then the front door slammed shut and footsteps trudged along the hallway toward us.

'Why's it so dark in here?' Mark called out.

I shot a look at Tom, our eyes widening. There was no time for anything—no time to take Scarlett away, no time to think of something to say, no time to change a thing.

Mark arrived in the doorway and flipped the light switch, brightness flickering above us.

'This place is a mess. Why is Scarlett on the table?'

He moved closer, glancing at Mom, who had not yet looked at him. 'Why is Scarlett on the table like that, Cathy? What's that on her—oh my God! What's—' He wiped her face with his hand, then tried again, this time using the blanket, becoming more desperate with every wipe.

'Oh no,' he cried. 'Oh no.' He picked her up and held her bloodied body to his chest. 'Oh no!'

He turned to Mom. 'Cathy! What have you—' Then he caught sight of the microwave and he knew.

'Oh my God. My baby!'

Mark took Scarlett into the living room and sat on the couch, hugging her, rocking her, trying to comfort her, calling her name. He stroked her head as if he was trying to lull her to sleep.

I caught Mom looking at them, there on the couch; her face was relaxed now. Relieved, probably, that Scarlett was finally asleep and Mark was doing his part to take care of her. That's all she'd wanted, after all.

She stood. 'I need to start on supper,' she said, opening the refrigerator.

Tom cast his eyes at me, scared, and I shook my head at him. *Just leave her.*

Mom stood staring into the open refrigerator as if she'd forgotten why she was there.

'Cathy,' Mark shouted from across the room.

'Darn it, I need to go to the store,' Mom said into the cold.

'Cathy!' Mark placed Scarlett on the sofa and stormed into the kitchen. He grabbed Mom by the shoulders and spun her around, staring at her in the face, seething.

'You killed her, Cathy. You killed our daughter!'

Mom looked toward the couch like she was confused about

what he meant. He pushed her against the fridge and her head thudded on the hard metal.

'Stop it!' I called out. 'Stop it, Mark.'

He turned to me, his eyes brimming with fury. He let Mom go, but then came at me, grabbing me around the neck. 'You're gonna find out how this feels, Cathy.'

He bent me backward over the counter squeezing my neck. I tried to prise his hands away but they were so strong, so full of hate. His eyes burned, his breathing hard. His grip was so tight I thought he might break my neck.

Then I remembered the potatoes. I reached out my hand, feeling for the knife on the cutting board. I pictured it halfway along the counter. I reached further, stretching my fingers until I found the edge of the board. I managed to sidestep a little along, touching the knife. But Mark pulled me away.

Then, suddenly, Mom was on Mark's back, trying to pull him off me, screaming at him to let me go. I could feel the struggle going on above me, but his grip stayed firm. Then, without warning, he let go.

I fell to the floor, gasping for air, looking up just in time to see Mark punch Mom in the face, sending her flying backward onto the tabletop with such force that the whole table screeched across the tiles.

With Mom on the floor, Mark turned back to me. Dropping to his knees, he reached for my neck again, squeezing for what felt like an eternity. Then all of a sudden a loud bang reverberated through the kitchen and a flash of white light ricocheted off the walls. Another bang followed immediately after; another blinding flash of light. Mark's grip on me slackened and the whole weight of his body fell onto me. I looked up to find Tom standing over us, Mark's gun in his hands.

I held his eyes with mine. I didn't speak but tried to convey everything I wanted to say with my face—my relief and my thanks and my fear all in one. I pushed Mark off and ran to Mom, who was still on the floor. She looked disorientated, blood spilling from her nose. But she was okay.

Then, like Paul Atreides in *Dune*, I had a glimpse of the future—Mom locked away in prison, Tom in juvenile detention, me in the foster care system like those kids in *The Pinballs*. Even my twelve-year-old brain understood what I had to do then. I had to protect the people I loved. People wouldn't understand what had happened in the kitchen if we told the truth. A calmness descended on me and time seemed to slow down.

I peeled the warm gun from Tom's trembling fingers, wiped it over with a wet dishcloth and then dried it with the dish towel. I placed it on the table.

I helped Mom up, sitting her in a chair.

'Mom? Mom! Mark killed Scarlett,' I told her.

'What?' she said. 'No.'

'Yes—yes he did.'

She looked around the room, confused. 'Where's the baby?'

'Mom, listen to me! Mark killed Scarlett, then he tried to kill me, so you shot him. Do you understand?'

She eyed the gun on the table but didn't respond.

Tom picked up on what I was saying and came to her side. He held one of her hands. I took the other. They were cold and damp to touch.

'Mom, you have to listen to me now. You have to do what I say.'

I was aware of how loud those gunshots were and that people would no doubt come soon. I looked at Tom. He nodded; he understood what I was trying to do.

'Mark killed Scarlett,' I said again. 'He got angry because she wouldn't stop crying. He hit you. Then he tried to kill me. But you stopped him. You got his gun out of the safe and you shot him.'

She looked at the gun on the table, blinking rapidly.

'You had to protect me,' I told her. 'And yourself. So you shot him. Understand?'

Something changed in her eyes. Somewhere deep inside her addled brain, something switched on. She took the gun and held it in her hands.

She nodded, just as a loud knock sounded on the front door.

I sat at the bus stop now. The rain continued to fall around me and I knew that I was not okay. I had never been okay. Not since leaving Queenscliff or, more likely, since my dad died. It hit me now like a car speeding through a red light, spinning me around and around, bumping me into every other car in range.

I'd tried to cushion myself from it all, covering my head with my arms to protect it from the blows. Booze, an early marriage, losing myself in writing and then this idea that I needed a child to make my life complete, always wondering if some genetic light switch would flip on for me.

It was too heavy now. In a single day, I'd lost Scarlett, I'd lost Tom and I'd lost my mother. Mom survived, of course, but she was no longer a complete person. When we first got back to the States she was institutionalised for a few months. But even after that, after all those years in Ely with Aunt Jem, it was as if she wasn't there. She took pills, and I never knew where the drugs ended and she began. She moved through life so slowly and so invisibly, carrying her trauma around like a bowl of hot soup filled to the brim, careful never to falter lest she should spill a drop and have her insides splash to the floor. Sometimes I hated her for it. Sometimes I hated myself. I had seen she was struggling with Scarlett and I'd done nothing.

I never imagined that my own mother, my beautiful, funny, happy, lively mom, would become unknowable to me. She died in a nursing home in 2014, her mind spongy from dementia, but really I'd already lost her in Queenscliff. The ghost of her was stuck here. Now her body lay alongside Scarlett's in a cemetery in Minneapolis.

I stepped into the downpour, letting it wash over me. I walked down Hesse toward the beach, and as I crossed the foreshore reserve, the rain faded to a sprinkle then stopped, leaving the pathway glistening.

I reached the bench under the black lighthouse and sat, overlooking the shipping channel and the pier where I'd been so many times with Tom in '92. A tanker slogged its way through the heads and a slim, orange pilot boat darted across the water to meet it, to ensure its safe passage to shore.

I didn't know if Mom had become confused and put Scarlett in the microwave when she'd meant to put in the bottle or if she was just desperate to stop the incessant crying. I never asked her, and it was one of those unanswered questions I'd had to live with. Maybe she didn't know herself.

I had absorbed the impact of these events, but they'd reverberated inside me, contained, unable to escape. They ate away at me from the inside out without me even knowing it, like a disease that lies dormant in your bloodstream for years until something triggers an attack. I'd told the lies of what happened that day so often that they had congealed inside me as truth.

Writing had been my sanctuary and my prison. It had given

me a structure from which to fashion a life. But in another way, it had provided a hiding place, a distraction from the one thing I really needed to do. Filling my life with words left me nowhere to go, no space to experience pain. But Mercer Street was always there, lying in wait.

Tom, too, must have had to close down a part of himself to survive. He had been put in an impossible situation, where he'd had to kill a man. That was bad enough, but then my lie had silenced him, so he could never seek help. How loud that silence must have been; how long he'd had to carry it on his shoulders. Maybe it had grown too heavy. Maybe it had pulled him all the way to the floor of the bay.

'I'm sorry, mate,' I whispered into the wind.

I climbed down the wooden steps, blown over with sand, and made my way along the beach, the undulating line of damp erased and re-created each time a wave came in. I stood on the pier, looking out across the bay, completely open, as if the world no longer had edges. A seagull flew down and perched on one of the balustrades, twitching its head, looking out to sea and back again. Since childhood, I'd hoisted upon myself the obligation to live a life big enough for three people—Dad, Scarlett *and* me.

Enough for three.

But that, of course, was impossible.

The seagull twitched one more time, and I watched as it flew away, high into the blue sky toward the bright white sun.

40

The next morning, I stood at the hotel reception counter, my bags at my feet, while Leon's printer churned out my bill.

'You look different,' he said.

'I do? Suntan probably.'

He shook his head. 'It's the salt water. It heals. Although your nose, and that gash on your lip, they look nasty.' He folded the A4 page from the printer into three. 'Sometimes the hero must go on a journey so he can discover what he always knew to be true.'

I smiled at his appreciation of story theory.

He handed me my receipt. 'Stay in touch,' he said. 'Follow us on Insta.'

'Okay,' I said. 'Yeah. I think I will.'

'I'll be looking out for your next book.'

My manuscript would need a complete rewrite. I'd have to start again. No, it wasn't starting again. Like Adam said, a failure is not a failure—it's a lesson that brought me one step closer to where I needed to be. The goal had not changed, but my relationship to it had. I had asked too much of my writing, put too much pressure on it to deliver something that it never could do on its own. I'd expected too much in return. Writing *is* the return. Like the fun of paddling out to Swan Island with Tom: it didn't really matter if we got there or not.

I headed through the hotel's main doors. Outside, the heat had gone out of the air. Adam was by the rental car, on his bike, with both feet planted firmly on the ground.

'You're a wuss,' he said.

'Adam . . .'

'No goodbye?'

'I thought it was best.'

'For you, you mean.'

This kid was smart beyond his years.

Adam rocked on his feet, the wheels of the bike moving an inch forward, an inch back with each small rotation.

'I've got something for you,' I said.

I reached into my messenger bag, felt around, found not what I was looking for but pulled it out anyway. I handed him my last full pack of Big Red.

'Wow,' he said without expression. 'Thanks.'

'You're welcome. But that's not it.'

I scrounged around until I felt the smooth exterior of Tom's lure.

'Your dad gave me this when we were kids. *For luck*, he said.'

Adam stepped off his bike and lowered it to the road.

I held the lure in my hand a moment and then passed it to him.

'It represents friendship, given from one mate to another. I want you to have it. From me to you.'

'Okay.' He sounded not entirely impressed, but respectful. He turned it in all directions, examining it from multiple angles. Then, peering at the underside, he squinted to see it more clearly.

'What's *wabi-sabi*?'

'What?'

I took the lure back. On the underside, Tom had written WABI-SABI in black uppercase letters. It had faded from the surface, as it had faded from my mind. Tears trembled in my eyes.

'Words to live by,' I said, passing the fish back. 'Look it up when you get home.'

Adam nodded. 'Sure you don't want it?'

'I don't need it anymore.' I motioned to his bandaged arm. 'How's the cut?'

'Three stiches. I've had worse.'

I nodded. 'Just remember to take care of it, okay?'

He sniffed, which I interpreted as a sign of acknowledgement.

'I mean it. These wounds we get . . . you can't let them fester.'

This time he closed his eyes and nodded.

I reached out to shake his hand goodbye but he grabbed me around the waist instead, tightening his grip. I flattened my hand around the back of his hair, cradling his head to my chest. When he stepped back, he turned away to hide his eyes.

'See ya, Drew.'

'Bye, my buddy.'

On the flight home, a deep sleep quickly claimed me—the first time ever on a plane. I dreamed about my parents often. I found them in all kinds of places in these dreams: parks, the state fair, rowing on lakes . . . in some kind of alternative dimension, or wherever you go when you die. But wherever they were, I dreamed that they were there together, the age they were when I was born, passing the time while they waited for me.

Scarlett would have been twenty-six now, finished college, starting her career, maybe in a relationship with someone special. Would she have Mom's hazel eyes or would they be more of a deep brown, like Mark's? Would her hair have stayed black? Would she wear it short or long? I'd never know.

But this dream, on this plane ride, was about Tom. We were twelve, on the beach, our bare feet sinking into the sand, the pier in our sights.

'I found a cool word,' he said to me.

'You did?'

'Yeah. It's *wabi-sabi*.'

'What the heck's wabi-sabi?' I asked.

'It's Japanese.'

'What's it mean?'

'It means that nothing in life is perfect, so why try to make it that way?'

I wasn't sure what he was getting at but didn't say so.

'See the bay out there?' he said. 'The best bits are right in front of us, it's just that they're hidden under the broken waves.'

I looked at those waves, coming apart on the surface, imagining the beauty of the marine world underneath. Everything seemed alright then. Words had made everything okay again.

Tom slapped me on the back. 'Or some shit like that.' He nudged me with his shoulder. 'Race you to the pier?'

He broke into a run and I took off after him, sprinting toward the bright light together.

Author's note

In 2007 I travelled to New Zealand for a wedding, and while I was there I caught up with my childhood friend, Tom. We'd spent a year together as twelve-year-olds, living in the same place overseas where our dads had been posted for work. That was the extent of our time together as kids, but I continued to think of him as my best friend throughout high school.

I saw Tom a few times in the years that followed—once as sixteen-year-olds in New Zealand, in London when we were nineteen, another time in Minneapolis, once in Melbourne—but we hadn't stayed in regular contact. We were both married by then, and had two kids each. But this trip to New Zealand in 2007 was the first time I'd met Tom's son, David. The physical similarities between Tom and David didn't strike me at first, but the essence of Tom was clearly there in his son—the way he moved, the way he spoke, his personality. He embodied my boyhood friend and I realised then how much I'd missed that time in my life, that friendship with Tom.

My wife and I flew to Queenstown the next day for the wedding, but the flight was diverted further south because of bad weather. I distinctly remember the three-hour bus ride from Invercargill to Queenstown. It was dark, and the rain was hammering against the bus windows as we wove our way along the mountain road between the two towns.

That's when I had the idea for this book—a story about a man who, at the wake of his childhood friend's funeral, meets his friend's son for the first time. The meeting brings back memories of their shared childhood and something that happened way back then to bond them forever. Something neither of them had fully dealt with.

I sat on this idea for fourteen years, only starting to write it in 2021 when I found myself with a book contract for the first time and only a year to write a novel from scratch.

The real Tom and I never had such tragedy in our time together. And, I'm happy to tell you, he is still very much with us, living in Illinois with his Minnesotan wife Cathy.

Tom is doing great, but if any of the material in this book has brought up issues for you, please talk to someone about it. In Australia, you can always reach out to support services like Lifeline on 13 11 14 or Beyond Blue on 1300 22 4636.

Acknowledgements

I want to first thank Tom Wolfenden and his family for inspiring the events and characters in this book. I also want to thank Bianca Simpson, my first reader, and the many Queenscliff residents, shopkeepers and local businesspeople who answered my pesky questions about their town. In particular, I'd like to thank Diana Sawyer from the Queenscliffe Historical Museum, Barb and Barry Griffiths, Carole and David Hutchison, Matt Davis and Jayne Tuttle from The Bookshop at Queenscliff, Carmel Christensen from *The Rip*, Peter and June Negri from the Queenscliffe Maritime Museum, Tanya Burns from the Burnside bait and tackle shop, and staff from Queenscliff Primary School—Richard, Sylvia and Helene. And for reading the manuscript for local accuracy: Michelle Gardiner, Michael Moore and Peter Smallwood for Queenscliff; and Dawn Frederick for Minnesota.

I am ever grateful for the dedication, passion and patience of my dream team at Pan Macmillan Australia: Alex Lloyd and Bec Lay. Thanks also to Ali Lavau for her astute copyediting and to Christa Moffitt for her stunning cover design.

Thanks, too, to the brilliant authors who provided generous endorsements for this book: Gabriel Bergmoser, Kylie Ladd, Peter Papathanasiou and Hayley Scrivenor.

And to my family—Rosie, Maddie and Ben—thanks for riding all the waves with me.

Resources

Once I got stuck into this manuscript and began to understand where it was headed, I realised I needed to do a heap of research. I'd like to particularly acknowledge the following writers and resources, all of which I found helpful and some of which inspired scenes and stories that appear in the book.

Books about Australia from a foreigner's perspective:
  Into the Rip by Damien Cave
  How to be Australian by Ashley Kalagian Blunt

Books about postnatal depression/psychosis:
  I'm Fine (and other lies) by Megan Blandford
  After the Storm by Emma Jane Unsworth

Books about Gulf War syndrome/illness:
  Against All Enemies by Seymour M Hersh
  Impotent Warriors by Susie Kilshaw

Articles about Gulf War syndrome/illness:
  'Gulf War illness and the health of Gulf War veterans: research update and recommendations, 2009–2013' by the Research Advisory Committee on Gulf War Veterans' Illnesses, 2014
  'Recent research on Gulf War illness and other health problems in veterans of the 1991 Gulf War: effects of toxicant exposures during deployment', published in *Cortex* by White, et al., 2016

The 'Sea-Change Mystery' series of novels by Dorothy Johnston (set in Queenscliff)

Articles about professional envy by Kathryn Chetkovich, Abby Mims and Nathan Rabin

'A Way with Words' radio show / podcast

MORE FROM MATTHEW RYAN DAVIES

Things We Bury

Three siblings, reunited in their home town, are struggling to deal with the fallout of a car crash that almost killed their father. This, on top of everything else life is throwing at them.

Josh is trying to save his marriage and hard-won TV career in the wake of a painfully public sexual harassment scandal. But is he really as innocent as he says?

Jac, perennially single, is getting married – unbeknownst to her family. But will the private war she's been waging since leaving the town sabotage this relationship, too?

Dane, ever honest and dependable, is running the family business while their father is in hospital. But not everything is above board. Can he look the other way for his dad's sake?

A mysterious list of names. Long-buried family secrets. Old, festering wounds.

What will happen when everything buried is dragged to the surface?

'An acutely observed, utterly compelling family drama.' MARK BRANDI

'So compelling, so well written, so damn clever. I am already desperate for his next book.' SALLY HEPWORTH

'Only a truly gifted novelist could pull this off, and Matthew Ryan Davies has written a beautiful, moving family drama.' MALCOLM KNOX

'Jeez, this family. Their stories. It's like an addiction. It gets into your veins and it is very hard to quit them.' JOHN BIRMINGHAM

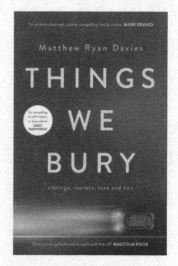